THE BOOK CLUB MURDERS

The Book Club Murders

ALAN GOREVAN

Alan Gorevan

For Erika,
who changed everything

Chapter 1

Izzy O'Brien left her old life behind on a Thursday afternoon in late February. She drove down the coast from her apartment in the city and arrived at her aunt's house thirty minutes later, during a rainstorm that rolled in off the Irish Sea and turned the sky the colour of a nightmare.

She parked next to the kerb and killed the engine. For a moment, she sat and listened to the frenzied rain pounding against the windscreen.

Her phone had been ringing almost constantly during the drive, so she'd been forced to put it on silent. Now she glanced at it.

27 missed calls.

All from Adam. Why wasn't he at work? Izzy had hoped to have more time before he noticed her missing.

This was a disaster.

The house lay halfway down a narrow residential road off Dun Laoghaire's main street. The other end of the road sloped down towards the harbour. On a clear day, the view would be pretty, but right now Izzy only saw a churning mass of rain blurring into the sea.

She was on her own, with nothing more than a Fiat stuffed with black sacks containing her possessions. Everything she'd accumulated during her thirty years sat in the car. It didn't look like much.

Her aunt Elaine had died ten weeks earlier. Her former home was one in a row of terraced houses, with two floors above ground and a basement half submerged. The walls were a faded cream. In contrast, the black paint on the door looked fresh and glossy.

Although the front garden was paved, it featured one of the palm trees which were dotted around the area. Combined with the spectacular view of Dublin Bay, the trees gave Dun Laoghaire a tropical feel when the sun was shining.

For most of its history, the place had been an unremarkable fishing village. Construction of the harbour in the early nineteenth century changed that. So did the railway which followed soon afterwards. It connected Dun Laoghaire to the city, twelve kilometres north.

A lot had changed, though, and Dun Laoghaire's glory days were behind it.

Izzy remembered Adam's confusion when he saw the place name written down.

"What's that when it's at home? How do you pronounce it?" he'd said in his thick Glasgow accent, a dark curl falling over his forehead. That had been on their third date, when Izzy invited him to her apartment for lunch.

"Most people pronounce it *done leery*, but if you want to be more Irish you can say *dune leery* and write the 'u' with a fada. Like this."

She scrawled 'Ú' on a piece of paper.

"A fada? Is that right, aye?"

"It is, aye," Izzy said with a laugh.

Imitating each other's accents had been a running joke from the start. She found it cute the way Adam pronounced *house* as *hoose*. In turn, he mocked the way she said 'r'. Like a pirate, he pronounced it *arr*. For her, it was *ore*.

The joking was over now.

Izzy braced herself and stepped out of the car. The hard rain bounced off her face and neck, hammering her fake-leather jacket and drenching her jeans. She shivered, her thin body struggling to stay warm.

She locked the car and approached the wrought iron gate to the house. When she pushed it open, the gate creaked loud enough to be heard over the rain. Izzy's aunt had been sixty-three when she died. Not old, but maybe old enough that she might have appreciated a little help maintaining the place.

That's what today has been missing. A little guilt trip.

Izzy jogged up the half a dozen steps to the door. She decided to reacquaint herself with the place before bringing her stuff inside her new home.

She slid the key into the hole. It turned in a smooth, easy motion, which was good because the longer she stood there, the colder and wetter she was getting. Her long brown hair was no doubt becoming frizzy, which she hated.

Frizzy Izzy the girls at school used to call her.

The door opened very smoothly. Elaine had got all the doors in the house replaced a couple of years earlier, opting for beautiful and expensive walnut. Izzy thought it was a waste of money, but Elaine hadn't been a fan of alarms, and replacing the doors was a security measure as well as an aesthetic choice. She said they'd stop a bullet.

Stepping into the gloomy hallway, Izzy wiped her wet hands on her jeans. She was shivering uncontrollably. Outside, it was about ten degrees, but the house felt even colder. The dark navy paint on the walls didn't help.

Closing the door, she paused by the staircase. Like the hall's floor, the steps were varnished oak. A brutal, unforgiving surface. She touched the banister, forcing herself to feel its smoothness on her fingertips.

She stared at the bottom of the staircase.

Elaine had died there.

Izzy gasped as someone pounded on the door behind her.

A thundering voice came from outside. "Izzy? Open up."

Adam was here. The outraged tone was enough to tell her it was him, even if his accent wasn't.

The doorbell rang three times in quick succession. Holding her breath, she crept towards the front room next to the hall. It had been Elaine's favourite place to read. Izzy walked to the bay window and peered out.

The net curtain should have been enough to hide her, but she kept close to the side of the window, in case she was wrong.

Adam stood on the doorstep. He was wearing a grey T-shirt and jeans and his curly black hair was a mess. How could he be here now? He must have left work early and arrived home right after she'd left.

And he'd come right after her.

What rotten luck.

When he raised his arms to bang on the door again, his T-shirt lifted up to reveal his toned stomach. Izzy watched his muscular arms as he banged on the door. She hated how physically strong he was.

Adam shouted, "I see your car. Open up."

Of course he saw it. His own *McGregor Fine Foods* van was parked right behind her Fiat.

She waited, her stress level rising like water, over her knees, past her chest, up to her neck. About to drown her.

Adam slipped his phone out of his pocket and tapped on it. A moment later, Izzy's phone lit up. She let it ring silently for the twenty-eighth time and watched as he paced on the doorstep.

His face scrunched up in a mask of rage, distorting the knife scar that ran across his left cheek. A souvenir from youthful scrapes in Maryhill.

The rain continued, plastering Adam's clothes to his body. When he glanced at the window, Izzy backed away, scared he'd see her. She caught a glimpse of his clenched teeth as he returned the phone to his pocket.

"What are you doing? Talk to me, Izzy."

At that moment, sirens screamed nearby. Maybe up on the main street. Adam cocked his head at the sound. He hated the police with a passion.

With relief, Izzy watched as he walked down the path and out the gate.

Adam paused next to her car. He glanced back over his shoulder, then put a fist through the driver's side window.

Chapter 2

Tess Smith led her friend, Kate Long, into Conference Room Three, on the fifth floor of Harrison Barney Todd's gleaming office building. The city centre was right outside the law firm's window, O'Connell Street a one-minute walk away. You could see the junkies from here. Hell, you could *smell* the junkies from here.

Kate strutted over to the long table.

"Take a seat," Tess said.

She perched at one end of the table. She was normally at ease in this room, in every part of the building, actually. That was natural when you spent as many hours in a place as Tess spent here. As a new partner in the corporate law division, she officially worked forty-eight-hours a week. Unofficially, she lived in the office.

For once, though, she felt uncomfortable.

Kate lowered herself into the seat at Tess's side, her chestnut hair looking ridiculously glossy. She crossed her impossibly long legs, the slit in her floral dress revealing a million miles of perfect skin.

Fuck, Tess hated her, even if they were book club buddies. She wasn't sure they'd be buddies after this.

Kate said, "Are you sure you—?"

"Wait a minute."

Tess had just spotted her assistant, a girl named Britney, whose birth year – no, the very evening of her conception – could probably be pinpointed to the release of a late '90s pop song.

Upon reaching her early thirties, Tess had begun to feel an increasing distaste for those in their twenties, especially when they were carefree and statuesque blondes.

She knew she was no beauty. She had a flat figure, a mouth full of sharp, little teeth, and a head of thin, red hair, which no one – not even Tess – liked. Her attempts over the years to label it strawberry blonde had fooled no one.

Britney walked along the corridor beside the glass wall of the conference room. A tray was perfectly balanced in one hand. She knocked on the glass door, then opened it and strode over with a huge grin.

Tess made a mental note to make her work till midnight.

"Your cappuccino," Britney said, putting the cup down in front of Kate, "with organic almond milk, as requested. And a green tea for you, Tess. May I bring you ladies anything else?"

"No," Tess said.

Britney gave a nod, then left the room.

Meanwhile Tess sipped her tea. It was so hot that

it burnt her tongue. She changed her mind about making Britney work till midnight. Better make it two in the morning.

Kate broke out laughing.

"Is she a robot? Why was she so polite?"

"She thinks you're a client," Tess said.

She felt a pang of guilt. Tess never skived off on the job and she felt conflicted about stealing time away from work, even a few minutes. But she'd known Kate had an audition in the city centre. Another one of those bullshit Irish crime shows that no one watched.

"Organic almond milk?" Tess said.

Kate laughed at that. "I don't even drink coffee. But the aroma is nice."

She lifted the cup with one hand. Lowering her head, holding her beautiful hair back with her free hand, she inhaled deeply.

Tess grimaced, watching her. There was something obscenely sensual about the way Kate did everything. But that was why Tess needed her.

She cleared her throat. "We can continue now."

"Right," Kate said. She lifted her head and gave Tess a disgusted look. "What was I going to say? Oh, yeah. So are you batshit crazy?"

"Come on, I doubt it would be the first boyfriend you ever tried to steal."

"Yeah, well, I was never *asked* to do it before."

Kate recrossed her long legs. They were tanned presidential orange and waxed to perfection. Not a hair in sight, unlike the dense undergrowth that hid under Tess's expensive but unflattering pantsuit. Tess occasionally hacked at that grass with a razor, but her skin was sensitive, and she always suffered a flare-up that left her legs pink and blotchy.

Tess didn't even dare to think about what might be growing from her armpits. The hair there must be long enough to plait by now. She'd need a chainsaw to cut it.

A thoughtful expression passed over Kate's face.

"You've been living with Gareth for what – a year and a half?"

"Two."

"How's the sex life?"

Tess shifted in her seat. She took another sip of tea, but it was still too hot. Her tongue throbbed as it became swollen. Britney would be working till four am, Tess decided.

"Gareth and I don't have much time for that. I work long hours. When I get home, I'm tired. I just want to sleep."

"Well, there you go." Kate said. Her face assumed the smug expression of a doctor who had made an easy diagnosis.

"It's not about sex."

"It's *always* about sex."

Tess shook her head, though she felt a prickle of doubt. At that moment, she hated Kate, with her hourglass figure, glossy hair, perfect make-up, and all the other eye-fluttering crap.

"I saw the way Gareth looked at you last time we

had the book club at my place." Tess shuddered at the memory. Her boyfriend had been staring. It turned her stomach. "I want to have a child, to get married. It's a serious commitment."

"Why bother?" Kate flicked her hair back. "All that stuff is overrated."

"You're the one who's married."

Kate shrugged. "If Stephen didn't treat me right, I'd be out of there like a bullet."

"Anyway, *I* want to get married and I want a husband I can trust. I thought that would be Gareth, but lately he's made me so suspicious. He never lets me see his phone. He always has it on silent when we're together. And when I catch him texting, he gets this guilty look and hides the phone. He tells me he's just checking how well his stock market picks are doing."

"I thought he was into greyhound racing."

"No. He's done with gambling. Now he's only interested in investing."

Kate rolled her eyes and gave an exaggerated yawn.

"It's bad enough that he's a schoolteacher without him having boring hobbies too. Ditch him."

Tess sighed. "But what if I'm wrong?"

"You bought the house by yourself, right?"

Tess nodded. Her salary had allowed her to buy a nice house with a sea view. The downside was that she spent all her time at the office, so she wasn't able to enjoy it much.

"Why don't you confront him?" Kate said.

"He could just tell me what I want to hear. I need

proof. If he's the kind of guy who could cheat, who could be swayed, I want to know that now, before I marry him."

"And you immediately thought of me?" Kate's expression hardened. "So that's what you think I'm like?"

Duh.

"Of course not," Tess said. "But come on. He was staring at you the day you came to my place. And you're an actress. If anyone's going to test him, it should be you. Tell me, how did the audition go?"

Kate rolled her eyes again. "Like you care."

"Sorry. This thing is driving me crazy. I can't think of anything else. My work is suffering. I haven't slept for a fortnight. I mean, I barely sleep anyway, but now I'm not sleeping at all. If you could—"

"Alright, alright. But if I do this thing, I'll do it right. I mean, if I set out to steal your boyfriend? No offence, but it's case closed. I'll get the job done."

Tess said, "Then at least I'll know the truth."

"Okay. It's a deal."

Kate rose from her chair. She even did that in a sexy way. Tess stood up too.

"Do you have another audition or are you going home?"

"I've only had one audition this entire month. It's not like my schedule is crowded."

"That's too bad."

Kate said, "I'm going back to Dun Laoghaire. Since

my evening is clear, I might start my little project right away. Is Gareth at home?"

"He should be by the time you get there. He doesn't like to hang around at the school once classes are finished."

Kate winked. "Then I might have an answer for you tonight. The book club is, what, eight o'clock?"

"Is that tonight? I'm not sure I can make it."

"You always bail on us, Tess. Don't do that tonight. I'll have an answer for you. That's what you want, right?"

Tess nodded miserably. "Yes."

An answer was what she wanted.

Chapter 3

When Adam had gone, Izzy hurried out of the house, down the steps and through the gate. The cold rain hit her again, making her slender body shiver. Looking towards the T-junction with the main street, she caught sight of Adam's van vanishing around the corner.

Her chest tightened as she walked over to her car. The window he'd punched was broken and smeared with blood.

Adam had been bad-tempered before. He'd been jealous, clingy, and controlling. But he'd *never* been violent.

Not to her, at least.

Shock gave way to anger. How *dare* he terrorise her?

"Are you okay?"

A woman's voice startled Izzy. Using her fingers, she combed the hair out of her eyes, and caught sight of a woman crossing the road, holding a huge umbrella over her head.

She looked to be in her mid-thirties, with wavy blonde hair so pale it was almost white. Her eyes were puffy, set close together on either side of a long, narrow nose. She wore a light purple cardigan over a white T-shirt, plus white trousers.

As she drew closer, she foisted the umbrella over Izzy too. Izzy caught a whiff of sweet perfume. The woman was beautifully made up. She wore chunky jewellery on her wrists and around her neck.

"You're getting drenched." The woman had to raise her voice to be heard over the rain.

"I'm fine," Izzy said.

"I couldn't help hearing the commotion."

"It's nothing."

In response, the woman looked at the Fiat's window. Blood was dripping down the broken glass.

"It looks like something."

"My ex," Izzy said, because she had to say something.

"I'm Louise Murphy. I live across the road."

Izzy tried to reply but broke out in a fit of coughing.

Not now. She'd had a bad morning, coughing until her sides ached.

Louise winced in disgust at the coughing, as if she thought she'd catch some terrible disease. Izzy was sick alright, but no virus or bacterium was responsible.

It was worse than that.

She turned towards the house, planning to get a drink, before remembering that she hadn't brought her stuff into the house yet. Was she going to be able to find a glass? She could feel her face growing pink as the coughing got worse. It felt like she'd cough up her lungs.

"Come to my place," Louise said. "I'll get something to soothe your throat."

Izzy gave a reluctant nod. They crossed the road together, with Louise craning her neck away from Izzy.

The gate outside Louise's house was painted a cheerful blue. Whereas the front garden of Elaine's house was paved stone, empty of life, Louise's had grass on both sides of the path to the door, and there were plenty of flower beds too. They were still mostly bare, but a few daffodil stems poked out of the soil, a hint of yellow visible at the tops.

As with Elaine's house, this one had half a dozen steps up to the entrance. Izzy followed Louise up them.

Inside the hall, a golden Labrador stood wagging his tail.

"Baxter hates the rain," Louise said. "He refuses to go walkies when it's wet."

Louise shook the rain off her umbrella, and stood it against the wall.

The hall was bright and airy, with pale pink walls and an elegant oval mirror inside the door. Izzy wiped her feet on the mat, then followed Louise to a well-equipped kitchen. This room too was bright and spacious, with large windows and light colours.

The worktop was covered in flour, margarine, eggs, a measuring jug, and an electric whisk. The air smelled of apples and old showband tunes were playing on a radio. It was like stepping into a different world, one far removed from the tension and silence Izzy knew.

She caught a glimpse of a tidy back garden through the window. Then Louise was pushing a glass of water into her hands. It felt icy.

"Can I have some warm water, please?"

"Of course."

Why did this stuff have to happen at inopportune moments? Izzy's boss, Mr. R, had noticed her difficulty lately, and he didn't look happy. No one wanted a waitress who struggled to carry orders and who coughed up her guts on a regular basis.

Louise turned on the kettle. Before it boiled, she turned it off again and topped up Izzy's glass.

She gestured for Izzy to sit down at the table. Clearly, Louise had been using the chair at the far end of the table, as a magazine sat there, open on a page with dessert recipes. The second chair had an apron thrown over its back, so Izzy chose chair number three, which was behind the door to the hall.

Louise closed the door so it wasn't in her way. Then Izzy sat down and sipped the water, finding the temperature just right.

Louise sat across from her. She waited patiently until the coughing eased.

All Izzy could hear was the hum of the fridge.

"Sorry about that," she said.

"It's fine." Louise broke out in a wide smile. "Did you buy that house? I didn't know it was up for sale."

"No. I'm Izzy O'Brien, the previous owner's niece. I'm moving in."

Louise frowned. "We were all so shocked at what happened to Elaine. I mean, to end her days like that... I'm so sorry."

"Thank you."

"Now that you mention it, I think I recognise you from the funeral."

"I'm sorry but I don't remember. I was such a mess that day."

"Of course."

Izzy noticed birthday cards on the shelves next to the kitchen table.

"Are those yours?"

"I was thirty-five yesterday."

"Really? You don't look a day over twenty-five."

"You're a terrible liar." Louise grinned. "I like that."

Izzy decided it was time to leave. "Thank you for the drink, but I better go."

Louise wagged her finger in front of Izzy's face.

"Not so fast. Are you going to tell me about Rambo out there? You need to report what he did. The Garda station isn't far from here—"

"Oh, no. It's not like that. He's not a danger."

Louise's eyebrows shot up. "That's not how it looked."

Izzy drank the last of the water in her glass. She hated being seen in such a state, with her health issues and her car crash of a relationship exposed. "I moved out of our apartment today. I... I left when he wasn't home."

"You poor thing." Louise reached across the table and took Izzy's hand in hers. "It sounds like things are far from ideal. Are you sure he isn't violent?"

"No. He's just an asshole." Izzy felt the heat come to her face. "I'm sorry."

"Believe me, Izzy, I've heard the word before, and I've met the type too."

"Glad it's not just me."

"Izzy, do you know anyone around here?"

"No. I lived in the city centre."

Louise leaned forward. "I want to ask you something—"

But Izzy didn't get to hear the question, because at that moment a door slammed. There were a few quick steps.

Then the door from the hall burst open.

Chapter 4

Around the time he parked outside his apartment building, Adam McGregor began to feel the pain in his shredded knuckles. He'd been oblivious till now, his outrage at Izzy's actions trumping all physical pain. Then, suddenly, the pain was *there,* and it was agony. Flaps of skin hung loose, and Adam could see the exposed flesh underneath, oozing blood. The more he looked at it, the sorer it felt.

He got out of the van. The apartment block rose above him. His gaze zeroed in on the second-floor balcony, third from the right. The balcony of his and Izzy's home.

But not anymore.

Everything had been going so well these last few years.

Although he'd grown up in a block of flats in Glasgow, which superficially resembled his current home, the two places were completely different.

Home in Scotland had been Maryhill. Everywhere had a place like that. In the U.S., they were the housing projects. In Ireland, council estates. In Glasgow, they were the schemes. The poorest, most deprived parts of the city.

Where Adam grew up, the neighbourhood's walls were graffitied with the names of local teens who'd gone to prison for murder. You were taking your life in your hands if you went out after dark, especially if you were a man. That was how Adam had earned his scar. A slash across the face by a lad from a rival gang. Typical Saturday night brawls in the schemes.

Adam had got out of there. He'd built a new life, started his own company and got a girl. Things were going so well... until now.

A bitter taste filled Adam's mouth, as he thought of how he'd fled Dun Laoghaire like a loser. He was glad none of the lads from Glasgow had seen that. He'd never have been able to hold his head up again.

Adam cracked his neck, looked around the car park.

The sound of a copper's car in Dun Laoghaire had spooked him. It made him think of PC Jim McDaid from Police Scotland. Adam hadn't thought of that bastard for a while, but he'd never forget McDaid's walrus moustache and garlic breath, as he slapped cuffs on Adam's wrists and whispered, *You're done, you wee bastard*, before shoving Adam into the back of his car.

Even now, the memory of it sent Adam into a rage. The injustice of it, horrible, making him gag, like oil in his mouth...

Adam hadn't known exactly what he was doing when he broke the glass in Izzy's car and jumped in his van. And he'd no idea where he was going as he drove away.

He should have been taking Izzy home with him, but instead she was holed up in her aunt's house, *laughing* at him.

With a final glance at his gory fist, Adam walked across the car park, entered the building, and made his way up the stairs to his floor.

He let himself into the apartment and closed the door. The place felt just like earlier, when he arrived home.

He'd left work early to surprise Izzy. It turned out he was the one getting a surprise. As soon as Adam set foot inside the place, he'd been struck by how empty it felt. Izzy should have been there, but she wasn't. He'd called her name, got no answer, and then seen that stuff was missing. Clothes, shoes, laptop. Her precious handbags, which she spent so many hours making.

She hadn't said a word to him.

Just vanished.

There was only one place she could have gone, so he'd followed her straight to the house she'd inherited from her aunt.

Well, that hadn't worked out so well.

Adam made his way to the kitchen, grabbed a bag of ice from the freezer, and held it to his knuckles.

The bouquet of flowers he'd bought Izzy sat on the counter.

He went back to the sitting room, seeing that Izzy

had left behind the set of accountancy books he'd bought her. He'd expected a little gratitude, but no. She'd hardly opened the books. It was like she wanted to be a waitress forever. She never even listened to his suggestion that she study bookkeeping while working at his company.

His heart felt physically sore, as if a pro boxer had taken it out of his chest and gone ten rounds with it.

Izzy had to come back.

This was crazy.

She couldn't walk out on him. He wouldn't be made a fool of by a woman.

He made his way to the bedroom, to the dresser on Izzy's side of the bed. The drawer had been full of her stuff. Some was still there. Some was gone.

Adam pulled the drawer out of the unit and up-turned it on the bed. All that was left was junk. She'd taken everything she needed.

Except...

Adam's heart soared as he realised that Izzy hadn't taken *everything* she needed. He smiled bitterly.

She'd be back.

And he wouldn't let her get away again.

Chapter 5

When the door of Louise Murphy's kitchen burst open, it swung towards Izzy so fast she thought it would hit her side. However, a rubber stopper on the floor protected her. The door hit the stopper and bounced back. It swung towards a large man who halted its movement with his hand.

He stepped into the room. Six foot one, six two. Impressive girth on him too. The guy had a beard and long, rust-coloured hair flecked with grey.

Not noticing Izzy, the man glared at Louise as he placed a fancy-looking gift box on the kitchen table. More than a foot wide and long, with red and blue stripes. A ribbon was tied around the box and a little white card rested on its lid.

"You're not going to believe this," he said.

Louise said, "Robert—"

"Listen to this." He plucked the card off the box with a delicate pinch of thumb and forefinger. With the card held in front of his eyes, he read, "Returning your gift. xxx."

Robert put his hands on his hips to emphasise

his indignation. He was squeezed into jeans that had clearly been bought when he was in better shape, and he wore a red plaid shirt, like he'd just finished a shift as a lumberjack. A beer gut hung over his belt, making him look heavily pregnant.

Louise said, "What does that mean? Where did you get it?"

"On the doorstep."

"We were only outside a moment ago—"

"Yeah, well, look at this." Robert untied the ribbon and removed the lid.

Louise leaned closer so she could see the contents of the box. Izzy did too. A pile of dog shit sat inside.

Izzy caught a whiff of it and gagged at the smell.

Louise put a hand to her nose.

"Are you crazy? Get that off the table."

"You know this is Melanie's work, don't you?"

"Robert—"

"I'm sick of her. Blaming Baxter every time a dog takes a dump on her grass. Does she think Baxter is the only dog in Dublin? Has she done a DNA test? And look at the ribbon. I mean—"

Louise raised her voice. "Robert, this is our new neighbour, Izzy."

The man went still, then slowly turned to face Izzy's end of the table. He gave a sheepish smile when he saw her.

"Sorry. I didn't know anyone was here." He held out his hand. "Nice to meet you."

Izzy said, "Maybe we... don't need to shake hands."

Robert nodded. "Right. Sorry."

Louise said, "For god's sake, would you wash your hands?"

"Yeah, as soon as I get rid of this." Robert picked up the box and brought it to the back door. He said over his shoulder, "One of our neighbours is a real piece of work. I guess you'll meet her soon enough."

He stepped out into the garden.

"I'm so sorry," Louise said. "What must you think of us?"

She jumped up and grabbed a bottle of antibacterial spray and a handful of tissues from a box on the counter. She sprayed copious amounts of surface cleaner all over the table. Izzy snapped her head back to avoid getting sprayed in the face.

Not seeming to notice, Louise wiped the surface with a handful of tissues. She dumped the tissues in the bin, then lathered up her hands and scrubbed them with a nailbrush. Her hands were pink and raw when she came back to the table.

Izzy heard Robert drop the box into a bin outside. He came back inside, passed his hands under the tap so fast they hardly got wet.

"You want some tea?" Robert said.

His eyebrows were dark, and his eyes were bright. He looked about forty, which would put him five years older than his wife.

"No, thanks," Izzy said. "I better go. I don't want to take up any more of your time." She got to her feet, took a step towards the door. "Thanks for the water. Nice to meet you both."

"I'll see you out," Louise said.

They walked down the hall. Izzy opened the door and stepped outside. Rain pattered on the street more lightly now. She turned to Louise, noticing the older woman's expression. It was hard to identify. Embarrassment, maybe.

"You have a lovely home," Izzy said, just to break the awkward silence. "So stylish."

Louise beamed. "Thank you. As an architect, I do enjoy living in this house, even if we're only renting it."

"An architect? Wow."

"Well, I'm on a career break at the moment, but that's my background."

Izzy nodded. She was about to turn away when Louise thrust her umbrella into Izzy's hands. "Take this. And listen, I run a little book club with a few friends from around here. I'd love you to join us."

Izzy shook her head. "I'm not sure—"

"Please say yes. We'd love to have you."

Maybe she could drop by for ten minutes.

"When is it?"

"Tonight, at eight o'clock. Right here in my house, so you've no excuse. You only need to cross the road."

"I'll see. I'm just moving in, so I need to unpack." Izzy shrugged. "Plus, I haven't read whatever book you'll be talking about."

"Oh, don't worry about that," Louise said, with laugh. "Most of us probably haven't either."

"I'll think about it."

"We're reading *A Study in Scarlet* by Arthur Conan Doyle. It's the first ever Sherlock Holmes book. Tess, the legal eagle of the group, suggested this one. You'll love her."

"Okay. Thanks."

"Don't forget that the library is just down the road. Do you know it? The dlr LexIcon?"

Izzy knew it. dlr stood for Dun Laoghaire-Rathdown, the name of the local administrative area, which swept from the Dublin Mountains down to the sea. And LexIcon was Dun Laoghaire's huge and relatively new library.

The County Council's decision to create such a space had been a matter of pride for Elaine, even though she hadn't been involved in the project. She had worked down at County Hall organising events in the region's public parks.

"My aunt was a regular visitor," Izzy said.

"Of course. Today's Thursday, so it's open till eight. I can show you the way if you like."

"No." The word came out more forcefully than Izzy had intended, but she was starting to feel exasperated. "Thank you, but I know where the library is. Over there, right?"

Izzy pointed diagonally, behind Louise's house, towards the sea.

"That's it." Louise smiled. "Remember, eight o'clock,

my house. You don't need to bring anything. Just come along, and we'll have a laugh. We always do."

Izzy opened the umbrella and walked away before Louise tried to reel her in again. She hurried across the road, past her car and its smashed-in window. Her running shoes slapped against the wet ground.

She let herself into Elaine's house.

"Home sweet home," Izzy said, just to break the silence.

The hall's hard wood floor and dark navy paint weren't any friendlier now than they'd been the last time she saw them.

Chapter 6

Melanie Flynn had only been home a couple of minutes when her phone rang. She was in her bedroom, hanging up her jacket, and thinking of running a bath.

It had been a long day at the salon, with one particularly difficult client, and the last thing she'd wanted to come home to was a big fat dog turd sitting in her lawn.

Robert did that just to annoy her. Brought that stupid Labrador to her garden and made him do his business on the lawn.

Melanie loved to take photos in the garden when the weather was good. She was sure that was why Robert made his dog crap there.

She walked across the room to her dresser, where she'd left her phone. Louise's name appeared on the display.

Melanie ran a hand through her hair, which had been freshly cut into a bob and dyed purple by Amy, one of her best employees at the salon.

Melanie thought about not answering the phone.

Just ignoring it. Truth was, though, she was starting to feel a little guilty about what she'd done.

She accepted the call.

"Louise, I'm sorry. I was just so angry."

"No, *I'm* sorry. I swear, I keep telling Robert not to walk Baxter anywhere near your house. I know he loves your garden. It's the nicest one in Dun Laoghaire. You know what a big softie Baxter is. He wouldn't do his business in your average garden. Nothing but the best will do for our Baxter."

Melanie laughed. "Yes, we all know how fussy he is." She sighed. "I shouldn't let Robert wind me up."

"Join the club."

They both laughed.

"That said, I'm not sure I'll come to the book club."

"What? We need you. Robert won't be home tonight. He's meeting some friends at Fitzgerald's."

Melanie wasn't surprised that Louise's husband planned to go to the pub. It was about as much as she expected from him. She was only surprised that he had found friends to accompany him.

"I don't know."

"Come on, Melanie. You know we all love having you here. Our celebrity book blogger. How is it going? Did you gain many new followers this week?"

"Nearly another thousand on Instagram," Melanie admitted. She knew Louise was only buttering her up. Despite herself, though, she couldn't help taking pride in her progress. "I was running a giveaway, so that got me some more."

"You're doing so well."

"Now I have thirteen thousand followers on Instagram. Only ten thousand on Twitter. The same on Facebook. And my blog is getting a lot of hits."

"All that in only a year? It's amazing."

Melanie's smile widened into a grin. It *was* amazing. Her social media had really taken off in the last few months. She'd only planned to share her love of books, but her account had exploded. Now people chose what to read based on her opinion.

"I don't know about amazing but..."

"Don't be so modest. Come along tonight and let us know your secrets. We have a new member."

"Oh? Who is it?"

"All will be revealed tonight."

"Huh," Melanie said, her curiosity aroused. "Keeping me in suspense, eh?"

"Have you finished the book?"

"Just a couple of chapters left. I'm going to finish it in the bath."

"You read so fast, I'm sure you'll be done in five minutes. How many books did you read last year? Two hundred?"

"One hundred and ninety-six," Melanie said. "Some of them were short, though."

"I wish I got through a quarter of that."

"Again, I'm sorry, Louise. I bought the box to put your birthday present in. And then, I just – I got mad."

"It's fine. Don't worry. I'll see you at eight, okay?"

Melanie smiled. "Okay."

As she ended the call, a car pulled up outside the house. She walked to the window and looked out. Her husband, Tom, stepped out of the car, swung his laptop bag over his shoulder and walked up to the door. He looked so neat in his suit and tie. But he wasn't afraid of showing his individuality too.

The sides of Tom's head were shaved to the scalp, while the top was long and flowing, a rich brown. He had a thick moustache which he'd taken to waxing neatly. Though his eyesight was perfect, Tom liked to wear a pair of stylish glasses.

A silver ring was set into each pierced ear and a tattoo of a snake coiled up the side of his neck, the creature's tongue just about concealed by the collar of his shirt. His suit trousers were cut short, showing funky multicoloured socks.

As soon as she heard the door open downstairs, she shouted down to him.

"Tom? I need you."

Without waiting for an answer, she stripped, then brought her photographic equipment to the bathroom and began to fill the claw-footed bathtub. It was one of her favourite features in the house.

The whole bathroom filled her with joy, ever since she and Tom had got it remodelled the previous year. It was all white tile, white ceramic, white painted ceiling. Nice and bright and clean, and it matched her social media vibe.

Tom's footsteps came up the stairs.

"Babe?"

"In here."

Tom appeared in the doorway. Though he was almost as short as her, they tried to hide that when they took pictures together.

Melanie thought it was important to reveal a bit about yourself when you were posting online. And people seemed to like Tom. He was more photogenic than her.

She bent over the bath to check the water's temperature.

Behind her, Tom whistled appreciatively.

"Oooh, this is what I like to come home to." Tom padded across the room and put his hands on her shoulders. Those strong hands were great at loosening the knots in her shoulders. But right now, Melanie needed him to do something else.

She straightened up, turned to face him. His smile widened as his eyes ran up and down her body. Her purple hair was almost the last thing his eyes registered.

"Cool 'do, babe."

"Ugh, you stink."

Tom sniffed his armpit. "Yep. Give me a second and I'll get in the tub with you."

"I have a better idea."

Melanie handed him a bottle of food dye and a battery-powered torch she'd ordered online. It had a circular bulb that gave a soft glow.

She turned off the water, grabbed her phone and

her hardback copy of *A Study in Scarlet*, and stepped into the tub.

"Aw, come on, Melanie. Not another photoshoot?"

She settled herself on her back. The water was perfect. She was careful to keep her phone and book from getting wet.

"You can add the dye now."

Tom sighed.

"Can't I just look at you for a while? You're so beautiful."

"No time. I want to post this online before the book club meeting, and I still have to think of a caption."

Tom cocked an eyebrow.

"Thought you hadn't finished reading the book?"

"I'll do a review later. This is only a teaser."

Tom upended the little bottle of dye and let the red liquid pour into the tub around Melanie's toes.

"What are you doing? Up here, Tom. No one wants to see my feet."

"Sorry."

He began to pour it over her chest.

"Splash it on the side of the tub so it looks like a proper crime scene."

He jerked the bottle a little too vigorously. What little dye remained splashed onto the floor.

"Oops."

"For god's sake!"

"We can take a picture of the floor. It looks like real blood."

Melanie closed her eyes and counted to five before

speaking. She had trained herself to do this whenever her husband acted like a fool. Some days she seemed to do nothing but count to five again and again.

"No one cares about our floor, Tom. They want to see the *tableau*."

"The tableau?"

"Our crime scene! Me and the book. Just point the light at me. And hand me that razor blade."

He gave *A Study in Scarlet* a dubious glance.

"There's no bathtub suicide in the book, is there?"

"Who cares? It's about the vibe."

The dye had turned the water a bright shade of pink, which was not what she had wanted at all. A few filters would need to be applied before she could post anything online.

The water was still quite translucent, so she'd have to cover her breasts. That was an idea. She'd use the book to cover her chest, while the bloody water swirled around her.

"Take the phone, Tom."

Her husband grinned. He placed the dye bottle at his feet and took her phone with his free hand.

She held the book over her chest. "How does this look?"

"Good."

Sometimes Melanie thought of all the people who had wronged her. She liked to imagine killing herself to make them pay, seeing their faces and hearing them regret their wrongs. She liked to think of them coming to her funeral, full of regret, while she sat in the coffin laughing at them.

She closed her eyes and leaned the back of her head against the cool ceramic.

Snap, snap, snap. If Tom took a hundred pictures, one or two might be usable.

"Show me."

He knelt next to the tub, held out her phone so she could see. The photos weren't what she wanted at all, but they'd have to do. She pulled the plug. "Okay, now clear off. I want to have a shower."

"No time for a bit of hanky-panky?"

"Nope. Go and make dinner."

Tom trudged out of the room as the water and fake blood drained from the bathtub.

Chapter 7

Izzy walked through the ground floor of Elaine's house. She was glad to be alone again. In the dining room, she stopped in front of a framed map on the wall. It showed Dun Laoghaire around the turn of the twentieth century.

Kingstown, read the caption.

That was one of the names the area had been known by over the years. It was Dunleary for a long time, but was renamed Kingstown in 1821, back when Ireland was under British control, to mark the visit of King George IV.

The name was changed to Dun Laoghaire in 1920, during the War of Independence. There were still plenty of reminders of the colonial past, though. Place names like George's Street and Queen's Road.

Izzy turned away from the map. There was nothing else interesting in the dining room, just a dark wood table and chairs. Izzy suspected that Elaine hadn't used the room much.

She walked to the sitting room, which had a more comfortable and used feel to it. For a moment, she paused by the overflowing bookshelf to see if Elaine had a copy of *A Study in Scarlet*. No luck. Her aunt's tastes had been a little more highbrow than Sherlock Holmes.

There was something about the shelf, something weird, but Izzy wasn't sure what.

She winced. Her stomach pain was bad today. She did her best to block it out and distract herself by resuming her exploration of the house.

Izzy remembered running around these same rooms when she was five or six years old. Her cousin, David, had been a year younger. They loved chasing each other through the house while Uncle Andrew watched in amusement and Elaine tut-tutted.

A tightness gripped Izzy's chest when she saw a photo of Elaine, Andrew and David on the mantel-piece.

It had been taken in Cyprus only days before the accident.

The trip was meant to be a family holiday, but Izzy had refused to go. She'd been twenty years old, and asserting her independence mattered more than any-thing else. The decision to stay at home had saved her life.

What saved Elaine was that she'd been sick on the day of the accident. She remained in her hotel room while her husband, her son, and Izzy's parents went on the bus tour.

Izzy still remembered the call from Cyprus. Re-membered rolling her eyes when she heard the phone ring. Her parents had called her three times that week already. There was a long, long pause when she answered. Finally, Elaine's trembling voice crackled over the line.

"Izzy, there's been..." The sound of Elaine swallowing, before she forced herself to continue. "There's been an accident."

After tumbling over the edge of a cliff, the bus had rolled multiple times and come to rest a hundred feet below. Seven people had died, including Izzy's entire family, except for Elaine.

A decade later, Elaine was gone too.

Izzy shook off the memory and made her way to the kitchen. Finding a glass in the cupboard, she rinsed it, filled it with water, and slumped in a chair at the kitchen table.

She took her box of hydroxychloroquine out of her pocket, opened it up, and slid out the blister pack of a dozen 200mg film-coated tablets.

Sjögren's, the autoimmune condition she'd been diagnosed with, was more common than Izzy would have guessed. It was related to lupus and rheumatoid arthritis and it affected millions and millions of people, although Izzy had never heard of the condition until her doctor said she had it.

Her body was attacking itself, affecting her glands and, possibly, her organs. Hydroxychloroquine was the only thing her doctor could prescribe, but it made her dizzy.

She put the pills back in her pocket without taking one.

She looked around the room. The last time she'd been in this house was December. She and Adam came and cleared out some of Elaine's stuff. It was a blur now, but she remembered that they hadn't got much done.

The plan had been to return and finish the job soon afterwards, but Izzy stalled, despite Adam urging her to sell the place. The more he'd insisted, the more Izzy began to wonder about him.

A gloomy feel swept over the kitchen as the light began to fade.

Home, sweet home.

Izzy plugged the fridge in. She was relieved when the light inside came on and the machine began to hum. She tried the kettle and the microwave, and they seemed fine. Of course, it was only a couple of months since Elaine had died. Everything *should* be okay. Izzy hadn't even had the power disconnected.

She went out to her car and brought her stuff in, one black sack at a time, dumping them unceremoniously in the hallway. By the time she was done, her back had joined her stomach in screaming at her.

Her jeans and socks were soaking wet from the rain, so she found dry clothes in one of her plastic bags and changed into them.

She hadn't even been upstairs yet, and she wasn't very enthusiastic about changing that. A vague sense of claustrophobia had begun to choke her. She wanted to get out of the house.

Perhaps she would check out the library, like Louise suggested, and afterwards she could visit the super-market to pick up something to eat. That was better than standing around waiting for Adam to come back.

*

Outside, Izzy crossed the road, passing Louise's house quickly. The rain had eased off but it was cloudy and there was a strong wind. She ducked down the lane and soon reached the library. A long, sprawling building, full of unusual angles, clad in red brick on one side and granite on the other.

Izzy passed through the revolving door. On the other side was a massive space with a high ceiling and huge windows. Every surface was varnished wood.

There were surprisingly few books visible, but Izzy hadn't been in a library for years. The place certainly had plenty of computers, however, and self-checkout machines.

She walked past a huge staircase. Chairs faced towards the windows on the left side. Half a dozen old folk were sitting in this area, a few of them reading newspapers, one or two with their heads buried in novels. It was hard not to imagine Elaine sitting there, reading and looking out over the small park next to the library.

Izzy noticed that the seats were flanked by shelves of crime novels. She looked in the C and D sections but found no Conan Doyle, so returned to the staircase, climbed it, and came out in another huge room at the top.

A few librarians were sitting at desks in front of her.

Izzy walked up to the huge window at the end of the building. The view was spectacular, taking in the harbour and the East Pier in the foreground. Farther away, she could look across Dublin Bay to Howth, north of the city.

To the side of the stairs, there was an area with dozens of study spaces facing the window. Books lined the remaining walls. Izzy soon found a volume of Conan Doyle's complete Sherlock Holmes novels and stories.

Grunting when she felt its weight, Izzy hauled it to the nearest librarian's desk.

A thirty-something woman, with mousy brown hair down to her shoulders, looked up. She gave Izzy an inquisitive smile, her eyes sparkling through a pair of thick-framed glasses.

"Can I help you?"

"I'd like to rent this book."

"We call it *borrowing*," the woman said. "No rent needed."

"Right," Izzy said. "I knew that. It's just been a while."

She handed the book to the librarian, who stared when she saw the cover.

"I don't suppose you know Louise Murphy?"

Izzy frowned. "She's the only person I do know around here."

"And is this a book club pick by any chance?"

"How did you know?"

The woman broke out laughing. It was a kind of hushed laugh she must have perfected, working where she did.

"I'm one of the regular gang. Louise sent a message around on the WhatsApp group a few minutes ago and said we've got a new member coming tonight."

Mystery solved. "Nice to meet you. I'm Izzy O'Brien."

"Dee Philips."

She looked vaguely familiar.

Izzy said, "I didn't actually say I'd go to the book club."

"Please do. We'd love to have you. You're Elaine O'Farrell's niece, aren't you?"

There was a rush of excitement in Dee's voice.

"Yes. You were at her funeral," Izzy said, beginning to remember.

"I was. We spoke briefly. Of course, you were very upset."

"Your mother... Paula... she was the one who found Elaine..."

Like Elaine, Paula Philips was a civil servant down at County Hall. The two women had worked together. Izzy remembered Paula coming up to her at the funeral. She'd presented herself as Elaine's best friend, though Izzy suspected that was a stretch.

"So can I borrow the book?" Izzy said, eager to avoid a conversation about her aunt.

"Sure." Dee said, "I take it you're not a member of the library?"

"I'm not."

"No problem. I'll get you signed up in no time. We just need some ID from you. Do you have your passport?"

That was when Izzy realised that no, she didn't have her passport. It was in the bedside unit at Adam's place.

"Are you okay?" Dee said. "You look like you just saw a ghost."

Without answering, Izzy turned and walked quickly to the exit.

Chapter 8

Kate Long kept a superior smile on her face as Tess walked her across the law firm's huge lobby. She added a little swing to her hips, her heels clacking as she crossed the gleaming marble floor. She could feel the security guard's eyes running over her body, admiring her. At the door to the street, Kate paused.

"See you later," she said.

Tess nodded grimly, then turned and walked away.

Once Kate was on the footpath outside, her face slumped into a grimace. Her skin prickled with a white-hot rage. She squeezed her handbag tight. Traffic sounds filled her ears but that wasn't the source of her anger.

Clearly Tess thought Kate was a whore. Kate was sure she was the first person Tess thought of when she decided she wanted to test her boyfriend.

The cold air prickled against Kate's legs. Her top was light, considering the weather, just a black blazer over her thin dress. The breeze seemed to pass right through her.

She was still burning with resentment when her phone buzzed with a text message from her husband.

I need to talk to you tonight, Stephen's message read.

Kate sighed so loudly that a man passing by paused to look at her. She ignored him and stared at the phone as another message from Stephen arrived.

It's important.

What was he on about now? She ran her fingers through her hair.

What a day.

She felt low after that audition. The casting director had kept her waiting for hours, then played with his phone during the thirty-second audition.

And now this? Her friend wanted to use her as a honey trap?

Her eyes burning with humiliation, she set off walking towards O'Connell Street, where she could catch the bus to Dun Laoghaire. The wide street was filled with its usual array of junkies, drunks, losers, beggars and idiots.

The digital display indicated that a bus would come in two minutes. Kate stood a little back from the stop so she wouldn't be too close to a noisy bunch of young men.

She wondered what the hell Stephen wanted to talk about now. He always seemed to want to talk. Kate blamed herself for this. She had once told him to express his feelings, to let it all out. She hadn't actually expected him to do it, but he really took her words to heart. What a pain in the ass that was.

Now that she thought about it, he'd been acting weirder than usual lately, but she'd put it down to the stress of his job. Stephen worked in public relations, dealing with some very high-profile people. Not so high-profile that they'd been any help to Kate, of course.

But what if it was something besides Stephen's career?

Was he ill? He seemed to have lacked energy lately.

Just then, a bus approached. The doors wheezed open as Kate joined the queue to get on. There were about twenty people ahead of her in the line and the bus already looked full. She'd probably end up standing the whole way home.

Checking the time on her phone, Kate realised that Stephen must be nearly finished with work. Perhaps she'd head to his office. It wasn't far away.

He might not be finished for the day. He often did overtime, saying he didn't mind, even saying his colleagues were like his family, but Kate might convince him to leave on time and drive them both home. That would be more comfortable than the bus.

Kate set off walking through the evening bustle, moving west along the quays, until she came to the Four Courts, then ducked up a narrow road towards Stephen's building.

The outer door was open, allowing her to enter the deserted lobby. It was nothing like the impressive lobby of Tess's firm. This one was cramped and worn, with a peeling linoleum floor.

Kate had been here once before. Stephen's company was on the second floor.

She rode an elevator up, stepped out, and walked past the unmanned reception desk. Nobody was at their desk in the open-plan office, but Kate heard cheerful voices.

She followed the sound down the corridor. The murmur of voices was interrupted by a smattering of applause.

Kate kept following the sound until she reached the doorway of a break room. Half a dozen people stood inside with their backs to Kate.

Stephen stood behind a table, cutting a cake. His colleagues, all well-groomed young professionals, were gathered around him.

Stephen looked dashing in his pale blue shirt and dark trousers.

"You have no idea how good this feels," Stephen said. A lopsided grin was plastered across his smooth face as he leaned over the cake, drawing the knife through it to cut the first slice. His blond hair had grown longer lately, and a long strand of his fringe fell over his eyes. He pushed the hair back with one hand, his smile only growing wider.

Kate hadn't seen him look so happy in ages.

"We're all so proud of you," a woman said.

Kate stepped forward and read the words, "Happy birth" written on the cake in icing.

Someone had printed huge individual letters on A4 sheets and strung them across the ceiling.

H-E-L-L-O-S-T-E-P-H-A-N-I-E.

"Well done," someone called.

Stephen put the first slice of cake on a plate and held it out to someone. "Cake for my dear friends," he said.

At that moment, his eyes locked on Kate's.

The plate slipped out of his hand and fell on the table. Someone gasped and another person laughed. Stephen's gaze remained locked on his wife. Everyone else followed his gaze.

"Hi everyone," Kate said. She stepped forward, forcing herself to smile. Stephen's colleagues stepped out of her way. "What's going on?"

Stephen stared at her. The chocolate-smeared knife was still held in his hand. Everyone remained silent, so silent it seemed they were holding their breath.

Kate said, "I got your text messages. Is everything ok?"

"Yeah. Great."

"So?"

He took a breath. "I didn't want to tell you like this—"

"Who's Stephanie?"

"She's... It's... Okay, so I've been preparing a speech, but—"

"What kind of speech?" Kate couldn't help interrupting, though she wasn't sure she wanted to hear her husband's answer.

Stephen blinked rapidly a few times.

"So, like all human beings, I... I want to live *authentically*... For a while now, a long while actually, I—"

"What?" Kate's stomach churned. Her face flushed, then the heat became icy cold. "What are you babbling about?"

She became aware that everyone else was slipping out of the room, avoiding eye contact as they passed her. After a moment she and Stephen were alone. Stephen swallowed loud enough that Kate could hear it.

"This is going to be hard for you to hear, but I've come to realise that I'm... I'm a woman."

"What? *What* are you saying to me?"

Stephen swallowed again. When his prominent Adam's apple bobbed, Kate felt like ripping it out of his throat.

"Oh, man." Stephen gave a giddy laugh. "It feels so good to say it. *I identify as a woman.*"

"I don't give a shit if you identify as a fucking potato. You're my husband."

Stephen put down the knife and came around the table. His hands reached out to Kate.

"Don't touch me," she said, backing away.

"Kate—"

"A minute ago, I was a sex goddess and now—"

"You were what—?"

"Shut up. And now you're telling me I'm married to a woman? Am I lesbian all of a sudden? You decided you're a woman and now I'm gay? Is that it, you bastard?"

"It's not like I *decided* to feel this way."

Stephen's tone was mildly reproachful.

"I'm such an idiot," Kate said. "How could you marry me?"

"I love you. Please believe me. I love you."

"But you're a woman, right? Are you going to leave me for another man?"

"That's not what this is about."

Tears came to Kate's eyes. "You want to leave me?"

"No. I already said *no*. Now... let's take it one step at a time. This all must be quite a shock."

"You turned into a woman and now you're leaving me?"

"Kate—"

Her hands were shaking. Her voice was too. She couldn't believe what she was hearing.

"Do you remember your wedding vows, Stephen?"

"Yes."

"Do you remember that bit, *Till death do us part*?"

Stephen nodded slowly. "Yeah," he said. "I remember that."

Chapter 9

Once outside the library, Izzy slowed to a brisk walk. She was furious at herself for leaving her passport at Adam's apartment. She'd have to return for it some time, but not now.

She made her way to the main street. There was a grittiness to it that reminded her of the city centre. Shabby old buildings lined both sides of the street. Plenty of the shopfronts were boarded up and copious vegetation grew from the chimney pots.

Izzy walked past a shop covered in Chinese characters. It had a poster showing a woman getting acupuncture.

She stopped when she came to another shop that looked similar. *Zhao Traditional Chinese Medicine.* A price list on the window indicated a dizzying array of treatments.

She'd heard varying reports about Chinese medicine. Everything from it being a cure-all to superstitious nonsense, with medicines that contained toxic substances such as mercury. But, at this stage, Izzy was ready to try anything. A year of chronic pain was sapping her will to live.

Swallowing her doubts, Izzy pushed through the door. A middle-aged Chinese couple manned the counter. Behind them, shelves were filled with dozens of glass jars containing herbs.

The man was talking in Chinese to a female customer. He wore a white doctor's coat over a grey shirt and baggy chinos.

The lady beside him glanced at Izzy. She was sitting at an angle on a swivel chair so Izzy could only see one side of her face. Small and birdlike, she had a narrow nose. Her tiny ear disappeared into lustrous black hair. She too wore a white coat.

"*Huān yíng guāng lín.*"

Izzy walked up to her. "Sorry. Do you speak English?"

The woman stared mutely back.

"I'm not sure if you can help me? I have a problem with my—"

The woman turned on her swivel chair. Izzy saw that she was holding a phone to her ear.

"Never mind," Izzy said. "I'll come back another time."

Shielding the mouthpiece of her phone with one hand, the woman called behind her.

Izzy was about to leave when a young Chinese man appeared from the corridor. He was tall, with a smooth face, prominent cheekbones, and messy black hair. Maybe in his late twenties. Wearing a long-sleeved T-shirt, jeans and runners.

He sighed, like he was doing this under duress, and came up to the counter.

"Help you?" he said. No trace of a Chinese accent. He sounded more Irish than Izzy did. "How may the Zhao family be of service? Oops, forgot my badge." The guy took a name badge out of his pocket and stuck it on his chest. *Dylan Zhao*, it read. "Here we are. Professional service."

Izzy gave him a summary of the symptoms she'd been suffering, her diagnosis, and how her doctor's prescription was making her feel worse. She took the packet of hydroxychloroquine tablets out of her pocket and set it down on the counter.

By the time she finished, the other customer had left, and the man had joined Dylan. A moment later, the woman finished her phone call and turned her attention to Izzy too. Based on the resemblance, Izzy decided the three people in front of her were father, mother and son.

Mrs. Zhao examined the pills, then glanced at Dylan and spoke in rapid Chinese.

Dylan opened a laptop. "Sjögren's is the English name?"

Izzy only nodded as he seemed to be talking to himself.

Dylan continued typing on his laptop. "Nasty bugger. Take a seat and we can do a preliminary examination."

"Now?" Izzy had only expected to make an appointment. She didn't realise she'd be examined.

"No better time," Dylan said. He walked to a bare wooden chair just inside the window. Under his watchful gaze, she sat down.

Mr. Zhao washed his hands at a small sink and then came over to this side of the counter and crouched in front of Izzy. *Wei Zhao*, said the badge on his white coat.

"Please, stick out your tongue."

She did.

Dylan said, "The tongue and face are closely related to the six *fu* organs and the five *zang* organs, so we examine their vitality, checking the abundance of *qi*."

Izzy could only grunt to show she had heard, as she was still sticking her tongue out. When Mr. Zhao had finished looking at that, he went on to examine her eyes, ears, nose, lips, throat, hair and skin. He took her pulse. Then he asked her a thousand questions. Questions about pain, sweating, lifestyle and diet. Even questions about bowel movements. He was nothing if not thorough.

"Do you agree with my doctor's diagnosis?" Izzy said when he was done.

Mr. Zhao was silent for a moment. Then he said, "We use a different system, which has its own terminology. I am sure that you have heard of *yin* and *yang*." He went on to explain his view of Izzy's condition, but she found the unfamiliar terms and ideas hard to follow. Mr. Zhao said, "Let me consult with my wife. She can prepare medicine that will help you to recover. It is part of your treatment, together with physical therapy. Do you wish to continue?"

Izzy nodded. She was willing to try anything.

Mr Zhao went behind the counter and spoke to his wife. As he talked, she began to take down some of the jars on the shelf and tip them into a container.

"What's he saying?" Izzy said to Dylan, who was standing next to her.

"The usual stuff." He rolled his eyes. "Your body is out of balance. Don't get me wrong. I'm sure Dad's right. I just hear it a lot, you know? Don't worry, though. This stuff works."

"You really think you can help?"

Dylan cocked an eyebrow. "Thousands of years of tradition can't be wrong. And it sounds like we couldn't do any worse than your doctor."

"How long will treatment take?"

"No way to tell," Dylan said with a shrug. "We need to see how it goes. Today we'll prepare the herbs. To-morrow you come back for physical therapy. The first session—"

Izzy pulled out her phone so she could make a note of what was being said. But when she saw the screen, a roaring sound filled her ears.

For a moment, it blocked out Dylan's voice.

There was a text message from Hannah, another waitress at the diner where Izzy worked.

Adam is here.

Chapter 10

As darkness fell, Adam McGregor had parked his van on a side street in the south inner city, around the corner from Shake, the diner where Izzy worked. He jumped out and slammed the door behind him.

A taxi shot past, nearly knocking Adam down. He shouted at the driver but the car didn't stop. Lucky bastard.

He walked towards Shake. The street was typical of Dublin's city centre, with its three and four-storey terraced buildings in red brick, most of them with a shop on the ground floor and offices overhead. Sometimes he hated the city, and this was one of those times.

Compared to Glasgow, it felt small and suffocating.

Adam hadn't been able to stand being alone at home, so he'd slipped Izzy's passport in his pocket and driven here. She'd need the passport some time. As long as he kept it with him, she'd have no choice but to meet him eventually.

Then he'd talk some sense into her.

Why was she doing this? Had he not given her everything she wanted? Constant attention, security and companionship. It killed him to think of her walking out on him. What would his friends say? Izzy was making a fool of him.

Well, he was going to her workplace now. Not to meet her, of course. He knew she wouldn't be there. But her friend, Hannah, might be. Adam wondered if she had put the idea of leaving in Izzy's head. He wouldn't be surprised. She'd never liked him.

Adam's shredded knuckles were sore now. He'd popped a couple of painkillers back at the apartment, but they did nothing.

Shake came into view ahead. It was modelled on American diners from the '50s. It was all curved chrome and shining neon.

Adam walked past the door, scanning the interior as he went by. He caught sight of Hannah serving a couple of people at a booth. You couldn't miss her big head, with all the hair shaved off.

Adam came to a stop. He was trembling with rage. He closed his eyes and imagined punching Hannah till she was dead.

That made him feel better.

He opened his eyes and pushed through the door of the diner. Elvis played on the bubble jukebox. The air was full of the smell of fried chicken.

The booths were covered in blood-red vinyl, which Adam liked. He had been here a few times when Izzy was working. In fact, it was how he'd met her. At lunch one day, Izzy had been his waitress. There was a vulnerability about her that made him want to take care of her.

He had charmed her, swept her off her feet. She'd moved in with him almost immediately, as the lease on her own apartment was nearly up. If only her aunt, Elaine, and her colleague, Hannah, had liked him. Instead, they insisted on meddling.

At the far end of the counter, Hannah was making a milkshake. Her eyes flitted from the blender to Adam, then quickly back to the blender.

Adam stood next to the sign that said *WAIT TO BE SEATED*. After a while, he got impatient.

"Hey," he said. Hannah didn't lift her head. Maybe she hadn't heard him over the music. "Hey, Hannah?"

His voice couldn't help betraying his anger.

Without lifting her head, Hannah turned and walked away from the shake machine, disappearing through a doorway marked *STAFF ONLY*. She was avoiding him. Maybe that was proof that this had all been her idea.

They'd met her socially a couple of times, and she'd always had a face like a lemon when she saw him. That was before he'd persuaded Izzy to forget about going to pubs. Much better for her to stay at home with him. There were so many creeps around.

He walked the length of the restaurant and went up to the door Hannah had just gone through. He tried the handle, found it locked.

"Hannah? We need to talk." Adam banged his fist against the door. It exploded in pain again. *Fuck.* He kept forgetting his wound. Blood was already soaking through his bandages. He switched to the other fist, banged again. "Hannah?"

A deep man's voice came from behind him.

"What are you doing? Get away from that door."

Adam turned to see a balding man about sixty years old. What little hair he had was combed neatly back. A white short-sleeved shirt covered his tubby upper body. A classic anchor tattoo covered one forearm. This was the famous Mr. R – Gino Romano, Izzy's boss. His eyes went straight to the scar on Adam's cheek, then quickly assessed the rest of him.

Adam said, "I need to talk to Hannah."

"You ain't staff," he said in a loud New Jersey accent. "Get away from there."

Izzy said Mr. R. was a real hard-ass. He used to be in the marines, back in the States. Though he'd gone a bit flabby with age, he still had the look of a guy who could handle himself.

Adam said, "Could you call Hannah down here?"

Mr. R squinted. "I know you, don't I?"

"Yeah, I'm Izzy's boyfriend."

"She ain't here today. What table you at?"

"I don't have a table."

"You ain't eating?"

"No."

Mr. R's arm shot out. His index finger jabbed at the door like he wanted to poke it from twenty feet away.

"Out."

"I—"

"Out."

"Arsehole," Adam muttered as he walked past.

"Say that to my face. I'll box your ears."

A surge of adrenaline pulsed down Adam's arms. He wanted to smack the bastard, but he stopped himself. Izzy was his priority. Getting her back.

Ignoring Mr. R., he walked past the booths and stools. Everyone was looking at him. Laughing at him. Adam felt his blood pressure soar. He pushed through the door to the street. Did it so hard, the door smashed against the wall.

The road was empty, so he stepped out onto it and looked back at the building. His eyes moved to the upstairs windows. Hannah was silhouetted against the window on the second floor, phone to her ear.

She must be talking to Izzy right now, poisoning her mind, turning her against him. He'd always suspected that Hannah was a dyke, and this just proved it. She probably wanted Izzy to herself.

Adam would make sure that never happened.

Izzy belonged to him.

Chapter 11

In the Chinese shop, Izzy leaned against the wall and read Hannah's text again. *Adam is here.* It could mean only one thing: trouble. She hit the call button and moved to the door.

"Back in a minute," Izzy called over her shoulder.

Dylan said, "Make it twenty. We need time to get your medicine ready."

She stepped out onto the street while the phone rang.

Though the air was still cold, it was no longer rainy. Darkness had fallen, though, and Izzy was momentarily blinded by the headlights of the cars and buses.

Why was Hannah taking so long? Izzy's pulse accelerated. What if Adam had done something terrible?

What if he had gone berserk?

Finally, Hannah answered, her voice breathless as she spoke. "Izzy?"

"What happened? Is he there?"

"It's the weirdest thing. I saw him walk by, like he was checking the place out. Then, a few seconds later, he came in and started calling my name. I thought he was going to cause a scene."

"What did you do?"

"The only thing I could do. I abandoned the customers and ran upstairs to hide."

Hannah gave a nervous laugh.

"Where is he now? Is he still there?"

Hannah sighed. "I don't know. Hang on, I'll look out the window. Oh, shit! He's standing on the street. I think he just saw me."

"Bloody hell."

"So you did it? You went to your aunt's house?"

"Yeah, but Adam guessed where I'd gone. He arrived there about two minutes after I did. He went crazy. Even put his fist through my car window."

"That's nuts."

"I know."

There was some muffled shouting on the line.

Hannah said, "I have to go. Mr. R. is calling me. Catch you later."

Izzy put her phone away and stood for a moment. She'd never thought Adam would react so explosively. It made her wonder how well she really knew him.

Since the Zhaos needed time to prepare her medicine, Izzy walked down the road.

She came to a bookshop, the kind of place that sold cheap out-of-copyright classics. They had plenty of Conan Doyle titles, including *A Study in Scarlet*.

Izzy bought a copy, slipped the paperback in her handbag, and continued to the supermarket. Walking around it, Izzy remembered that there was nothing in her aunt's house. She felt like grabbing everything she saw. Coffee, bread, meat, vegetables, tissues, toilet paper. And she'd better get something for Louise's birthday.

The aisles were busy with the after-work crowd. There were people everywhere. Strangers. It was dizzying.

What if Adam appeared out of the crowd? He'd grab her, squeeze her throat until—

Get a grip, Izzy.

She leaned against a freezer to steady herself. Coldness crept up her fingertips. She straightened up, did her best to shake off the anxiety, and made her way to the checkout.

Walking back down the road, Izzy's arms and back ached from the weight of her shopping.

Before her health became an issue, she and Hannah often had competitions at the diner, seeing who could carry the most food. It had been six months since Izzy had even pretended to compete.

Back at the Chinese shop, she staggered through the door as Dylan placed a bag on the counter.

"Ah, you're here. Your herbs are ready." He reached under the counter and pulled out some papers. "Now, we need to take your details. Let's get some forms filled in."

Izzy took a step towards him, feeling breathless and dizzy.

The bags seemed impossibly heavy. The world began to spin.

Dylan's frown was the last thing she saw before she blacked out.

Chapter 12

Kate stepped out of the taxi and slammed the door behind her. Standing on the footpath for a moment, she watched the car move away. Then she strode up to the entrance to the apartment building where she and Stephen – yes, *his* name was *Stephen*, damn it – lived.

She keyed in the door's code. The interior of the building was chilly and unwelcoming. Kate ignored the post boxes and walked straight to the elevator.

As the lift ascended, Kate fumed. She remembered the elevator ride up to Stephen's office.

Stephen. Stephanie.

She couldn't believe what that bastard was doing to her. She was in her prime. She could have had her pick of men and she had chosen one who was a woman.

Worst of all, Kate was the only one who didn't know.

Stephen's colleagues had been there, happy as hell, celebrating whatever the fuck it was called when a guy decided he was a chick. A coming out party? A gender reveal party?

Happy birth, the stupid cake had said.

Whatever the occasion was called, Kate hadn't been invited. Stephen was celebrating with the people who actually knew him.

Now she understood his text messages. He must have planned to break the news to her later. He'd celebrate with his friends and commiserate with his partner. They'd been having a grand time till she came along.

Stephanie.

"Fuck," Kate snarled, as the elevator doors opened, revealing her elderly neighbour, Mrs. Lynde, in the corridor, waiting to go down. Mrs. Lynde flinched.

Kate brushed past, nearly knocking the walking stick out of her hand.

She strode down the hall to her apartment and let herself in. It was exactly as she'd left it, and yet everything was different now.

Kate kicked off her shoes and walked down the hall to the kitchen.

She poured a glass of white wine, and knocked it back, her hand shaking all the while. The rim of the glass clicked against her front teeth. Her chest rose and fell in shallow, unsatisfying breaths.

Her phone rang. She pulled it out and checked the screen. Stephen. She rejected the call.

It rang again at once. She was sure it would be him again, but this time it was her mother. Kate knew she'd keep calling until she got some kind of answer, so Kate picked up.

"I can't talk," she said, and ended the call.

She powered the device down for good measure, then poured another half glass of wine and walked into the bedroom, her footsteps muffled by the rug on the floor. The duvet at Stephen's side of the bed was pulled down and the faint outline of his body was still visible on the mattress.

Should she have known earlier?

Were there clues?

Kate stepped out the door onto the balcony. The concrete footpath was thirty-five or forty feet below her. And beyond the neighbouring buildings, the dark sea churned.

Her marriage to Stephen had been rushed. She'd been on the rebound, eager to hurt her previous boy-friend, who had dumped her. Stephen had been so handsome, so kind, so goddamn clean and neat, that she should have known it would never work out.

He'd obviously had his doubts too. All those panic attacks, all that anxiety. He always put it down to stress, but now she knew what was behind his suicide threats. She winced thinking of all the times she had reassured him that he was a great guy, that he had a lot to give, a lot to live for.

Kate needed to vent. Lucky that tonight was book club night. She just needed to hold on a little longer. Then she could tell everyone what a bastard Stephen was.

She brought the glass to her lips. Another few mouthfuls of wine went down easy. She was getting a slight buzz from the alcohol now.

Maybe she'd walk the pier to kill the time till the book club. She loved the pier, especially at night.

Or maybe she'd do something else that would make her feel better. Something that would make her feel like a woman.

Kate had momentarily forgotten about Tess's request. But now it seemed like the timing was perfect.

She decided to check if Gareth was at his house. She'd told Tess she'd have an answer for her tonight, so why not do exactly that? And Stephen would see that Kate could have any man she wanted.

*

Adam smashed his phone against the steering wheel. Izzy still wasn't picking up. He was sitting in his van, just around the corner from the diner.

The skin of his face prickled hot and cold as he thought of how he'd been kicked out by Mr. R., how Hannah had ignored him when he called her name, how Izzy had walked out on him without a word.

All those losers were treating him like garbage.

It was Thursday and Thursday was poker night. He always had friends over. And Izzy was always sitting next to him, his own little good luck charm. She prepared the drinks and snacks and greeted everyone.

He couldn't do poker night without her, and there was no sign that she was about to come back. Not yet.

He quickly sent a text message to his friends.

Sorry, lads. Got a dodgy stomach. No poker this evening.

When he was done, he threw the phone on the

passenger seat next to him. He ignored the beeps as his friends replied. He didn't care what they said. Adam's only concern was getting Izzy back, so things could get back to normal.

He started the engine. He'd go to Dun Laoghaire again and set things right.

Chapter 13

Izzy found herself in a heap on the floor of the Chinese shop. Disoriented, dizzy. She closed her eyes but that made it worse, so she blinked rapidly, trying to clear her blurry vision.

"Oh man, she fainted."

Izzy looked up to find Dylan leaning over her. He took her hands, pulled her up.

"I'm fine," she said, though she hardly managed to get the words out. "I didn't faint."

"Yeah, right."

Mr. Zhao pulled a chair out from behind the counter and Dylan helped her to sit in it, like she was feeble. Mrs. Zhao pushed a cup of tea into her hands.

"I'm fine, really," Izzy said.

The biggest danger was that she'd die of embarrassment, but Mrs. Zhao was practically tipping the tea into her mouth, so she drank it.

The family were all standing staring at Izzy. She gave herself a moment to let the dizziness pass.

"Your body is out of balance," Mrs. Zhao said in

a thick accent. The woman's birdlike face was stern. "We need to restore the balance."

Izzy nodded. When she was feeling better, she accepted a clipboard and pen from Mrs. Zhao. She set about filling in the form for new patients, then paid for the medicine.

"You should not carry so much," Mrs. Zhao scolded her, glancing scornfully at her shopping bags. "You will hurt yourself."

Izzy tried to keep the irritation out of her voice. "I can carry my shopping."

"No, you cannot!" Mrs. Zhao snapped. "You need to protect your health."

She spoke to Dylan in rapid Chinese, then stormed off down the corridor. Scary lady, Izzy thought. She stretched and felt her mind clear.

Dylan said, "I'm to escort you home when you're ready."

"It's not necessary. I can carry my things the rest of the way. It's not far."

"Good luck telling my mom that," he said. "I've never had much luck changing her mind about anything. And what about them?" Dylan pointed to two huge bags standing on the counter. "Can you carry the medicine too?"

Izzy looked at the bags.

"I guess you can help just this once."

Dylan took her groceries and let her carry the two bags of medicine. They turned out to be light, despite their size.

"Thank you," Izzy said to Mr. Zhao, who was sitting behind the counter tapping away on his laptop. She gave a nod that almost turned into a bow, a gesture she immediately regretted.

Dylan broke out laughing. "No need to kowtow."

They stepped out of the shop. Dylan pulled up the hood of his jacket as if he didn't want anyone to see him.

Izzy led the way. She walked quicker than usual because of Dylan's long stride and the bored expression on his face. They passed the church and the old shopping centre on the corner of Marine Road.

"It's not much farther," Izzy said.

"Whatever."

Dylan was still walking behind her. She slowed her pace a little so that he came up alongside her.

"Do you work with your family full time?"

He broke out laughing. "God, no. I'm just helping out while I'm home."

"What do you mean?"

"I went back to college to do an MBA. It's pretty intense, but it's only for one year. I need to save money on rent so I'm living with my family again."

"That's cool."

"Not really. I used to be in a band. *That* was cool, except I had no money. How about you? What's your ambition?"

"I don't really have one," Izzy lied.

"Nothing? No dream?"

"Uh, I like crafts," Izzy said. "I made this handbag."

She showed him the silver bag with its gold-coloured chain, and a gold heart on each side. Dylan looked unimpressed and they walked for a while in silence.

"What kind of music do you play?" Izzy said eventually.

"Folk rock, mostly. Bob Dylan. That kind of thing. I was named after him. My dad's a big fan."

Dylan seemed to look everywhere but at Izzy. Was she such bad company that he couldn't wait to get away from her? She felt her cheeks redden.

She said, "I can take the bags if you want to turn back."

"No. My mom would kill me if she found out. And she *would* find out. Dun Laoghaire is so small. There's always someone watching you."

"Does your family live near here?"

"Right over the shop." They reached the turn to Izzy's street. "There used to be a lady who lived along here. A real weirdo."

"Really?"

"People would find her walking around in her pyjamas in the middle of the night. How creepy is that?"

"She lived along here?"

"Yeah, I think it was that one," Dylan said, pointing at Elaine's house.

"I guess I'm the new weirdo," Izzy said. "She was my aunt. I live here now."

The smile on Dylan's face fell away.

"Oh, I didn't—"

Ignoring him, Izzy turned in at her gate and made her way up the steps. She unlocked the door, stepped into the hall and dumped the medicine on the floor. She took the groceries from Dylan.

"I'm sorry, I—"

Izzy cut him off. "Just tell me what to do with the medicine."

"Okay," Dylan said. "There are small bags inside the bigger bags. That's one day's dose. You take one of those packets, empty it into a saucepan and boil it up for forty or forty-five minutes. Make it good and thick and drink it down."

"Got it."

"And come to the shop tomorrow for physical therapy. Twelve o'clock."

"Fine."

Izzy slammed the door in his face.

She went into the front room and peered out the bay window. Dylan stood on the doorstep for a moment, looking forlorn. Then he made his way down the path to the gate. Outside, he paused, seeing the broken window on her car. He looked back at the house one more time before leaving.

Chapter 14

In his study, at the back of the house he shared with Tess on Crofton Road, Gareth Gillen powered up his computer. He slumped at the desk and gave his stress ball a few squeezes, but that didn't help his mood.

For a moment, he was lost in thought, gazing through the open doorway to the front room, and the sea view it enjoyed. The house looked out on the harbour. *Thanks, Tess.* If they'd relied on Gareth's teaching salary, the view would have been different.

Average, actually.

What an awful word that was. And what an awful thing to be. Gareth knew he was exactly that. He stood five foot ten, weighed a hundred and eighty pounds, earned a respectable but unspectacular salary, was not quite handsome but not particularly ugly either, had fair hair and a fashion sense so close to the middle of the road that Gareth was amazed no one had painted a white line down his chest.

Average.

But not for much longer.

He checked his inbox, deleting one e-mail after

another. They were from the usual people. The credit card company telling him he'd maxed out his card, the bank saying his loan was overdue, and a debt collection agency, warning Gareth for the last time that they'd have him in court if he didn't discharge their client's fees.

He broke out in a sweat.

Shakespeare, the Brontës, Charles Dickens and Jane Austen stared down at Gareth from the fancy wooden shelves that lined the room. Novels and plays he had taught in class a hundred times at Saint Brendan's Secondary School, and which now bored him.

After loosening the top button of his cotton shirt, Gareth went straight onto Google Finance and checked how his favourite company, Scanning Solutions International, was doing.

He typed its symbol, SSI, into the search bar, and a chart popped up, showing that the stock was trading at $0.03 on the NASDAQ. Shares had risen nicely since Gareth bought into the company earlier in the week, and quarterly earnings results were due to be announced tonight, after the market closed. Who knew how high the price would go then?

Gareth loved the stock market. It was much better than betting on the horses or going to the greyhound track. The stock market required *skill*.

After a few missteps, which cost him a lot of money, he'd sought expert help. Say hello to former hedge fund manager Lauren Blitzoff. Gareth paid an eye-watering subscription fee to get her stock recommendations by e-mail.

Her first e-mail had been about SSI, a small tech company that was about to become huge. Their proprietary scanning technology could determine the constituents of any material within seconds just by firing a beam of light at it and doing a few fancy calculations. Ms. Blitzoff approved.

Imagine every police force and customs official on earth being equipped with an SSI scanner. This is the BIGGEST opportunity I've seen in all my years on Wall Street and I don't say that lightly.

This is an investment that could change your life. I only choose the BEST stocks for my personal portfolio.

You might wonder if it's worth being so picky. Does being a smart cookie pay off?

Well, it's the reason I could retire at 27 and devote my time to helping small investors outperform the Wall Street elite.

But enough about me...

Let's talk about YOU. Would you like to retire young and IN LUXURY? How are you going to spend your time?

Does owning a yacht sound good? A Maserati? How about TEN of them?

By the time he'd read the newsletter, Gareth had almost been able to taste the money that would soon be flowing to his account. He just needed to get a bigger chunk of change to play with, since he'd already burnt through his savings (and a small home improvement loan from the bank).

One day, in the staff room, he'd heard Maggie Connell, the principal, lamenting that one of the school's dropouts had been seen associating with Billy "Chisel" Cooney, a local loan shark.

Cooney's name was vaguely familiar. Gareth recalled that Cooney was a distant cousin of Melanie, one of Tess's friends, so he probably wasn't as bad as Maggie Connell was making out.

Getting in touch hadn't been hard. Cooney operated out of Ale House, a bar just half a mile outside town. But his interest rates were tough. Gareth's loan was due today, but he couldn't pay it back without selling his shares, and he didn't want to sell his shares before SSI announced its results.

Earlier, Gareth had tapped out a text message.

Hi Billy. How are you? Is it okay if I pay you back tomorrow? Just let me know if there's an extra fee. Happy to pay it. Cheers, Gareth.

He'd heard nothing back until... The doorbell chimed.

Gareth cursed under his breath. His heart racing, he walked out to the hall. He tucked his shirt into his trousers and opened the door. A skinny teenage boy with a thuggish look stood on the step. Shaved head, tracksuit. Scowl a mile wide.

He looked vaguely familiar. After a moment, a name bubbled up in Gareth's mind.

"Darren?"

It *was* him. Gareth hadn't seen the kid since third-year English. Darren had been the worst student in Gareth's class. He'd left Saint Brendan's the following year. Darren must be seventeen now.

Darren said, "You have the money?"

"The *money*?" Gareth stepped out onto the doorstep. "Darren, what—"

Darren punched him on the nose. Gareth fell back, more astonished than hurt.

"What the hell?"

Darren punched him again, this blow hitting him right on the cheekbone.

"You're hurt, Mr. Gillen." Darren's thin lips barely moved as he whispered the words.

Gareth stared at his pimply face. "I'm not hurt. I'm wondering what the hell you're doing."

"*Act* like you're hurt."

"Why would I do that?"

Darren tried to hit him again, but Gareth saw it coming this time. He grabbed the boy's fist, stopped it in mid-air. He grabbed Darren by his tracksuit top and was about to deck him when he heard laughter.

A voice said, "Let the boy go."

At the end of the driveway, a man dressed in a black T-shirt and black jeans stood smoking a cigarette. Its red dot was the only thing Gareth could see clearly, as the man blended into the darkness of the evening.

Then he stepped forward and a little light fell on his face. Gareth felt a chill as he recognised Chisel

Cooney. He hadn't seen him since their meeting at the Ale House a week earlier.

Cooney leaned on the metal gate. He was stocky, with a huge head and no neck. His T-shirt revealed bulging muscles. He wore nothing else on top, despite the cold night. Heavy work boots poked out from the ends of his jeans, polished to a mirror. The sides of his head were shaved down to the skin, but his hair was long on top.

He held a golf club casually over one shoulder.

Gareth saw now that there were two even larger men behind him, standing next to a black SUV. Bald and big. Huge meaty guys with heads as big as footballs and arms like tree trunks. They wore black jeans and black leather jackets and identical expressions, which told of few brain cells and much violence. They looked indistinguishable so Gareth assumed they were twins.

Darren wriggled free of Gareth's grasp and punched him in the mouth. Gareth staggered back, tripped over his own feet.

He fell back into his own hallway, hitting the floor hard. Darren stepped inside and kicked him in the ribs.

Gareth heard heavy footsteps approach. He looked up in time to see Chisel Cooney appear in the doorway. He blew a smoke ring.

"Nice house," Cooney said. "I'm looking for a new home myself, you know."

Gareth said nothing.

"You're late," Cooney said.

"I just need a little more time. I sent you a text message."

Please. Just give me one more day.

Cooney stepped into the hall. He glanced at the shelf, where a photo of Tess and Gareth stood. Cooney picked it up gently. The golf club was still in his hand. He now held it like a walking stick, though he didn't need one. The man was about forty and built like an ox.

"You owed me fifty thousand?"

"Yes."

"Now you owe me a hundred."

"*What?* I can't, I—"

Cooney didn't even look his way, just put the photo back on the shelf and patted it gently, his thick fingers brushing Tess's face.

"Nice life you got here. Nice house. Nice *lady*. Everything is so nice."

Gareth swallowed.

If his investment worked out the way he thought it would, he would have enough money.

"Okay," he said. "One hundred thousand. I'll have it."

"I know you will. You see, respect is everything in this business. I can't let someone make a fool of me."

"Oh, no. I wouldn't."

"Shhh," Cooney said. His thick face twisted into what might have been a smile. "Do you know why they call me Chisel?"

Gareth shook his head. He wondered if he was allowed to stand up.

"I don't like chisels," Cooney said, "if that's what you're thinking. My old man did, though. Sometimes I talked back to him. He didn't like that. Once, during dinner, he got so mad at me that he a stuck a narrow-headed chisel through my hand. Pinned me to the kitchen table with it, he did. Said he wouldn't take it out till I apologised."

Cooney paused and held up his hand so Gareth could see the scar on his palm. His voice dipped as he continued.

"I was stubborn too, I guess, so I didn't apologise. My father made me sit there with the chisel through my hand for three hours. I pulled it out myself after he went to bed. The day I turned seventeen he was found dead. Someone stabbed him in the neck with a chisel. Funny old world, isn't it?"

Gareth said nothing.

"I don't compromise. It's a weakness of mine, I suppose, but I won't tolerate disrespect."

"I-I didn't mean any disrespect."

"I think you'll agree that we did you a service by loaning you the money and by coming here to remind you of your commitments."

"I guess so."

Cooney nodded to Darren who came closer. "Then say *thanks* to the boy," Cooney said.

The blood in Gareth's veins began to boil. But what could he do? This wasn't about hurting Gareth. If they'd wanted to do that, the big lads would have done it. Or Cooney himself, with that damn golf club.

This was about humiliation. About reminding him how little power he had.

"Thanks," Gareth said through gritted teeth.

Chapter 15

Elaine's house was icy cold and bathed in darkness. Izzy groped on the wall for the light switch. She found it, flicked the hall light on, and made the mistake of glancing at her phone. There had been 52 missed calls from Adam.

He was never going to give up.

Izzy had one more day off work. Then she'd be returning to the diner and Adam could walk through the door any time he liked. He could slide into a booth and sit there all day every day, and there was nothing she could do about it.

Izzy dragged her shopping to the kitchen, her back aching with every movement. She popped a chicken curry into the microwave and turned it on.

While waiting for her food to heat, she searched the cupboard for a saucepan so she could cook the medicine. She opened one of the bags from the Chinese shop and pulled out a packet. The contents looked like a mixture of dried plants and twigs. It gave off a bitter, unpleasant odour.

She emptied the stuff into the saucepan, covered

it in water from the tap, and stuck it on the hob. Once the water was boiling, Izzy covered the saucepan and let it simmer while she collected her food from the microwave.

Eating was a slow process. Saliva wasn't something she'd ever thought she'd miss until she had none. She sat at the table with a cup of water, slowly working her way through the meal while she opened *A Study in Scarlet* and read the first few chapters.

The odour from the medicine became more pungent as it cooked. Forty-five minutes later, she'd finally struggled to the end of her meal.

By then she figured the medicine was done. She turned off the hob and poured the thick black sludge through a sieve into a mug. Its smell was foul, but when it had cooled a little, Izzy drank it all.

The medicine tasted revolting and it took all the willpower she had not to gag.

This stuff better work, she thought.

After scrubbing the saucepan, she made her way to the staircase. Its hard, unforgiving wood chilled her. She hurried up the steps, eager not to linger.

The first room along the hall was Elaine's bedroom, decked out in turquoise and pale pink, colours that always brought Elaine to mind.

Elaine's clothes still hung in the wardrobe. Looking at the room now reminded Izzy what a half-hearted job she and Adam had done of clearing the house out.

Adam kept encouraging her to finish clearing the place and sell it. The money would have helped their financial situation. Though he didn't tell her much about it, she believed that Adam's company was struggling, and Izzy's waitressing salary didn't go far.

But the relationship had already been moving so quickly. They were living together only a few weeks after meeting.

That was exciting, as was their engagement. Adam had proposed on a night out, with both her friends and his friends watching, as he went down on one knee.

Saying *yes* had been wild and thrilling and stupid. Hannah had been right when she warned Izzy things were moving along too fast. At the time, Izzy had thought Hannah was jealous. And anyway, Izzy was swept up in the moment. Life seemed so full of possibility.

Elaine's death had made Izzy slow down and question everything.

They'd argued, made up, argued again, made up again. And Adam grew increasingly more insistent that she sell the house.

Thank goodness she'd resisted.

A framed photo next to the bed caught Izzy's attention. It showed Elaine with a priest – Father Peter Brennan? – outside the church. Why was it there? Izzy looked at it in confusion for a moment, then set it down where she had found it.

Next door to Elaine's room was the bedroom belonging to Izzy's cousin David. It had been left more or less as he'd left it when he went to Cyprus, never to return. Izzy took a quick look, then closed the door again.

She continued down the hall to the spare bedroom. The single bed was made, with a bright blue duvet cover and pale blue sheets. That would do.

Izzy went back down the stairs, cringing when she hit the midway point, and cringing more when she neared the bottom. She didn't think she'd ever be able to pass that point without imagining Elaine's neck breaking.

Chapter 16

Kate was not drunk. She told herself that after tripping over her own feet and falling flat on her face. This was just after she left home, as she was walking down the lane to Crofton Road. She was distracted by the movement of the evil-looking sea and managed to snag one foot on the other.

She was *not* drunk, though.

Only merry. Or she would have been, if that was possible, given the day she'd had.

She got to her feet, and continued on, walking just as quickly as before. The evening air had a chill that reached right through both her jacket and the thin fabric of her dress. Goosebumps broke out on her bare legs.

As she reached Crofton Road, a train rumbled past. The track was hidden behind a granite wall on the other side of the road, but she was reassured to know it was there.

The possibility of movement, the idea that she could go places, was one of the things Kate had always liked about Dun Laoghaire. You could head north or south along the coast on the DART (Dublin Area Rapid Transit) train, head inland by bus or car, and there was always the sea. Wales was not far away. When the weather was good, Kate had occasionally seen the Welsh coast with the naked eye.

She shivered, pulling her jacket tighter around her, as she walked up the road. Stepping over a cigarette butt trailing a thin line of smoke, she climbed the steps to Gareth and Tess's house.

Was Gareth any good in bed? Kate laughed to herself, suddenly excited. It didn't matter. Right now, she wanted to feel a man's eyes on her, wanted a man to make her feel desired.

She jammed her index finger on the doorbell, though she only heard a faint peal of bells. She waited impatiently, shivering against the cold. There was no movement from inside the house.

She stepped to the side and peered through the window. A net curtain hung on the inside of the glass, so she couldn't make out a lot, but she did see a light on at the end of the hall.

Kate was about to bang on the door with her fist when she caught sight of movement within. It was so subtle she almost missed it, but something in the hallway moved. A figure, partially silhouetted against the dim background light.

"I can see you, Gareth. Open the damn door."

It opened a little, and Gareth's face appeared in the crack. Kate was gratified when his gaze ran briefly over her bare legs, but his face betrayed no interest, and his watery eyes moved quickly to her face.

"Tess isn't home from work yet."

"That's a shame," Kate said. "I needed to see her before the book club tonight. Does she have a spare copy of our pick?"

"I have no idea. Doesn't she read everything digitally now?"

"I'm not sure. Can I come in and wait?"

"I have some work to do. I'm marking essays."

"I can help." Kate winked at him. "Although I was a pretty terribly student. Maybe I need more schooling."

Gareth's face betrayed not even a hint of a smile. Had every guy's dick fallen off or what? Kate used to turn heads everywhere she went. How could that change so quickly?

Okay, the schooling thing was a bit strong, not to mention clichéd, but come on. It was *self-consciously* bad.

"You should catch up with Tess at Louise's place."

Gareth began to close the door. Only the fact that she jammed her foot in the way stopped it. Her slightly impaired reflexes meant that she kicked the door while she was at it, smashing the nail on her big toe.

She howled in pain, bent over and looked in horror at the nail. Half of it had fallen off. The rest was loose and bloody. She pressed it down vainly but that made it hurt even more. She hopped on one foot.

"Fuck! That was your fault, Gareth."

"What are you doing kicking the door? Are you the Gestapo or what?"

"Why were you shutting it in my face?" she countered.

"Sorry. I'm busy marking—"

"You should be sorry. I need a plaster. And have you got antiseptic?"

"Aren't you being a little dramatic?"

"I'm *hurt*."

This drew a loud sigh from Gareth. "Fine, come in then."

He opened the door wider. Despite the pain, a flash of triumph coursed through Kate as she limped past him.

"Go on into the sitting room," Gareth said.

Kate hobbled through the door. The room lay in murky darkness. But the connecting room, Gareth's study, was brightly lit and the door was open. Obviously, Gareth had been working there.

Kate turned on the light and limped across the room to the couch. Gareth walked to the front window. He peered through the glass.

"Damn," he said, looking out. "Is that Dee?"

"I don't know." Kate shrugged. "Who cares?"

"Maybe she saw us together." Gareth quickly closed the curtains.

"Are you ashamed to be seen with me?"

"Of course not."

A little heat came to Kate's face as she sank into the couch.

"Back in a second," Gareth said. "Let me find the first aid kit."

Kate looked around while she waited. Tess had made a nice home for herself. There was no doubt about that. All those billable hours at her law firm sure paid the mortgage. Kate had been here a few times for book club meetings, but otherwise Tess never invited her over.

Of course, Tess was hardly ever home. You could tell. There was an impersonal feel to the room, with its fancy armchairs, and abstract paintings on the wall. The place did smell good though. A bowl of potpourri on the mantelpiece gave off the warm smell of orange and cinnamon.

The windows were well insulated. Much better than the walls in Kate and Stephen's apartment. She couldn't hear the trains from here.

Soon Gareth was back. He sat on the couch next to her. He had a look of concentration on his face as he opened the kit and scanned its contents.

"What happened to your face?" Kate said. Now that Gareth was closer she could see his face was pink and his nostrils were bloody.

"Don't worry. It's nothing."

Kate took the opportunity to lean back and sideways in the couch, and swing her leg up, resting her injured foot on Gareth's thigh.

He flinched, then brought his attention back to the task at hand.

"What kind of papers were you marking?" Kate asked.

"Papers? Oh, I... uh, they're..." He looked up, but not at Kate. His eyes seemed to blur into the distance.

"It's not a hard question, Gareth." Kate jiggled her foot up and down on his leg. "It's not hard, is it?"

She gave her most coquettish laugh. On cue, Gareth's face flushed.

He cleared his throat. "Just English essays. The usual boring stuff. Honestly, I'm sick to death of it."

She waited in silence while he cleaned her wound and wrapped a plaster around the mangled nail. Thank goodness her toe was hidden, because it was repulsive enough to kill any kind of mood.

And right now, Kate wanted some fun.

Then she could tell Tess about it, and Tess would be *grateful*.

What a deal.

"All done," Gareth said.

"My hero."

She stroked his upper thigh with her foot. How long had it been since Tess teased him? Probably never. She was a straight-to-business kind of woman. Kate was sure they had efficient clinical sex.

"Why don't you fix us a drink?" Kate said.

Chapter 17

Izzy tried to brush away morbid thoughts. Every time she was near the staircase, she thought of her aunt's final moments.

She always imagined it the same way. Elaine, losing her balance, tumbling down the stairs, smashing against the hard wooden steps as she somersaulted, until an unfortunate landing broke her neck.

Elaine was thought to have died on the fifth of December, so she must have been dead for two days when Dee's mother – Elaine's colleague, Paula – called to the house. She'd been worried as Elaine hadn't shown up for work or answered her phone. Obviously no one answered the door to her.

It was another couple of days, on December ninth, when Paula reported her concerns at Dun Laoghaire Garda Station. An officer called to the door, got no answer, and phoned Izzy to see if she knew anything. When she said *no*, the officer got a locksmith to open the door, and found Elaine's body at the foot of the stairs. It was speculated that she'd been sleepwalking when she fell.

All that time, Izzy had been oblivious, going about her ordinary life, working at the diner and spending the rest of her time with Adam.

She hated to think of how selfishly her life had continued while Elaine lay dead and unmissed.

Izzy went to the front room. She remembered the niggle she'd had earlier about Elaine's bookshelf. The vague feeling that there was something wrong with it. Izzy went and stared at the shelf, trying to figure out what it was.

It took her a moment to realise that it was the way a set of worn hardback books on the middle shelf all seemed to be the same thickness.

Exactly the same thickness.

Jane Austen, Charles Dickens, Samuel Beckett, and many other familiar names. Their books couldn't possibly all be the exact same length.

She pulled out a copy of *Crime and Punishment* by Fyodor Dostoyevsky. It looked very old and worn until she picked it up. As soon as she handled the book, she realised that it was not as old as it looked. In fact, it was in pristine condition. The wear was a deliberate illusion.

Opening the book, Izzy saw that there was no printed text inside. Instead, it was a notebook. Actually, a diary.

And her aunt's spidery handwriting filled the pages.

Izzy pulled another volume off the shelf – purportedly a copy of *Wuthering Heights* – and found that this too was a cleverly disguised diary, full of her aunt's writing.

Izzy slipped it back onto the shelf. There were dozens of volumes. Izzy had had no idea that her aunt was such a prolific diarist.

She brought the volume with the *Crime and Punishment* cover over to the nearest armchair and sat down with it. She flicked through the pages and saw that this volume covered a section of the previous year.

She paused when she got to Halloween.

October 31ˢᵗ

It happened again last night. I'm still mortified as I write this. Woke up in bed with dirt on the soles of my feet. Went outside and saw footprints in the grass. I'm really losing my marbles. I had hoped I only went as far as the gate but no...

<u>I ran into Louise on my way home for lunch to-day. She asked if I remembered anything about last night. She said she found me wandering the street in my nightie and was afraid I'd freeze to death. It was certainly a bitterly cold night. She managed to get me in the house and back to bed while I was still asleep.</u>

Thank God she helped me, but how embarrassing... I hope it stops soon. It's been years since I went walkabouts like that.

When I mentioned it to Dr Mullen last week, during my regular check-up, she said stress might be the trigger. She asked if there was anything on my mind. Naturally I said no.

Izzy stopped to process what she had just read.

Dylan had been right. Elaine really had been sleep-walking around the neighbourhood. And it had been serious enough that she'd told her doctor.

Izzy felt a momentary pang of guilt. This stuff wasn't meant to be read, but she couldn't resist.

When did Izzy tell Elaine about Adam? About a week earlier? She flicked back a few pages, curious to see if it was mentioned.

October 26th

I gave Izzy a call tonight as I hadn't heard from her in ages. I waited until eight as I hoped that was a good time to catch her. I'm sure she's busy with work and everything.

Was surprised when she mentioned she's seeing someone. She was reluctant to get into it, but once she started talking about the fellow she didn't let up.

Apparently he's a Scotsman named Adam McGregor. An entrepreneur, it seems, with his own food company. Izzy said to look for McGregor Fine Foods in the shop – but only the little artisan places, as the supermarkets have thus far refused to stock his line of pastries.

She had to end the call after a few minutes as she has plans with him tonight.

I really hope this one is different to the others. Izzy sounds absolutely smitten, but it wouldn't be the first time, would it? Poor girl. She tends to choose duds.

Izzy closed the diary. She was embarrassed and guilty and somewhat resentful.

What would Elaine have thought if she'd seen

her today, fleeing her apartment? Running away from Adam?

Yeah, she had a history of choosing duds.

Izzy checked her phone and saw it was getting late. She really didn't want to go to the book club. The only thing worse would be staying here alone all night.

Waiting for Adam to come back.

She went to the kitchen, slipped *A Study in Scarlet* into her handbag. She slipped Elaine's diary in next to it. There was something both comforting and disturbing about the diary. It was a little piece of her aunt, all that Izzy had left of her, and she wanted to keep it close.

She hurried to the bathroom so she could splash some water on her face before going to her first ever book club meeting.

Chapter 18

When Tess got the text message, she was still in the office, papers splayed out on her desk. Her computer screen glared at her. Outside, on the main floor of the office, many of her junior colleagues were still at their desks.

Britney had just arrived with another double espresso. She tapped her knuckle on Tess's door, then brought the coffee over.

Tess remained stony-faced.

She noticed how Britney's make-up still looked perfect, though she'd been working since dawn. No bags under her eyes, either. Ah, the joys of being twenty-something. And she smelled good. What perfume was that? It was a crime when your assistant wore a nicer perfume than you.

After talking to Kate, Tess had dissolved into a distracted mess. It was impossible to pay attention to her work, and Tess hated that.

She could only think of Gareth.

Would her boyfriend fail the test? Would he succumb to Kate's charms?

As Britney set the cup down, Tess saw that she'd put a heart-shaped chocolate on the saucer. Typically thoughtful and affectionate of her.

"Do you need anything else, Tess? A glass of water?"

"No."

"I hope I'm not overstepping," Britney said. "But is everything okay? You look a little – off?"

"Off? I look a little *off?*"

Britney recoiled. "I'm sorry, I—"

"Do I comment on your appearance, Britney? This firm has a policy when it comes to personal remarks."

Which everyone ignored. Especially the partners. But so what?

Britney's face fell. "I'm so sorry. I didn't mean anything. I just— I was concerned. Forgive me."

Tess decided she'd make her work all night, every day this whole goddamn week.

"I need you to go over the Maxwell file. Summarise where we stand on it in a memo. Be sure not to miss anything."

Britney nodded slowly.

This was a horrendously complicated corporate restructuring that Tess had been meaning to untangle for weeks. Well, now was as good a time as any to make some progress.

"Sure. I'll get right on it in the morning."

"I need your memo for 8 am."

Suck on that.

Tess's assistant didn't let her dismay show. She even forced another smile.

"Absolutely. I'll get right on it." She gave a laugh. "I might need some coffee myself."

With that, she turned on her heel and strode out. Her nonchalance made Tess even angrier. Women like Kate and Britney drove her nuts.

When Britney was gone, Tess returned to her own work. At least, she tried to. She had been gazing at the same documents for two hours. She'd read the same few words a hundred times and they still weren't soaking in.

Her phone pinged. Tess snatched it up at once, gripping the device tightly in her clammy hands.

The fate of her future with Gareth was on the line.

She swallowed and read Kate's text.

I've got an answer for you.

Tess waited for another message. Why didn't Kate say what the answer was? What good was a message like this?

She downed her espresso and threw the chocolate in the bin. Then she waited. She stared out the window.

The lights of a plane moved slowly across the sky, going in to land at the airport. A plane full of families, maybe. Coming back from holidays in the sun.

When was Tess's day in the sun? When was her family time?

After five minutes, she couldn't stand it anymore. Out of patience, she dialled Kate's number. Waited while it rang. One, two, three rings. No answer.

Was Kate's phone on silent? Or was it buried in her

handbag, ignored while she and Gareth got down to business?

She dialled Gareth next. His phone didn't even ring, just went straight to voicemail.

Were they in bed together? Tess hadn't asked Kate to go that far. But Pandora's box and all that. Kate might have started flirting with Gareth only for it to get out of hand.

Tess's mouth flooded with bile. She bent over the bin and puked into it.

Gareth had been so distant lately. And he seemed... resentful?

She wiped her mouth and checked the time. She had to find out what was happening. Rising from her chair, she turned off her PC and flicked off the light, then put on her long black coat before walking out.

Tess caught the sideways glances her colleagues threw at her. Leaving so early was unlike her. She knew that. But so was asking someone to seduce her boyfriend. Sometimes you had to take a chance.

*

At home, Tess parked in the driveway behind Gareth's car and hurried up the steps to her door. The drive had seemed interminable. Tess had heard nothing further from Kate, and her calls had gone unanswered.

Was Kate in the house? Had she *really* got an answer? What if the answer was *yes*, if Gareth was distracted because he no longer loved Tess? Was he ready to move on to the first woman who fluttered her eyelashes at him?

Maybe he already had.

Tess's hand shook, making getting the key in the lock difficult. She ground her teeth and finally managed to get the door open.

The light in the hall was on.

"Gareth?"

Only silence greeted her. She stepped into the sitting room. There was no one there.

A first aid kit sat on the coffee table. Was Gareth hurt? Tess felt more freaked out by the minute.

"Gareth? Are you there?"

She walked through the whole ground floor.

Nothing. No one.

She went upstairs. There was no sign of anyone there either.

In the bedroom, Tess scrutinised the bedsheets. Were they tussled more than normal? Was that a hint of perfume Tess detected? She didn't know anymore.

She took out her phone and called Gareth again.

He picked up on the fourth ring. Tess could hear ambient noise in the background. Faint music. The murmur of voices. The clink of glasses.

"Hey. Tess."

"Where are you?"

"I decided to pop into Fitzgerald's."

"You're at the pub? Why?"

A pause. "Just, you know, felt like it. You don't mind, do you?"

What she minded was the false cheerfulness in his voice. It was completely unconvincing.

"But why?" she said.

"I just fancied a drink."

"We have drinks. We have plenty of drinks at home."

"I wanted to get out of the house."

The bonhomie was gone from his voice now, replaced by irritation. Tess felt like she was about to puke again.

"Are you alone?"

"Well, the bar isn't empty." Before Tess could ask what that meant, he said, "You've got your book club tonight, haven't you? I didn't think you'd mind."

"I don't."

"Okay. I'll see you later then."

The line went dead.

Was Gareth drinking away his guilt?

Tess took a breath and headed for the door. She'd have to go to Louise's house. Hopefully Kate would turn up there and Tess could soon find out just what she had done.

Chapter 19

It was seven fifty-eight when Izzy hurried out of the house. She'd done the best she could to make herself presentable, but her hair was an ugly brown mess, frizzy and not even clean. And none of her clothes looked good on her now that she'd grown so thin.

At least she'd managed to put on some deodorant and change into a clean jumper and a plain white dress. Over that, she wore a denim jacket with a furry lining, and she was glad of its warmth.

Shivering, she gripped the handle of her canvas tote bag. Inside, she had two bottles of Chardonnay and a birthday card for Louise. Her shoulder bag contained her copy of *A Study in Scarlet* and Elaine's diary.

Her first ever book club meeting.

Izzy didn't feel ready for it. What would she say? She'd only read a few chapters of the book. Sure, it had been fun to see how Dr. Watson met Sherlock Holmes. They were two of the most famous characters in literature. But she had nothing smart to say about the book. She'd never been academically gifted, and she felt sure the others would think she was an idiot.

As she approached the footpath on the other side of the road, a large man walked past. Seeing the big belly and scraggly beard, Izzy recognised Louise's husband, Robert. Absorbed in lighting a cigarette, he didn't notice her as he headed in the opposite direction.

Behind her she heard the roar of an engine and saw a van coming down the street. A white van.

Adam?

Izzy felt a stab of terror.

She stepped up onto the footpath behind Robert and made her way through the open gate of his house.

The van probably wasn't Adam, right? She shouldn't get paranoid. Still, her stomach churned as she climbed the steps. She felt like she was running again. The van had stopped up the street. Adam could be sitting in it, waiting for her.

Izzy saw a shadowy form moving along the footpath.

Her heart nearly stopped.

She waited, terrified, until the figure stepped under a streetlight and Izzy saw that it was a woman. Maybe she was coming here, to the meeting?

There was no backing out now. Izzy pressed the doorbell, heard it ring.

The other woman turned in at Louise's gate, climbed the steps, two at a time. The light from the sconce lit up her face as she got to the top. Her face and her thick-framed half-circle glasses, were familiar.

It was Dee, the librarian. She wore a long, padded coat that covered her whole body. It was like she was wrapped in a duvet.

Dee smiled. "Hello again."

Izzy remembered running out of the library, after realising her passport was still at Adam's place.

"Sorry about earlier. You must think I'm a lunatic."

The librarian shook her head. "I just hoped you were okay. What happened?"

"I'm fine." Izzy returned the other woman's smile. "It was nothing."

The door opened and Louise appeared in the doorway. Louise had changed into another stylish outfit since Izzy had seen her earlier. A long, colourful top over another pair of pale trousers. As before, her face was beautifully made up, and innumerable pieces of jewellery sparkled in the light.

I'm so not ready for this, Izzy thought.

Louise's face lit up when she saw them.

"Come in. Tess and Melanie are here. We're only waiting on Kate."

Chapter 20

Robert Murphy caught the heavenly smell of beer as soon as he pulled open the door of Fitzgerald's. He entered the pub, noticing Gareth Gillen sitting at a table by the door. The English teacher was by himself, staring at his phone.

Rock music played low over the speakers. The lights were low too. It looked kind of quiet tonight, and the mood seemed depressed. Was that Tom Flynn at the end of the bar?

He turned his attention back to Gareth. It was a long time since Robert had seen him here, especially on a school night. He noticed that Gareth's face was a little swollen and pink.

"You okay?" Robert said. "Who beat you up?"

Gareth glanced at him, then quickly turned his attention back to his phone. "Nobody. I'm fine."

An almost empty glass stood on the table. Tall, round glass, sparkling liquid inside. A wedge of lemon and lots of ice crowding the alcohol.

"Gin and tonic?" Robert couldn't help letting a little scorn into his voice.

Gareth looked up again. "No, I'm okay."

"I didn't ask if you're okay. I asked what you're drinking."

"Don't worry about it."

Robert snorted. "Did I say I was *worried*? I don't want to get you G&T if you're having vodka and soda." He stroked his beard thoughtfully. "Not that it makes an awful lot of difference. I mean, they're both women's drinks. Why don't you have a beer? You know, like a man?"

Gareth didn't crack a smile, but Robert's words did have an effect. He blinked rapidly.

"Jesus," Robert said with a sigh. "Alright, fine. G&T it is."

He strode down the bar to where Jimmy, the barman, stood polishing a glass.

"Alright, Jimmy. Give me a bottle of Corona. Straight out of the fridge. None of that room-temperature stuff like last time. And a G&T for the lady."

For the benefit of a couple of older guys on high stools, Robert puffed up his chest and sighed to show that he was making this purchase under protest.

Jimmy said, "You've got some nerve. How dare you?"

"How dare I what?"

"How dare you show your face here again after Saturday?"

"What happened on Saturday?"

Jimmy's hair flopped from side to side when he shook his head.

"How can you not *remember*?"

Robert thought back. He had come here at the weekend, but there had been nothing out of the ordinary. He'd met a couple of friends and sunk a few cold ones – actually, room temperature ones – and that had been it.

"What? It was a good night, except the beer was warm."

Jimmy flung the cloth over his shoulder and placed the glass he'd been polishing down on the bar.

"A good night?"

Robert nodded, rubbed his round belly. "I made a few investments in the old bank here. I remember that much."

Jimmy gave a humourless laugh. "Do you remember how you left?"

"On my feet?"

"Barely. I found you in the toilets."

"So what?"

"You were pissing into a hand dryer. Do you remember that?"

Suddenly Robert did remember. "I was a little confused. Those new dryers look a lot like urinals."

"So that's why you peed in it?"

"I don't know if I actually peed into it."

"When I found you, you were waving your dick at the sensor."

Hey Jimmy, this is the best blow job I've ever had!

Yeah, it was all coming back now.

He recalled Jimmy grabbing him by the collar and

dragging him to the door while he laughed and struggled all the way.

Robert cleared his throat, aware that the older guys sitting at the bar had broken off their conversation.

"That's not exactly my recollection," he said. "I was just a little confused."

Jimmy continued. "Somehow, you managed to fall asleep while standing on your feet, drying your dick in a hand dryer."

A chuckle came from one of the older men. Robert ignored him.

"Did I do anything else?"

"Plenty, but the dryer incident is enough."

"Give me a break, Jimmy. So I got a little sloppy? I'm sorry. I'll make up for it." Robert fished his wallet out of his pocket and dropped a twenty on the bar. "I only popped in for one tonight, while Louise hosts her book club. Don't make me walk up the road to O'Connell's. I'd prefer to support your fine establishment."

The truth was that he couldn't walk up the road to O'Connell's because they'd barred him.

Jimmy seemed to consider it for a moment. Then he grabbed the money.

"You better be on your best behaviour."

"Of course."

"Otherwise, I'll kick you out on your ear."

"I'd expect no less."

While Robert waited for the drinks, he glanced at Tom Flynn, sitting with one of his friends at the end of the bar. The two of them were drinking some kind of craft beer Robert didn't recognise. Tom was wearing thick-framed glasses though everyone knew his eyesight was 20/20.

"Damn hipsters," Robert muttered.

Tom looked up.

"What was that, Robert?"

"Your wife gave me a nice present today."

Tom looked at him blankly. "What's that?"

"A box of shit."

Tom and his friend cracked up. Tom said, "Good for her. One of these days I'm going to staple that dog's ass shut."

"Try it, you motherfu—"

"Robert!" Jimmy was back with the drinks. "I thought you were going to behave. You want to drink here or not? No fighting."

He folded his arms.

"Sorry about that," Robert said. He glanced at Tom Flynn, who was looking even more smug now. Robert ignored him. "Thank you, Jimmy. You're a gentleman, sir."

"Stay away from my hand dryers."

"Yeah, yeah."

Robert brought the drinks to Gareth's table and sat down. The guy was still staring at his phone and barely seemed to notice.

"Here we are, buddy."

Up close, Gareth's eyes were bloodshot and watery, and he really did look like he'd got a couple of smacks in the face.

Gareth downed half the drink in one go.

"Seriously, what the hell happened?" Robert said. "Is Tess beating you?"

"Like you care."

"That hurts, Gareth. I care."

They used to be pretty good friends before life got in the way, but after a few years as a teacher, Gareth started acting like a real know-all.

Gareth lifted his phone again. Robert snatched it out of his hand.

"Hey, give that back."

Ignoring him, Robert put the phone in his own pocket.

"You can look at your stupid phone later. Tell me why you're such a mess. Is it a woman?"

This actually made Gareth laugh. Robert took a slug of Corona, watched as Gareth drained his fresh drink.

"It doesn't matter."

"Cos if it is a woman, hell, I've had my share of troubles. Like to think I've learnt a thing or two from it all."

"Really?"

"Sure. Louise and I have been through a lot. I think every married couple has." He didn't mention that he and Louise had been sleeping in separate bedrooms for over a year. She said it was because of his snoring but Robert wondered if she was just sick of him. "And if it's something embarrassing, I'm familiar with that too. Shit, not five seconds ago, Jimmy told everyone at the bar that I stuck my dick in a hand dryer."

Gareth sighed. "I've got bigger problems."

"Like what? You'll feel better if you tell someone."

"I don't know about that."

Chapter 21

Izzy and Dee followed Louise into a large room, with two huge couches and two armchairs, all set in a circle. A low coffee table in the middle of the room was covered in crackers and skewered squares of cheese.

A woman in a dark suit, with a sour expression, sat on one couch. She ran a skeletal hand through her short hair.

The woman on the other couch had a short bob, dyed a brilliant purple, and wore baggy jeans and a short leather jacket. She unwrapped a scarf from around her neck and put it on the couch beside her.

"It's hot as hell in here," she said, fanning her face with her hand.

Louise put an arm around Izzy.

"Ladies, this is Izzy O'Brien, our new neighbour. Come and say hi."

First on her feet was the purple-haired woman, who turned out to be about five feet tall.

"I'm Melanie. Good to meet you."

Grinning, the woman threw her arms around Izzy.

"She's the popular one," Louise said. "A social media queen."

"I'm not really." Releasing Izzy, Melanie shook her head, but she clearly enjoyed the description. "I'm actually a hairdresser."

Izzy said, "Then I desperately need your services."

She hadn't been thinking any such thing until she said it, but the idea of a change excited her. A new hair style for a new beginning.

Melanie beamed. "I have an opening in the morning. Come along and we'll get you seen to. My salon's up on George's Street. It's the one called Pamper."

"And this is Tess," Louise said, as the short-haired woman in the suit came over. Izzy shook her hand, finding it as cold and limp as a dead fish.

Louise said, "Tess is the brains of the group. If you ever find yourself in legal trouble, you know where to turn. She chose our book pick tonight. The Conan Doyle. She—"

Tess interrupted. "Have you heard from Kate?"

Louise frowned. "I'm sure she'll be here in a minute. It's just gone eight. You know how she is." Louise gave Izzy another smile. "Kate is the late one."

Dee said, "I thought she was at your place, Tess."

Tess glared at the librarian. "What do you mean?"

"I passed your house an hour ago. I thought I saw Kate inside."

There was a long silence.

"Are you sure?"

"Maybe it wasn't her," Dee said with a shrug. "Weren't you expecting her?"

Tess didn't reply.

"I'm sure she'll be here soon," Louise said. "What's everyone still doing standing? Sit down and relax."

Melanie patted the armchair next to her couch. "Sit next to me, Izzy. I want to hear all about you."

Izzy took her place next to Melanie. Now everyone was seated except Louise.

A beautiful paperback of *A Study in Scarlet* sat on the coffee table in front of Melanie. Izzy saw that Louise had some large architecture books piled on the shelf under the coffee table.

Tess checked her phone, then put it in her jacket pocket again and looked around impatiently while Dee took a well-worn hardback of *A Study in Scarlet* from her bag. It had a library barcode on the side.

"We better add Izzy to the WhatsApp book club group," Dee said.

They all took out their phones and exchanged numbers. As they finished, Baxter pushed open the sitting room door and ran past Louise, dodging her as she tried to grab him. He ran around the table, licking any hands he could reach and wagging his tail.

"Get that stupid dog away from the snacks," Melanie said.

Louise frowned. "Come on, you naughty boy." She grabbed Baxter's collar, and dragged him out of the room. "Back in a second. I'm going to give him his dinner."

Louise pulled the door to the hall shut behind her.

For a moment, everyone was silent. Tess stared into space, seemingly lost in thought. Melanie was busy munching on a cracker. Izzy felt Dee's eyes on her. She was sure the librarian was about to ask her about herself.

She was saved by the doorbell's ring.

Izzy heard the front door open and close.

A moment later, the door from the hall burst open and a very drunk woman staggered into the room.

Chapter 22

Across the table, Robert stared at Gareth as the English teacher took a sip of G&T. Their second round had just arrived and Gareth was quickly working his way through his drink.

Robert said, "So what's the problem?"

"Keep your voice down, will you? Have you ever had... you know, less going on downtown than you want?"

"Downtown?"

"Yeah." Gareth nodded to his crotch. "Downtown."

Robert was distracted when he noticed a slice of lime squeezed into the neck of his beer bottle. If Jimmy wanted to turn Fitzgerald's into a classy pub, he was going to have to do better than that. Robert pushed the lime down into the beer and took a sip.

"Trouble downtown? Absolutely not," Robert said. He stroked his beard thoughtfully. "Never. Everything is in working condition."

"Well, you're lucky. I've lost my mojo. I'm feeling so blah about everything. My whole life is so fucking mediocre."

"What's the big deal? You're too tired or drunk to pitch a tent. Who cares?"

Gareth lowered his voice even more. "What if you weren't tired or drunk? That's the problem."

"Then you're with the wrong lady," Robert said.

He recalled other nights, years ago, when he and Gareth used to sit at a table like this, in a crappy pub like this, and tell each other everything while they drank beer till closing time.

"Damn, I miss grabbing a beer with you," Robert said. "Anyway, you know what your problem is?"

"What?"

"You're going to kick yourself." Robert laughed. "Your problem, my friend, is stress."

Gareth gave an exasperated sigh. "I thought you had a good idea."

"I do. Are you stressed at the moment?"

"Well," Gareth said slowly. "Perhaps. Things are busy at the school. And there's... other stuff."

"You need to get on top of that shit." Robert took a slug of lime-flavoured beer. "Stress is a killer. And that's not the only thing you need to worry about. Look at me. I think I'm getting early-onset dementia or something."

"Why would you think that?"

"I'm misplacing stuff left, right and centre. Half the time, I can't find my clothes. Jeans, T-shirts, jackets, you name it. They just go missing. No idea what happened to them." He shrugged. "Anyway, another round?"

Without waiting for an answer, Robert pushed his stool back from the table and stood up. He spun around and walked straight into Tom Flynn.

Tom was holding an e-cigarette in his hand and was heading for the door, clearly heading outside for a bit of vaping.

The two men collided.

Robert's deposits of fat largely insulated him from the impact, but Tom bounced off him and fell over.

"What the fuck?" Robert said.

Tom got to his feet. The two men glared at one another.

"Watch where you're walking," Tom said. "Are you blind?"

"It was an accident."

"*You're* an accident."

"Don't talk to me like that."

"And your mutt's an accident."

Robert raised a warning finger. "You leave Baxter alone."

"That stupid dog takes one more dump on my lawn and I swear to God, I'm going to go over to your place and squat on your grass myself. Let's see how you and Louise like it."

"I bet Melanie would be there, taking a photo so she can stick it on Instagram."

"Don't you talk about my wife."

"Fuck your wife. I saw her review of *Pride and Prejudice* last week. Guess what? Jane Austen called. She said the review is two hundred years late."

"Shut up."

"And Melanie hurt her feelings with that three-star rating. Jane is suicidal after hearing that the famous Melanie Flynn thinks the book is overwritten."

"I'm *warning* you."

Tom gave him a shove.

Robert snorted, turned to Gareth. He was sitting silently at his table, cradling his empty glass in his hands, and watching the two men.

Robert said, "Can you believe this shit?"

Gareth's eyes darted around, as if he didn't want to be drawn into the conflict. But after a moment's hesitation, he got to his feet.

"Alright, let's settle down," Gareth said, putting on his teacher's voice.

"You shut up, too," Tom said.

"There's no need for that. Let's behave like civilised men."

Tom's face contorted into a sneer. "You think you're so smart, don't you, teacher boy? 'Civilised men'? This isn't an English class and you're not smart at all."

"I never—"

"If you're so smart," Tom said, crossing his arms, "define the word 'until'."

Confusion clouded Gareth's face. "Until?"

"The word 'until'. Tell me what it means."

"Until? It's like... when something happened in the past... and..." He faltered. "No, wait, it's when you've got something that's—"

"Nope," Tom said triumphantly. "That's not the

definition of 'until'. That's a bunch of gibbering non-sense. And you're an idiot." He uncrossed his arms and broke out laughing. "And you're meant to be teaching our kids. Thank Christ I don't have any."

Robert's temper had begun to simmer. Now it boiled over.

"Hey Tom," Robert said.

"What do you wa—?"

Robert's knuckles connected with Tom's mouth before he could finish the word. It was a snappy blow, and Tom dropped to the floor for the second time.

The bar erupted in noise. There was a screech as Tom's friend pushed back his barstool and came running.

Before any of them got there, Tom staggered to his feet.

"You're going to pay for that," Tom said.

Gareth grabbed Robert's arm. "Let's get out of here."

"I'm not running away."

"You shouldn't have hit him."

"He was being a jerk," Robert said.

"I know, but still."

Tom's friend came to a stop beside him. He helped Tom up, then cracked his knuckles and stepped forward.

Robert grabbed his empty beer bottle, hit it against the side of the table, lopping its neck off.

"Okay, who wants to eat glass?"

Chapter 23

Izzy watched the new arrival stagger into the room. Kate must have been freezing, as she was wearing a short, thin dress. Beautiful as it was, with its floral pattern, it looked very light. Her black jacket seemed unsuitable for the weather too.

The ladies stood to greet her.

"You guys are not going to believe the day I've had," Kate said, straightening her back like a drill sergeant about to address her soldiers.

Tess blinked quickly. "What happened?"

Louise said, "Kate, this is Izzy, our new member."

"Hi." Kate leaned over and held out her hand. Izzy shook it, then backed away as Kate continued speaking. "You're not catching me at my best, Izzy. Forgive me. But I've just found out that my husband is a woman."

"What do you mean?" Dee said. "Who said that?"

"He did. I mean, she did, if I want to honour his pronouns. I mean, her pronouns. Fuck! Stephen has decided he's actually Stephanie. And I'm giving him too much credit. He didn't tell me at all. I went to meet him at his office and his colleagues were all celebrating his sex change or whatever. What do you think of that?"

There was a lot of noise all at once. Gasps. Expressions of surprise. Questions. Only Tess and Izzy remained silent. Tess seemed lost in thought.

"I need wine," Kate said, piercing through all the other voices.

Louise said, "I have some very nice teas, fruit juices—"

"*Wine*," Kate said. "What's a book club without wine, anyway? You always pull this crap when you're hosting, Louise. Please, give me wine. If you have an IV drip, plug it directly into my veins."

Louise frowned. "I'm not sure if I have all that much wine."

Izzy said, "I brought a couple of bottles."

She'd placed her tote bag on the floor next to her seat. Now she lifted it up, removed the bottles and held them up so the others could see.

Kate came over and threw her arms around her. Izzy gripped the bottles tighter, trying not to drop them.

Kate said, "I love this girl already. Corkscrew and glasses, please, Louise."

"Alright, fine." Louise sighed. "Give me a minute."

When Kate had released Izzy, and dropped into the chair next to her, Louise took the bottles.

"They were for your birthday," Izzy said. She handed Louise the birthday card too.

"You're so kind."

"Can I help you with the wine?" Izzy said. "I'm a waitress."

"Are you really?" Louise gave her a big smile. "Well, not tonight, you're not. You're a guest in this house. Sit down and relax."

Izzy did sit down, but she was far from relaxed. She watched Louise leave with the wine.

Kate crossed her long legs and sat elegantly in her seat, her back perfectly straight, not sinking gracelessly into the cushions the way Izzy had done. She ran a hand through her glossy, dark brown hair and Izzy caught sight of a pretty turquoise bracelet on her wrist.

Tess stood for another moment before sinking wordlessly into her seat, still scowling.

"Wait," Melanie said. "Tell me again, Kate. What happened? You went to Stephen's office and found everyone celebrating the fact that he's now a woman? And he didn't tell you anything about this?"

"That's about the sum of it. They even had a cake for him, and a banner strung across the ceiling. Did he tell you guys? Did you *know*?"

"Of course not," Dee said. "I can't believe it."

Louise appeared with a tray. It had tall wine glasses, a corkscrew, and a cup of water.

"I'm so sorry, Kate," Louise said as she pulled the cork out of the first bottle of wine. "I'm shocked."

"I can't believe he did this to me."

"She," Melanie said. There was an uncomfortable

silence. "What are you looking at me like that for? We should start calling her Stephanie."

Kate said, "But *she's* not *Stephanie. She* is my husband, Stephen."

"It's terrible for you, but she's a woman now and we'll just have to accept it."

"I don't believe you're taking his side," Kate snapped.

"*Her* side. And I'm not."

"Would you shut up with your stupid fucking pronouns? You know how fucking retarded you sound?"

"Don't you dare say *retarded.* That's an incredibly nasty word. You know my sister has learning diffi—"

"Everybody!" Louise said. "Let's take it down a notch. Okay? We're all friends here. Kate, here's your wine. Now, who else wants a glass?"

Everyone did except Izzy. It had been months since she'd had a drink, and she didn't miss it.

"I brought you some water," Louise told her. "I wasn't sure if you wanted wine or not, but I thought you might like some water anyway."

"Thank you." The mug was warm.

Dee said, "So what's going to happen?"

Kate shook her head. "I have no idea. I don't know if there's someone else. I mean, is that what prompted this? That he met a man? Or does he still like women? I have no idea. I just feel so stupid. It doesn't make any sense."

When Louise finished doling out the booze, she took the seat on the couch next to Tess.

"Have you been married long?" Izzy asked gently.

"Four and a half years. *Four and a half years* of my life have gone down the drain. My life is over."

Izzy had always thought that Elaine was happy in Dun Laoghaire because nothing much happened here, but maybe this seaside suburb wasn't as sleepy as Izzy had imagined.

She wondered what else she might be wrong about.

Chapter 24

Adam McGregor's rage turned from hot to icy cold while he sat in his van in Dun Laoghaire. The engine was off, the air as cold as water from a well.

A dark form padded across the road, lit for a second by the glare of a streetlight. Adam only caught the briefest glimpse of it.

A fox, maybe?

He watched the creature disappear into a garden. Adam was in such a bad mood that he felt like jumping out of the van and tearing the creature to shreds with his bare hands.

The driver's window was rolled all the way down.

He'd never felt so betrayed.

There had been Ruth, of course, but that was different.

The van was parked a few houses up from Izzy's place. His phone calls to her had gone unanswered. He'd left a dozen voice messages too, but she hadn't got back to him.

They were a couple, and she'd left him without a

word of explanation. She couldn't do that to him. He wouldn't let her.

He'd arrived here in time to see her leave her aunt's house. Obviously, she was up to something. Izzy had crossed the road, went a few doors down, and entered a neighbour's place.

Adam had been about to take a closer look when another woman came along and entered the same house.

What were they up to?

Adam was only certain of one thing. Izzy had been planning to abandon him for some time, and these women were involved. They'd put her up to it, maybe. And now they were gathering to celebrate.

For a second, the coldness in his chest turned hot again, the skin on his face prickling feverishly.

He ought to slice them up. That would teach them not to mess with him.

Ten minutes after Izzy went into the house, he'd watched another woman arrive.

How many of these witches were there? It was like the coven was having some kind of party. And Adam felt bitterly that it was all at his expense.

After everything he'd done for Izzy, this was how she repaid him? By abandoning him at the first opportunity?

By mocking him?

He patted the faint shape of her passport in his jacket pocket. She was his. She just needed to be reminded of that fact.

*

Jimmy the barman pushed Gareth Gillen and Robert Murphy through the door of the pub onto the street. He'd sprung into action as soon as Robert smashed that beer bottle, breaking up the fight before things got more violent.

The cool night air hit Robert almost hard enough to sober him up, though of course he wasn't drunk. He'd only had a couple of bottles of Corona, for god's sake.

"And stay out," Jimmy said.

Robert wheeled around.

"Wait up, Jimmy. I'm barred?"

"Yes, my dear Robert, you are."

"How is that fair? Tom started it."

"Your big mouth always causes trouble."

Robert tried for a note of levity. "Actually, I think it was my big dick, not my big mouth, that caused trouble last time. You know, with the hand dryer?"

"You're not funny." Jimmy scowled. "I should have barred you years ago."

"Come on."

"I'd say I'm sorry, but I'm not."

The barman disappeared back inside, letting the door swing shut behind him.

Robert walked over to Gareth, who had taken a few steps away. "Where should we go for our next drink—?"

"I'm going home."

"Are you kidding me?" Robert looked around. The main street was deserted, dark and the ground was wet. He felt very alone, all of a sudden. "You're going to ditch me?"

"I have work in the morning."

"So do I."

Gareth snorted a laugh. "I have to get up in front of a room full of teenagers."

"Oh, I see." Robert nodded to himself. "I'm just a humble train driver, but you're a *teacher*. You have a noble calling."

"I didn't mean it like that."

"This is why we stopped hanging around."

"What are you talking about?"

Robert jabbed Gareth's chest with his index finger. "You think you're better than me."

"I don't."

"Yeah, you do, you arrogant bastard. That's why you got so annoyed when you couldn't define that word, when Tom asked. What was it? Oh, yeah. *Until*."

Gareth's eyes narrowed. "I think you're the one who got annoyed, and I didn't hear you come up with a definition either."

"Of course not. I'm a train driver, not a brainiac like you."

"Robert, go home and take it easy."

"How can I? The whole book club is at my place. Your girlfriend is at my place. My wife is at my place. I've been kicked out of my own home."

"Is Kate there?"

"I guess so. Why?"

"Just wondering."

The way Gareth said it made Robert suspicious. He was holding something back. Did he have a crush on Kate?

"Do you want her?" Robert asked.

"Who, Kate?"

"Duh. I don't mean J-Lo. Of course, Kate. You're very curious about her."

"God, no."

"Huh," Robert said.

"You should go home," Gareth said. "It's your house too."

"Screw that. Let's go for a pint somewhere."

"Sorry." Gareth was already crossing the street. His dampened footfalls echoed off the buildings. "Another time, Robert. The drinks will be on me."

He turned slightly, waved goodbye, and hurried on down the side street. Off to his fancy house paid for by his rich lawyer girlfriend.

Gareth had been right about one thing, though. Robert should be able to stay in his own house instead of getting kicked out on the street.

He walked towards the church. He began to feel angrier as he went, thinking of all the injustices he'd suffered.

He only snapped out of it when he stepped into a puddle. Freezing water drenched his shoes and socks, making him gasp.

His angry shout carried down the dark street.

Chapter 25

After Kate had vented for a while, she started to calm down. She didn't look any happier, though. Louise passed the crackers and cheese around. The cheddar was rich and salty, which Izzy liked, but the crackers were very dry. She sipped water while Louise opened the second bottle of wine and topped up Kate, Dee and Melanie's glasses.

Louise was so busy playing the host she had hardly taken a sip or two from her own glass so far. And Izzy wasn't sure Tess had touched her wine. The lawyer looked shocked by Kate's news, and her cold eyes darted about the room, never settling on anything for long.

Kate slumped back in her chair with her freshly filled glass.

"What about you?" she said, looking at Izzy. "What's your deal?"

"Me? No deal."

"You said you're a waitress?" Kate spoke loudly.

"Yeah, at Shake Diner."

"Nice! Boyfriend?"

"Yeah – I mean no."

She'd had a boyfriend until this afternoon, if that's what Adam could be called. A fiancé, actually. But it was definitely over now.

Kate raised her eyebrows and recrossed her long legs. "Make up your mind. Which is it?"

"We've just split up," Izzy said.

She realised that she'd made the decision sound mutual, when it was anything but.

"Leave her alone," Louise said. "You know she only moved here today."

"Elaine was a cold fish, wasn't she?" Kate said. "No offence, Izzy, but your aunt kept to herself. Was she always like that?"

"I guess she was a private person. I hadn't seen much of her in the months before she died." A cold wave of shame washed over Izzy. "She didn't get on with my partner."

"That's enough prying into Izzy's life," Louise said, wagging a finger at Kate.

Kate ignored her. "So what do you do for fun?"

"I like crafts," Izzy said. "I made this bag."

Everyone's eyes went to the bag. Izzy was sorry she'd mentioned it. They probably only cared about expensive bags from fancy stores. Izzy was surprised when Kate's eyes widened in admiration.

"That's gorgeous. Can I see it?"

"Sure." Izzy passed the bag over.

Kate admired it closely, running her finger along the heart on the side. "Oh my god. It's beautiful. I need one. Can you make me one? You could be a big-name fashion designer."

"It's just a hobby." Izzy shrugged. "I don't want to be famous."

Kate peered inside the bag.

"What have we got here? I don't mean to pry but I see *A Study in Scarlet*. And *Crime and Punishment*. I love this book. Raskolnikov is such a cool character."

Izzy felt like snatching the bag back. She did her best to keep the irritation from her voice. "Actually, it's a diary."

Kate looked at her. "What do you mean? It's a novel."

"That isn't really *Crime and Punishment*. It's a diary disguised as a novel. My aunt's diary."

Kate took it out of the bag and flicked through it. Izzy had to stifle the urge to grab it from her.

"Don't even think about reading that," Louise said. "I'm sure it's private."

Kate shrugged and continued flicking through the pages. "Wow, your aunt wrote a lot."

"Yep. I just found it this evening."

"I hope you don't find any shocking secrets," Kate said. "Like that your aunt suddenly decided she was a man one day."

She slipped the diary back into Izzy's handbag.

Baxter began barking in the hall. Louise rose from her chair as the door to the sitting room burst open. Louise's husband came into the room.

"Hello, ladies," Robert said in a booming voice.

Baxter wagged his tail and ran around Robert. "How are we all doing?"

Louise frowned. "You're home early."

"I was wondering why I was never invited to join your club."

"Ladies only," Kate said.

"That's sexism."

"I don't care what it is, Robert. You're not joining us."

"You don't want me in your club, fine. But this is my house. I'm allowed be in my own house, aren't I?"

Louise sighed. "Of course, you are. Why don't you go upstairs until we're done?"

Robert gave her an indulgent smile. "I'm curious about what a book club is actually like. I've never been in one."

"You've never read a book either."

"Yeah, well. I don't have much time for that. What are you reading, anyway?"

"Sherlock Holmes."

"Oooh, I see Melanie has a very nice-looking copy of it with her. That's lovely. It's as beautiful as her perfectly manicured garden." He sniggered. "Have you read it or do you just take selfies with it?"

"I've read it three times," Melanie said in an icy voice. "First when I was thirteen and then again when I—"

"No need for your life story." Robert turned to Izzy. "And you? New girl, have you got the book?"

Izzy nodded towards her handbag, sitting in Kate's lap. "I bought it today. I've read a few chapters."

Robert's smile vanished. "What? You haven't finished it?"

Louise crossed her arms and shifted weight from one foot to another.

"For god's sake, Robert, would you stop making a show of yourself? I've never been so embarrassed in all my life. I'm amazed Izzy had time to find a copy of the book, never mind read any of it. She only arrived this afternoon."

"True," Robert said. "That's somewhat understandable, I suppose."

Louise sighed. "Never mind *somewhat understandable*. It's none of your business."

Robert pointed at Dee. "You?"

She held up a library copy of the book.

"You?" Robert pointed to Tess.

"Leave me alone," Tess said.

This made Robert laugh. "I guess you'll be sending me a cease-and-desist letter. Maybe a summons to court too. Have you read it or not, Tess?"

"If you must know, I'm listening to the audiobook. Stephen Fry reads it and he—"

"What about you?" he said, pointing at Kate.

"I read stuff on my phone."

"I'm asking if you have you read this book."

"Nope."

"What?"

Kate said, "Would you stop playing the buffoon?"

"Excuse me," Robert said. "I think this is a book club, and you should have read the book. You've got nothing else to do, do you? I mean, you call yourself an actress, but you've never actually acted in anything."

"You have no idea what you're talking about."

"It doesn't take a genius to know what a book club is."

"It doesn't take a genius," Kate agreed, "but it takes someone smarter than you, apparently."

"Get up." Robert grabbed Kate by the arm. "Come on, stand up."

"Let go, you idiot! Get your hands off me."

Suddenly everyone was talking loudly, and Baxter was barking like crazy and running in circles.

Robert yanked Kate out of her seat.

"It's a book club and you haven't read the book. You know what that means? You're *out*."

He dragged Kate to the door, then shoved her through it. They were both roaring at each other. Kate put up a spirited fight, but Robert was stronger.

Soon everyone was on their feet. Baxter was still barking, now even louder, and running in panicked circles.

Izzy had the sinking feeling that something terrible was about to happen.

Louise followed Robert and Kate out to the hall and everyone else followed after her.

Izzy arrived in time to see Robert open the door to the street and push Kate out. She stumbled down a couple of steps. Izzy had a moment of terror when she thought Kate would fall, but she grabbed onto the railing and steadied herself.

"And stay gone," Robert roared and slammed the door shut. He turned to the other ladies. "Now, that's how you run a book club."

Chapter 26

Stephanie found the apartment empty when she got home. The air was stuffy and there was no sign of Kate. She wondered if Kate had gone to her book club as usual.

She flicked on the lights and checked every room, just to make sure. She was definitely alone.

Maybe Kate had met her friends or else she'd headed to the pub instead. Her temper had been really something. Stephanie understood that finding out the truth that way must have been a shock.

Obviously Stephanie had planned to tell Kate. And she'd planned to do it tonight. She just wasn't sure *how*. She didn't want to hurt her.

Now she had to tell everyone else in her life.

Stephanie's parents would be even worse than Kate, if that was possible. They were hard-line Catholics who took the Pope's word as law. There were no gender reassignments in their family. It was going to devastate them.

Stephanie dreaded telling them.

After Kate stormed out of the office, Stephanie's

colleagues had been supportive. Many of them had hung around for another half hour, just chatting and congratulating Stephanie for her bravery. They were the best.

It was a small company, and those on Stephanie's team had known about her for a long time. She had never actually told them, but no one was surprised when she said, *I'm a woman.*

Wow, those words felt as nice as hot chocolate on a cold night. And hot chocolate was a damn fine idea. Maybe she should watch some RuPaul while Kate was out. She didn't think a show about drag queens would go down well with Kate right now.

Stephanie made her way to the kitchen, filled a mug with milk and nuked it for two minutes. While the microwave hummed, she searched the cupboard for the jar of cocoa.

She hadn't planned to tell her colleagues. It had just come out of her mouth at break time when they'd been discussing some stupid movie that Stephanie hated.

"I don't like it, but then I hate romcoms. Do you like them?" she'd asked her PA.

"Of course I like romcoms. I'm a woman."

"I'm a woman too," Stephanie had said.

She could have laughed off the slip of the tongue and continued with her day. But she hadn't. She'd repeated the words.

"I'm a woman. And I don't like romcoms."

There had been silence for a good five or six

seconds, which felt like hours. Then, to her surprise, Gary, the payroll clerk, had begun to applaud. It spread around the room until everyone nearby was clapping and whooping.

A lump had come to her throat. She swallowed and told them, "I'm a woman, and you can call me Stephanie."

The clapping grew in intensity. It was a real moment.

And that wasn't the end.

In the late afternoon, Stephanie had been asked to come to the break room by her supervisor. She'd messed up a few things during the day, what with being so distracted, and she expected to be reprimanded. But no.

Her whole team was waiting for her. There was cake, decorations, smiles and hugs.

Her boss said, "Cut the cake, Stephanie."

Kate appeared a minute later.

The microwave beeped three times, bringing Stephanie back to the moment. She spooned cocoa into the mug. The milk smelled funny. Damn, it had gone bad. She poured it down the drain.

What a day it had been.

Tomorrow, Jessica from Human Resources would announce the news to the rest of the company, and she and Stephanie would discuss the transition in more detail.

Stephanie wondered what she should wear. It would be her first day arriving at the office as a woman. She wanted to mark the occasion but didn't want to go too far.

After all, she'd only begun the social transition. Nothing physical had happened yet.

A chill passed down her spine and she thought, what if Kate told Stephanie's parents the news before she could? Maybe she ought to ring them now. Or should she just ring Kate, and see how she was?

Decisions, decisions.

Stephanie went into the sitting room. It was tiny, grey and sterile, like a metal box. She closed the curtains and turned on the TV, got RuPaul playing in the background, with the sound way down, then rang Kate.

No answer.

She called her parents next. Her mother answered the landline.

"Hello, Stephen. This is a pleasant surprise."

Her mother's tone told her that they hadn't heard the news yet. As they chatted, Stephanie decided to wait a little longer before telling her parents that they had a daughter.

*

Everyone crowded into the hallway as Robert pushed Kate out the door, then shut it behind her. Louise was shouting at him. Melanie and Dee were, too. Their voices blended into an ugly squawk, and Tess was only able to catch the occasional phrase.

"How dare you do that?"

"Let Kate back in."

"What a *jerk*."

Tess hung back next to the new girl. She couldn't quite believe what she was seeing, nor what Kate had said about Stephen.

It was only a few hours since Kate had come to Tess's office. During their meeting, she'd been so sensual, so full of her usual confidence.

Then she'd gone to Tess's house. Kate had done something, found *something* out. That was obvious from the text message Kate had sent, saying she had an answer about Gareth.

But a little while later, here Kate was, deflated and drunk, saying her own husband was a woman.

What the hell was going on? And what had happened with Gareth?

Tess needed to know the truth.

She strode towards the door, which Robert was blocking.

His expression was smug as he told Louise, "Kate's not coming back in here. She broke the rules of book clubs everywhere. She didn't read the book."

"I doubt," Louise said, "that Kate will ever want to come back in this house after tonight."

"Suits me," Robert said.

Dee, Melanie and Louise were all talking at once. And the dog, Baxter, was still barking, while he turned in nervous circles, unhappy with the commotion.

"Let me by," Tess snapped, pushing Dee and Robert out of the way.

"Sure," Robert said, backing to the side of the hall. "I don't believe you read the book either."

"Butt out," Tess said. "You're not a martyr."

"You don't have to go," Louise said.

Ignoring her, Tess opened the door and stepped out into the night. At first, she couldn't see Kate.

She hurried down the steps and the driveway, and looked towards the main street. No sign of Kate. She turned to the other side, towards the sea, and saw a figure disappear around the corner.

Tess was vaguely aware of her friends' voices behind her. She ignored them and hurried down the road.

Chapter 27

Izzy found it weird going 'home' to Elaine's house. It didn't feel like home, but nowhere did now. She would never return to Adam's apartment.

"Never," she whispered to herself, as she stepped into the hallway.

She turned and waved goodnight to Louise, who was standing at the gate, and who had insisted on walking her home. Not that it took more than half a minute to get from one house to another.

"Again, I'm so sorry."

"Don't worry," Izzy said. "It's not your fault."

"Robert is such a dummy sometimes, but he has a good heart."

Louise waved back and smiled as Izzy closed the door.

After Kate had been kicked out of Louise's house, and Tess stormed off, everyone else had made their excuses.

Dee and Melanie had left only moments before Izzy, and Louise had latched onto Izzy. Meanwhile, Robert had looked unfazed by the havoc he'd caused. The last time Izzy saw him, he'd been ambling casually towards the kitchen, as if he'd worked up an appetite.

Izzy didn't like the way he had ignored his wife's pleas to calm down, to let Kate back in. He didn't seem to respect Louise at all.

And poor Kate. She'd had a day to rival Izzy's.

Izzy walked down the hall to the kitchen. The pungent smell of the Chinese medicine still permeated the air. Izzy had the vague feeling she was forgetting something, but she had no idea what.

The house was so still, so quiet. She listened to the unfamiliar street noises. She supposed the traffic on the main road never stopped, though she was some distance from it here, so the noise was only a faint hum.

Izzy turned on the kettle. She decided to make a cup of tea and then read Elaine's diary—

The diary.

That was when she remembered her bag.

The book. The diary. She'd given the bag to Kate for her to look at. Moments later, the trouble with Robert had started, and she'd never returned the bag or its contents.

Luckily Izzy had kept her purse and keys on her. But what happened to the bag? Did Kate absentmindedly bring it with her when Robert dragged her from the house? Or was it left behind at Louise's?

Izzy tapped out a message to Kate.

Hi Kate. Hope you're okay. Just checking if you still have my bag?

It sounded a bit terse and selfish. Izzy agonised over how to make the message sound more sensitive, then gave up and tapped out a message to Louise instead.

Hi Louise. Thanks for inviting me to your house tonight. It was an interesting first experience of a book club. Did I leave my bag behind, by any chance? Kate was looking at it but I'm not sure if she took it with her.

Izzy hit send. She made her way upstairs, a chill running down her spine as she did so. Would she ever be able to use the stairs without feeling weird, without thinking of Elaine's death? And would she ever shake the fear that she might slip and fall too?

Izzy knew how precious life was, knew how easily everything could be taken away. Her parents' deaths had taught her that.

She went to the spare bedroom. As she'd seen earlier, the bed was made, and it looked like it had not been slept in. That would have to do until Izzy unpacked her own bedclothes.

After brushing her teeth, Izzy turned off the lights. She got into the unfamiliar bed and lay on her back, staring at the ceiling.

Finally, she managed to drift off to sleep.

A woman's face swam before her eyes. The image was always the same. Bulging brown eyes with dark rings underneath. Thin lips, closed tight, and adorned with a stud on the left side. Pointy nose, narrow brows, and brown hair scraped back in a severe ponytail, held by a blue band. A fake diamond stud in one ear. Her face well-lined, though she was only twenty-three.

Ruth.

Izzy didn't wake up till the next morning, which was when they pulled a body out of the sea.

Chapter 28

On Friday morning, Dee walked along the paved walkway called The Metals, which linked the coastal towns of Dun Laoghaire and Dalkey. She was making her way towards the library. Yesterday's storm had passed, and it was a cool, dry morning with a sky of pale blue. Dee breathed in the scent of the sea and sighed.

Two hundred years earlier, the granite used to build Dun Laoghaire's piers had been brought from the quarry in Dalkey in the south. Trucks carrying the stone were pulled by horses along The Metals.

It was a pleasant enough place to walk, with granite walls on both sides. The modern railway line was below it.

Dee was ready for a day behind the librarian's desk. However, as she approached the library, a fuss at the near end of the East Pier caught her attention. There were patrol cars and flashing lights.

Dee had never been able to resist the lure of a juicy bit of gossip, and she prided herself on knowing things before anyone else. For instance, when she'd got home the previous night, she'd had to tell a few discreet friends about Stephen becoming Stephanie, about Robert going nuts (again), and about the arrival of the new neighbour, Izzy.

Something even juicier was happening now, and Dee couldn't help taking a closer look.

When she came to a gap in the wall, she walked through it, and crossed the road quickly.

The whole pier was sealed off. Two patrol cars, a Garda Technical Bureau van, a Harbour Police SUV, a Dublin Fire Brigade engine, and an ambulance were all parked in a cluster. A line of young Gardaí stood grim-faced in front of crime scene tape. Dee had never seen such a presence before.

A small crowd had gathered. The pier was a popular place for a walk, even on a chilly February morning, and most of those standing around had probably come for their daily stroll.

Dee cut through the crowd, looking for a familiar face who might know what was going on. She spotted Bridie McGlynn, an older neighbour, standing near the fire engine, with a hand over her mouth.

"Morning Bridie. How are you? What's happening?"

"They've pulled a body out of the water."

"No!" Dee felt a thrill of excitement.

Bridie pointed to the side of the pier close to the land. Over there, a path led along the outer wall of the pier for a while, and you could go down to the seaweed-covered rocks if you liked.

"They've brought a stretcher and a body bag down

there to put it in. The forensics lads are photographing everything."

"That's shocking."

Bridie nodded. "They aren't saying anything, so we don't know who it is yet. If the body was in the water all night, I wouldn't fancy having to identify it. You know how rough the sea was."

Dee imagined the body being dashed to pieces on the rocks which lined the shore, being smashed against the side of the pier.

She stood there a while longer, but Bridie had no more information, and Dee couldn't hang around all day. She had a job to get to, so she made her excuses and left. There was no point asking the officers anything. Dee knew from experience that they were usually tight-lipped spoilsports at times like this.

But she would talk to her brother later. He was a Garda and, although he was stationed in Drogheda, he might be able to find out the identity of the poor soul who was dead.

She hurried to the library, greeting colleagues as she made her way to the first floor.

She threw her bag on the floor, then continued on to the end of the room, where an enormous window overlooked the harbour.

From here, she could see the scene even better.

Bridie had been right. Beyond the emergency service vehicles, white-coated Technical Bureau people were scouring the seafront down at the rocks.

Dee let out a soft squeal of excitement when she

saw them wheeling a stretcher towards the ambulance. The body bag was black and gave no clue about its contents.

"Dee?"

Who was in the bag? A man or a woman?

Someone she knew or a stranger?

"Hello? Earth to Dee?"

Dee turned at the sound, realising that her supervisor was standing right behind her.

"They've found a body," Dee said.

Her supervisor scowled and brushed some imaginary flecks of dust from her blouse.

"Well, that's none of our business, is it? Come on, the training session is about to begin."

"I'll be right there."

"*Now*, please."

Dee would never have become a librarian if she'd realised quite how much time was spent away from her beloved books. There was endless IT training, and event management stuff, as the library rented out rooms for meetings and conferences. Not to mention the fact that they hosted art exhibitions and readings by authors, but never anyone Dee liked. They hadn't had Nora Roberts or Stephen King come and visit, only local writers no one had ever heard of.

Dee gave the seafront a final look, but the ambulance was gone. She'd missed the part where the body was loaded into it.

"Damn it."

She turned her back on the window and began to

walk across the floor when her phone rang. Dee didn't recognise the number displayed on the screen. She answered anyway.

"Hi Dee. It's, uh, Stephen Long," said the voice on the other side of the line.

"You mean Stephanie, right?"

There was a weak laugh. "I wasn't sure if you'd heard the news yet, so I didn't want to confuse you."

"Oh, we've all heard the news."

"It was a big thing, coming out like that. I'm not sure Kate took it very well."

"What can I help you with?"

"Actually, it's about Kate. I was wondering if you've seen her. She didn't come home last night."

Chapter 29

Izzy was disoriented when she woke up on Friday morning. The room was unfamiliar, and the bed felt different to her own. This mattress was soft, and it creaked whenever Izzy shifted her weight.

It took a moment to realise that she was in her aunt's house. The duvet was heavier than the one she was used to, but Izzy was glad of that, given that she hadn't figured out the central heating yet.

Light shone through the gap between the curtains. Izzy stretched and took a moment to orient herself before climbing out of the bed. She dressed quickly in jeans and a warm jumper while the icy air nipped at her skin.

Once she was clothed, Izzy opened the top window. The house needed fresh air running through it.

This would be the first day in months that Izzy hadn't been weighed.

First thing in the morning, Adam usually had Izzy step on his electronic scales. It started as a joke when Izzy mentioned losing a kilogram. Her autoimmune condition made her thin and weak. Adam had pulled out the scales and had her step on them. The next morning, he did it again.

Before she knew it, getting weighed and evaluated was her morning routine. Another one of Adam's many routines and rituals that had to be followed.

Adam's mood for the day, how well or badly he treated Izzy, was set by how far she strayed from a hundred pounds. He considered that the right weight for her. For some reason, he didn't like the metric system and never used it, so Izzy couldn't use it either.

She dreaded his reaction when she strayed more than a pound above or below one hundred.

But she had to get healthier. She *wanted* to gain weight.

It was refreshing not to have to worry about the scales this morning.

Izzy checked her phone. Her notifications lit up like a Christmas tree. Calls, texts, voicemails. All from Adam. She dismissed the notifications and resisted the temptation to check what Adam had said.

Screw you, she thought.

The stairs creaked as Izzy descended them.

She gripped the banister tight, feeling the smoothness of the wood under her skin. Every step looked so hard, so brutal.

She shivered, still having not managed to shake off her squeamishness, the thought of a fragile human body smashing against the wood.

In the kitchen, she drank a glass of water and

thought about breakfast. She yearned for a big fry-up. Eggs, bacon, toast with lashings of butter.

Screw you, Adam, she thought again.

She'd seen a couple of cafes on the main street yesterday, and she figured one of them must be able to give her what she wanted. It would be nice to be waited on for a change, and she'd be sure to leave a decent tip, not like some cheapskates who came into the diner.

She flung on her jacket and looked around for her favourite handbag. She'd sit and read *A Study in Scarlet* while she ate her breakfast, and maybe have a look at Elaine's diary. A breakfast treat was just what she needed.

Then she remembered that she didn't have the bag or the book.

Had Louise replied to her text message? Izzy checked her phone again. There was indeed a reply from her, lost in the dozens of messages from Adam. Louise had sent it late the previous night when Izzy was already asleep.

Hi Izzy. Sorry again about Robert. I can assure you that our book club meetings aren't normally like that. I hope you aren't put off. No, I didn't see your bag here. I think Kate must have taken it with her. You can ask her today. Maybe give her a while to sleep off her hangover first.

There was also a message from Melanie confirming her appointment at the salon.

Izzy walked to the bookcase in the sitting room

and looked at the shelf where she had found the diary disguised as *Crime and Punishment*. She picked up another volume, this one disguised as *Great Expectations*. A quick flick through it confirmed that it was another instalment of Elaine's diary. This one covered July and August.

Izzy put it back on the shelf and picked up a volume that looked like a collection of Poe's writings. This diary seemed to continue where the *Crime and Punishment* volume left off, with its first entry being at the start of November.

Izzy flicked through it quickly. The last entry was near the back of the book. December fifth. The day Elaine died.

Izzy had to read this.

And she had to recover the other volume, though Louise was right about waiting a while before contacting Kate.

In the meantime, Izzy was going to enjoy a nice breakfast. She brought the diary with her, put it into her second-favourite handbag – a cute cream and brown number with a narrow leather strap – and slung it over her shoulder. She put on her jacket and grabbed her keys and purse.

As soon as she opened the front door, she saw the flowers.

An enormous bouquet sat on the doorstep, every kind of flower you could think of, all different colours, beautifully arranged and bound up in a clear plastic bag full of water.

A greeting card was tucked into them.

Izzy had been looking forward to finally having some time to herself. What a rare luxury. She was free aside from her appointments at the salon and at the Chinese shop.

But she'd only been out of bed ten minutes and Adam had already ruined her day.

Thinking of you was printed on one side of the card. She flipped it over to find a handwritten note.

I'm sorry I lost my temper, but what did you expect? You disappeared with no warning, took all your stuff, and MOVED OUT. What's going on, Izzy? Please give me a call. Love, Adam.

Izzy felt anger course through her. She binned the flowers and the card in the kitchen, then left the house. She paused by the gate but there was no sign of Adam. When did he bring the flowers? The thought of him being around here creeped her out.

She walked to the main street, thinking as she went that she'd have to get her car window replaced.

She soon came to an Argentinian café. Handwritten signs on the window listed items from their menu. The place did a variety of grilled pork sandwiches, which sounded amazing. But then she saw what she was looking for.

All-day breakfast inc. tea/coffee €6.95.

She stepped inside. The café's interior was narrow. A few empty tables, just inside the door, lay in sunshine. Other tables, farther back, were shaded.

An old man was reading a paper near the back. Two

staff members stood behind the counter along the side wall.

One of them came over as soon as Izzy entered.

"Can I sit here?" Izzy asked, pointing to the table closest to the door.

"Yes, of course. You want to see the menu?"

She ordered the all-day breakfast and tea.

"Coming right up," the waitress said with a big smile.

Izzy took a chair facing the street so she could watch people passing by. After a pot of tea had been brought, she took out Elaine's diary.

November 2nd

Another lousy day at the office. Word has clearly spread about my sleepwalking adventures. Paula kept saying she was sleepy, asking if I was sleepy blah blah blah. What a silly woman. If she were any less subtle, she'd be in a pantomime.

I know Paula's eldest daughter, who works at the library, has been blabbing about me. I don't know if she saw me sleepwalking with her own eyes (unlikely) or if she heard it from someone else. In any case, now she and Paula are telling everyone.

I think Paula wants to undermine me. She always wanted my position. She hates me being able to tell her what to do.

The fact that people are gossiping about me only makes me more stressed out. And according to Dr. Mullen, that makes another sleepwalking episode more likely!

I told Father Peter about it. As usual, he was a pillar

of support. We might go to Bray for a walk at the week-end and I really need it.

However, the sleepwalking – and gossip about the sleepwalking – are not the only things that are adding to my stress levels. There's also the man. The one who's been watching me. I saw him again today, this time standing by the Queen Victoria Fountain.

I wonder if I should be scared.

Chapter 30

As usual, the salon felt suffocating with the heat of a hundred lights, the noise of half a dozen hair dryers, and the buzz of conversation.

Melanie needed a break.

She made her way to the little office upstairs and dumped herself in the swivel chair at her desk. It was only morning, and she already felt like going to bed.

Give me strength, God.

Melanie spent very little time up here. Even though she was the boss, most of the time she was cutting hair alongside her staff. But sometimes during the day, she had to get away from it all.

Sometimes she went home.

When she left Amy in charge, she knew the salon was in safe hands, but today Amy was using an annual leave day to celebrate Chinese New Year. So, Melanie contented herself with a little break up here before she returned to the frontline. It was a tiny square office with a leaking window, damp walls and a computer that was nearly dead. But whatever. A few minutes alone made all the difference.

She often liked to give Tom a quick call and she did that now.

"Babe?" he said, picking up after a few rings. "We've talked about this."

"I know—"

"Can you *please* not call me when I'm in work?"

He said that his boss, whose desk was next to Tom's, hated it when people made personal calls on company time. Melanie thought that must be an exaggeration. His boss could hardly expect people to not answer their phones.

"Sorry, but I just wanted to check up on you."

Tom had been shaken by his encounter with Robert Murphy in Fitzgerald's the previous night. His shock had grown greater when Melanie told him about the scene Robert had made at the book club.

"I'm fine, babe."

Melanie said, "Are you sure?"

"I told you, I'm fine."

"You should really go to the Garda Station and get Robert charged with assault. I want to see that bastard in jail."

"No need. I'll handle it myself."

"But he brandished a broken bottle in your face. He could have killed you."

Tom laughed. "Robert Murphy? Kill me? I don't think so."

"Yeah, well, I worry about you. I can't help it. It's not just Robert Murphy. It's this town. I hate this place —"

"Please don't start, babe. Not now. I'm trying to work."

"I can't live in this kip any longer." Melanie felt like screaming. "I'm sorry but I hate this place."

"You don't mean that. You have friends here."

"Not really."

"You do. Louise, Dee, Tess, Amy, the other salon girls, your clients—"

Melanie couldn't keep the exasperation from her voice.

"I'm telling you I want to live somewhere else." She squeezed her eyes shut tight. "Sometimes I get so mad, I think I might lose my mind."

"What do you mean?"

Suddenly, Tom sounded alarmed. Good. She had to get his attention one way or another.

"Never mind. I better go."

"You already sent Robert a box full of dog dirt. Please don't do anything else crazy."

She smiled, trying to imagine what Robert's face would have looked like when he opened his surprise.

"Of course not. Anyway, I forgot to tell you last night, but I found some properties in north Dublin that sound amazing. I'll show you them later. I think we should talk to an estate agent. I swear, I'd move today."

"We can't just pick up and leave."

"Of course, we can. The house is rented."

"And the salon?"

Melanie stifled her irritation.

"I'll open a new one somewhere else. This place is getting me down. I feel depressed every day. Amy could take over the running of this place, and we can open another one somewhere else."

"Let's talk about it later. Don't do anything crazy. Your family's reputation is bad enough already."

"Don't remind me."

Melanie would never be allowed to forget that she was a distant cousin of Billy Cooney, the black sheep of the family. As far as Melanie was concerned, Chisel Cooney was another good reason to leave the area.

"I better go," Tom said. "Talk to you later."

"Okay. Love you."

The line went dead.

Chapter 31

The sky brightened. At her sun-soaked table, Izzy stared at the diary in her hands, trying to make sense of her aunt's words. A man had been watching Elaine? Why?

She heard the sizzle of a frying pan, the scent of frying bacon, and the sharp sound of eggs being cracked.

Izzy knew her food was on its way when she heard a toaster pop. But she continued reading.

I first noticed him at work yesterday. I saw him through the window. He was just the usual kind of scruffy fellow, wearing a dark hoodie and jeans. I didn't see his face. He was standing outside the DART station, where the bus stop is. I didn't pay any particular attention as I assumed he was waiting to catch a bus or else that he would go into the station and catch a train.

This morning I saw him again. He was standing at the Queen Victoria Fountain next to the station, staring at my window. It was slightly unsettling, although by lunchtime I had forgotten. I went down to the burger place.

As I walked back to the office, a fellow bumped into me. Hard. It was the man in a hoodie. I called after him but he didn't look back. As I write this, well after eight o'clock, my shoulder is still sore. That was how hard he walked into me.

<u>Update: Nearly ten o'clock now. He was here a few minutes ago, standing on the street, staring at the house.</u>

I thought about calling 999. But when I looked again, he was gone. Very unnerving, but perhaps it is a coincidence.

A shadow passed over Izzy's table, startling her.

It was just the waitress. She smiled. "Now, the all-day breakfast?"

Izzy put the diary down with some reluctance. She was shocked that someone had apparently been stalking her aunt. Why hadn't Elaine told someone? Why hadn't she told Izzy?

Izzy tried to recall where she had been on November second, the date of the entry, but she couldn't remember. It was certain to be one of two things: either she was working a late shift at the diner or else she was at home with Adam.

Izzy dug into her bacon, eggs, sausages, and hash browns. She was hungrier than she'd realised. Despite her dry mouth, she polished off everything relatively quickly, even soaked up every drop of egg yolk with her toast.

But as she was eating, she couldn't help thinking how she'd failed Elaine.

Had her aunt felt that Izzy wasn't there for her? Was that why she had never confided in her? In early November, Adam had still been treating Izzy like a princess. Izzy had been smitten. She didn't have time for anyone or anything else.

How selfish she had been.

When Izzy's plate was clear, she poured a fresh cup of tea from the pot and opened the diary again.

There were lengthy entries for most days. Apparently, Elaine had devoted a lot of time to her day job. She had recorded detailed thoughts on many work projects.

Izzy skipped past that stuff, looking for any mention of the stalker again, or of herself. She read snatches here and there that caught her attention.

November 4th

Called Izzy tonight but could not get through. She's probably working. I hate to interrupt her, especially when she's so busy. I know the lease on her apartment runs out at the end of the month and she's frantically trying to find somewhere else to live. I keep telling her she's welcome to use my spare room, but I'm quite sure she doesn't want an old lady cramping her style.

November 5th

Izzy texted me back. Said sorry, she was busy, and that she would call me next week.

November 7th

I posted Izzy the property section of the newspaper, where it lists some apartments she might want to view.

I hope she can find a suitable place soon. I must visit some estate agents' offices too.

Father Peter said he too would keep his ear to the ground.

November 8th

Izzy texted me, said thanks for the paper, but she looks up lettings online. The ones in the newspaper were probably gone by the time my post got to her. Of course, I'm a dinosaur. I asked if she wants to do something on Sunday, but she has plans with the Scotsman.

November 10th

<u>*I called Izzy as she hadn't told me whether she found a place to live. I asked her about it, and she hardly even seemed to know what I was talking about. She told me she's engaged. Good God. I was so surprised that I didn't know what to say – except to remind her that she has only known the Scotsman three weeks. Three weeks. I've had toothaches that lasted longer than that.*</u>

I sensed a note of irritation creeping into Izzy's voice when she realised I wasn't as excited about her engagement as her. She ended the call a tad abruptly. I do wonder if I should just keep my mouth shut. On the other hand, I'm Izzy's only family. No one else is going to talk sense into her.

The more Izzy read of the diary, the more miserable she felt. She remembered that phone call with Elaine. She really had been irritated that Elaine wasn't happy for her.

"Old maid," she'd said to Adam.

"Never mind her," was his reply. And they'd gone

to bed, Izzy thinking what a fool Elaine was never to have remarried after her husband's death.

"Yep, I got engaged to him," Izzy muttered. "Like a prize-winning moron."

She wondered about Elaine's references to Father Peter. Elaine had mentioned the parish priest to Izzy once or twice over the years, but it sounded like they knew each other better than Izzy had thought. And there was that picture of them together.

Izzy continued reading.

November 11th

I've been sleepwalking again. This morning, I woke up to find the front door wide open. God only knows what I was thinking, but I must have gone out onto the street again.

I found footprints in the flower bed, and my feet were muddy. It was a cold night too, but not icy, thank goodness. Somehow I returned to bed safely and continued sleeping.

I suppose I'm lucky nothing terrible happened. Someone could have come in and cleared the place out. Or slit my throat.

Izzy leaned back in her chair and sighed. When was the last time Izzy asked Elaine how she was, or if she needed anything, or if she just wanted to meet and have a chat? For a moment, Izzy truly loathed herself.

She wished she could hug Elaine and tell her she was sorry and that she missed her, because she did.

Izzy glanced out the window. A man was standing

on the footpath outside, staring at her through the glass.

It was Adam.

Chapter 32

Tess sat in her office, her U-shaped desk covered in files and papers. She stared unseeingly at the computer screen. Her short, unpainted nails clicked as she tapped her fingers on the desk. It was impossible to focus. Utterly impossible. Why had she even come to work? She could think of nothing but the previous night, and her stomach churned.

To complete the nightmare, her assistant, Britney, appeared with a cup of coffee. She had been in the office almost the whole night. The security guard on the door had confirmed that Britney only left at 4am and returned at 7:35 am.

Food, shower, change of clothes. Then back to the grindstone.

Tess had done that herself many times, and she'd suffered for it. Sagging skin, wrinkles, huge dark circles under the eyes, feeling like death.

Unlike Tess, Britney barely looked any worse for wear. No tiredness showed on her perfect face. No tetchiness in her manner. And the work Tess had requested Britney to do had been done, and done well, judging by the cursory glance Tess gave her Maxwell memo before flinging the file across the room. It lay in a heap on the floor, but Britney didn't seem to notice. Or maybe she was discreet enough to ignore it. That would be just like her.

Tess breathed in the bitter aroma of her espresso. Not quite as bitter as the choking scent of her own doubts and fears, but close.

"Anything else, Tess?"

I'll think of something.

But Tess only said, "You can go."

Britney shot her a toothy smile and left the room, shutting the door behind her, so that the murmur of conversation outside was cut off.

Silence.

The previous night, after Kate had been kicked out of Louise's house, Tess had hurried after her. Down by The Metals, she caught up. Kate had been in no mood to talk though. She'd been furious, tottering along on her high heels, with her bandaged toe and her wounded pride.

"Leave me alone," Kate screamed.

Tess held her hands up in a conciliatory gesture. "Just tell me what happened with Gareth. You said you had an answer."

"Everything's about *you*, isn't it?" Kate gave a maniacal laugh. Her eyes were wet. "If the world was ending, you'd still only care about yourself."

"Tell me what happened. I guess nothing, since not even your husband wants you."

A brief surge of satisfaction came over Tess. It felt good to lash out. She kept her rage buttoned down so much of the time.

The feeling vanished when Kate slapped her across the face.

"I won't tell you," Kate said. "How about that?"

She gazed at Tess's shocked face for a moment before storming off.

A cold rage had swept across Tess then. As she watched Kate vanish into the darkness, she felt like killing someone. She walked home in a rage.

When she reached the house, Gareth was back from the pub. She found him in his study, staring at his computer screen. A very obvious black eye was forming on his face.

"What happened? I saw the first aid kit."

Gareth said there had been a bit of a scuffle at the pub. Robert Murphy and Tom Flynn had got into a fight.

"I was caught in the crossfire," Gareth said.

Tess had unsuccessfully tried to unwind in the shower. Even the expensive body lotion she put on afterwards was unable to distract her.

She went to bed and read a detective novel until Gareth came to bed.

"Still awake?" he said. Tess got the impression that he'd stayed in his study late just so he could avoid talking to her.

"As you can see," she said.

When she asked about Kate, he'd been evasive.

"No, I didn't see her."

"She didn't come here?"

Gareth went pale. "Why would she come here?"

Tess pressed on. "Dee said she saw Kate here, before the book club."

"She's mistaken."

Tess felt like he was lying, both about his black eye and about Kate's visit. She couldn't get a handle on what was going on, and it was driving her crazy.

"How's the latest investment?"

Gareth perked up a little then. "I think it's going to skyrocket."

He seemed strangely excited. It couldn't be about the stock market. No one got excited over a five-hundred-euro investment, which was all Gareth said he'd put at risk. At work, Tess's hourly rate was almost that much.

So, what was Gareth *really* up to?

He got into bed and turned off the light. She listened to his breathing change as he drifted off to sleep.

Meanwhile Tess lay awake, looking at the back of his head. What was going on with him? Morning's insipid light had come without providing any answer.

Tess snapped back to the present moment when her phone pinged with a message.

It was from Dee on the WhatsApp book club group. *Girls, Kate is DEAD!!!!!*

*

Before Louise woke him, Robert was having the best

dream of his life. Like Santa Claus bringing presents, he was driving a sleigh through the air over Dublin. It was pulled by a team of thousands of flying poodles, all yapping away, while the lights of the city sparkled below. Robert threw apples over the side, aiming at his enemies' houses. There were quite a few of them and he was having tremendous fun trying to hit them all.

They'd get the fright of their lives. An apple shower from the heavens.

He spotted Tom Flynn's house. Melanie was lying in the garden, though it was covered in snow. He picked up and apple and—

Robert was shaken.

"Huh?" he muttered. The images began to fade.

"*Wake up.*"

He opened his eyes to find that it was morning. He was in bed and the room was bright with sunlight. Louise stood next to him.

"I was about to pour a jug of water over you."

"Why? What's going on?"

He stretched and yawned. He'd been dreaming about...Christmas, or something? The memory was already going.

"It's late," Louise said. She pointed at the clock next to their bed.

"I have a day off."

"Yeah, well I think there are plenty of things you need to do. You said you were going to get some paint for the dining room, didn't you?"

"Yeah, well—"

"You've been saying you'll do it for two years."

Louise pulled the duvet down. Icy air gripped Robert's exposed skin. He was only wearing a thin white vest and his favourite pair of boxer shorts, with *VIP AREA* printed on the front, and *EXIT ONLY* written on the back.

"Do you remember last night?" Louise said.

"Of course, I do. I wasn't drunk."

"Well, are you pleased with your behaviour?"

He could see that Louise was in one of those moods. She worried too much what people thought of her, thought of both of them.

"What are you talking about?"

"You made a show of yourself," Louise said.

Robert sat up, swung his legs over the side of the bed and stood.

"I asked you if you're happy with yourself, Robert."

He thought of the bar. Getting in a row with Tom Flynn, getting kicked out of the pub by Jimmy. Was that what Louise was talking about? No, she didn't know about that stuff.

"Help me out, will you?"

Before she could answer, it came back to him. The scene here in the house last night. The book club.

Robert flushed. He turned away so that Louise wouldn't see, making a show of looking in the wardrobe for a clean pair of trousers.

"Oh," he said evenly.

"Oh? *Oh?* You recall bullying my friends and kicking them out of the house?"

"I only kicked *one* of them out," Robert said. "Let's not exaggerate."

He pulled on his trousers, a pair he hadn't worn for a few months. Closing the button was a struggle. He'd gained a little weight lately and he thought it was starting to show. He had stretch marks at his sides, and a narrow line of dried blood along the beltline on both sides of his waist, where his trusty leather belt had cut into him.

With his trousers on, he tried to give Louise a hug, but she stepped away.

"I suppose it would be an exaggeration to say that your behaviour was appalling?"

Robert shrugged. "Nobody died," he said. It was his usual response when Louise overreacted to something.

Louise put her hands on her hips.

"Tell that to Kate."

Chapter 33

Izzy gasped at the sight of Adam. His eyes were pink-rimmed and dark, his face sickly pale. She only caught a glimpse of him before a group of elderly people appeared on the footpath outside. Izzy lost sight of Adam in the sea of bodies.

She waited for them to pass, but they stopped outside the café. Izzy heard French accents, saw a street map in one lady's hand. Her eyes darted around. Where was Adam?

Her breakfast churned in her stomach. One of the tourists pushed open the door and came into the café.

Putting Elaine's diary in her handbag, and flinging the bag over her shoulder, Izzy hurried to the counter.

"Excuse me?"

Izzy's waitress came over. "Was everything okay? If you'd like dessert, we have fresh—"

"Is there a back exit?" Izzy interrupted.

"No, only the front. Is everything alright?"

"I'll pay now," Izzy said quickly.

"Sure."

The girl tapped a few buttons on a card machine,

then held it out. Izzy tapped her card, then hurried to the door. The rest of the tourists were spilling in, looking cheerful and carefree. None of them seemed to notice that they were blocking the way, even as Izzy pushed her way through them, feeling more suffocated with each passing second.

She stepped out onto the street, scanned the area to the left. No sign of Adam. But he couldn't have gone far. She was turning to the right when a heavy hand landed on her shoulder.

"Izzy?"

Suddenly Adam was in her face. He held a huge bouquet of roses and was smiling as if nothing was wrong.

Izzy stepped back. "Get away from me."

"Whoa, take it easy, Izzy. I got you some—"

"No." She turned and launched herself down the footpath, narrowly avoiding a collision with one of the tourists.

"Izzy? Don't be silly. What are you doing?"

He wanted to charm her, to get her to go home. There'd be no escape then.

On legs as wobbly as jelly, she ran down the path.

Glancing over her shoulder, she saw Adam let the roses fall from his hand as he broke into a jog.

Izzy urged herself on. Faster. Dodging pedestrians.

Adam shouted her name.

She glanced back, saw him running at full speed now, arms and legs pumping like crazy, his taut, lean body ready for violence.

Izzy couldn't outrun him. He was in excellent shape and she was suffering from a chronic illness.

A taxi came up the road. Her only chance to get away. The light on top of the car's roof was on, showing that the cab was free.

She ran towards it.

Izzy didn't look back when Adam called her name. Didn't slow down. She threw herself in front of the car, forcing the driver to slam on the breaks.

She jumped in the back seat.

"You crazy?" the driver said. "You want to get knocked down?"

"Lock the doors."

"Where do you want to go?"

"Anywhere. Just lock the damn doors!"

A car horn beeped behind them. Through the front windscreen Izzy saw Adam moving swiftly towards them. He reached for the door handle.

The driver touched a button on the steering wheel. Izzy heard a click as the doors locked, a fraction of a second before Adam tried the handle.

"Hey," Adam snarled. "Open up or, I swear, you'll be sorry."

The driver hit the accelerator. Adam ran after them for a while, but he fell behind as the car sped up.

"You alright, yeah?" the driver said.

"Yeah," Izzy said, though she felt lightheaded. She took a few deep breaths, trying to steady herself.

I'm okay.

Her first thought was to go straight home, lock

the door and never come out again. But she had her appointment at Melanie's salon. Once she'd calmed down a little, she told the driver the address.

He turned towards the sea, then down Crofton Road, driving parallel to the train tracks, before reaching County Hall. The train station and bus stop were on her left, the Queen Victoria Fountain just past it. The fountain was surrounded by a circular structure consisting of elaborate ironwork arches covered in a dome. It had been built to commemorate Queen Victoria's visit in 1900.

Izzy thought of Elaine's stalker standing there, looking across the junction at County Hall. At Elaine's office window.

The driver continued to the salon and stopped right outside the door.

Izzy got out and stood on the footpath for a moment to compose herself. There was no need for Melanie to see her in her panicked state. A few long breaths helped ease her racing pulse to some extent. She checked her phone.

There were new messages on the WhatsApp book club group.

Dee: *Girls, Kate is DEAD!!!!!*

Louise: *Are you serious?*

Melanie: *What?!*

Tess: *Are you kidding me? What happened?*

Dee: *She was pulled out of the sea this morning.*

Louise: *Oh my god.*

Tess: *I don't ducking believe this spit.*

Tess: *Stupid autocorrect.*

Chapter 34

Stephanie made a cappuccino in the office kitchenette. She breathed the drink's aroma in deep. Today she was wearing her usual trousers and shoes, but a soft cotton shirt with a grandfather collar. It wasn't feminine, but it wasn't particularly masculine either.

The androgynous look wasn't quite the statement she'd wanted to make on her first day as a woman, but everything had happened so fast. She hadn't time to prepare her wardrobe. And until she got hormone replacement therapy, Stephanie didn't actually want to dress like a woman.

She took a sip of cappuccino and wiped the foam from her upper lip.

Despite the nerves, she had never felt so well. In the past, mornings were difficult. It was a drag getting out of bed, hauling herself to the city centre, and sitting at her desk staring at a computer all day. But today she felt full of hope and optimism.

Not having to talk to Kate last night had been nice too. The only thing that marred it was the uneasy feeling she'd got ever since phoning Dee. She thought

Dee might have heard from Kate, but she hadn't. But Dee had said she was walking by the pier and there was something going on there. Stephanie hadn't liked the sound of that, but Dee had already said she didn't know where Kate was, so Stephanie ended the call.

She brought the coffee back to her desk.

Now that her social transition was under way, it was time to think about next steps.

Nearly a year earlier, Stephanie had made an appointment with her doctor, during which she'd admitted that she didn't feel she was a man. The doctor had referred her to a psychiatrist, who diagnosed gender dysphoria, and, in turn, referred her to an endocrinologist.

Stephanie hated having to keep all that from Kate, but she had been scared of Kate's reaction. Obviously, she'd been right to be nervous.

Now the appointment with the endocrinologist was finally approaching, and Stephanie hoped she'd be able to begin treatment. She dreamed of oestrogen shots and, eventually, surgery. You had to travel outside Ireland for that. She had her eye on a clinic in the States. Maybe she could combine surgery with a holiday in the sun.

Her phone rang. Jess on the front desk.

"Stephen? Sorry, *Stephanie*. There are a couple of Gardaí here to see you."

"Gardaí?"

"Yes." Jess's voice went lower. "They look serious."

Stephanie swallowed. "I'll be right there."

She got to her feet and hurried through the office to the reception desk. Two uniformed officers stood there, one male, one female. They were grim-faced.

"Can I help you?"

The female officer said, "You're Mr. Long?"

Close enough.

"Yes, I am."

"Is there somewhere private we can talk?"

"Yeah. If you'd like to follow me."

The conference room was empty, so she took the cops there.

"What's this about?" Stephanie said once she'd closed the door. There was a moment's silence.

"You might want to sit down," the male officer said. "I'm afraid we have some bad news."

*

When the lunch bell rang, Gareth Gillen shot out of the classroom even before his students. He strode to the staff room, eager for his ham and cheese sandwich and a cup of tea. He ignored the kids streaming into the hallway from all the other classes. Let them fight. Who cared?

Whatever vocation he had originally thought himself to have, it was long gone.

He reached the staff room while it was still quiet. Only the geography teacher, Mrs. Slattery, and the art teacher, Mr. Harris, had got there before him. They were seated by the window, deep in conversation. And the principal, Maggie Connell, was pouring herself a cup of coffee in the kitchen area.

"Hello, Maggie."

Her eyes widened as she saw his bruised face.

"It looks worse than it is," he said with a chuckle, though inside he was still seething about what had happened the previous night. "I thought boxing would be a fun way to get some exercise, but no."

"You need to work on your defence," the principal said, before going to join Mrs. Slattery and Mr. Harris at their table.

Gareth poured his tea, then grabbed his sandwich from the fridge where he'd left it this morning. He brought them to a table far from the other staff members and sat with his back to them so he wouldn't be disturbed.

Excited, Gareth took out his phone. The NASDAQ was closed (with SSI up 51% at the end of the previous day's trading) and he'd already digested the company's earnings announcement before bed the previous night.

The results were better than expected, and the stock had nearly doubled in after-hours trading. Gareth would have to wait for the market to open properly before he could sell his shares.

Gareth had read the one article he could find in the financial press, which quickly appeared after the announcement.

SSI Beats on Top and Bottom Line.

Now, with shaking hands, he checked if there was anything new.

The first thing he noticed on the stock chart was

the big green number showing that the stock had ended the previous day up nicely. The second thing he noticed was the small writing in red, saying that the stock was down 60% in pre-market trading.

What the hell?

Beads of sweat broke out on Gareth's face. How could the stock be down? It had surged last night and announced spectacular results.

"Don't be a loner," Maggie Connell said. Gareth realised the principal was speaking to him. "Join us."

Gareth knew that was more an order than an invitation, but right now he didn't care.

"Give me a minute. I have an urgent e-mail."

He Googled news on SSI again and found a message on an investing forum. A user, commenting on the results, wrote, "Whoa, glad I never bought in. That rights issue just wiped shareholders out. Will watch for a dead cat bounce, but aside from that I'm gonna short this sucker."

Confused, Gareth found SSI's announcement from the previous night. He read it again, more carefully this time. The company had announced more than great results. It had announced its intention to issue millions of new shares to raise funds, diluting the value of existing shareholders' investments.

Wiping out Gareth's investment.

Chapter 35

Entering the salon, Izzy affected a calmness that she did not feel. She was shaken by her encounter with Adam. The news of Kate's death was a further shock, one she didn't even know how to process.

The salon was a long, brightly lit room with chairs and mirrors along one side, and a striking white and pink colour scheme.

The woman at the desk inside the door greeted Izzy with a smile. "Can I help you?"

"I have an appointment with Melanie."

"Just a sec." She swiped the screen of the tablet in her hand. A frown creased her face. "Hmmm."

"It's not in the book."

The voice made both of them turn their heads. In the light of day, Melanie's purple hair looked even more dazzling than it had the previous night. She was dressed in black leather trousers and a red tank top. It was a strong look, one Izzy was certain she herself would not have been able to pull off.

Melanie gave a strained smile as she walked over. "How are you?"

"A bit shocked, to be honest. I just saw the message about Kate."

Melanie nodded. "I can't believe it either. Come with me."

She led the way to the back of the salon, the farthest chair from the entrance, which Izzy was glad about. There was less chance of Adam passing the salon and seeing her inside.

She sat down.

"I called Dee," Melanie said. "But she didn't know anything more about Kate's death. She had a lot of ideas, of course, but nothing solid, and I don't like to repeat gossip."

"Of course."

"Dee said Stephanie called her this morning, asking if she'd seen Kate. Dee told me she was literally watching them pull the body out of the water when Stephanie rang."

"Oh my god. Is it definitely Kate?"

"I think so. That's what Dee said, and she has her sources."

"What a terrible accident. I *assume* it was an accident."

"What if it wasn't?" A hard expression sharpened Melanie's features. "If she killed herself because of what Robert did..."

"Surely not?"

Melanie shrugged. "All I know is that she was in a delicate state *before* he made that scene. He kicked her out on the street like a dog. No, worse than a dog. He'd never treat his precious Baxter like that."

"Robert does seem a little unpredictable."

"Louise makes excuses for him, says he's having a hard time because of that incident on the track last year. Some fellow walked out in front of the train Robert was driving. Splat!" Melanie shrugged. "Okay, crashing into that guy can't have been pleasant, but Robert wasn't much better before that."

Their phones both beeped at the same time.

Melanie had hers out of her back pocket first. "It's Dee. She wants everyone to come to her place tonight. Says she has important news."

Izzy had no idea what Dee's news might be, and Melanie looked none the wiser.

"Well, I guess we'll find out later," Melanie said.

"I'm sure she didn't mean me to come."

"Of course, she did." Melanie put a hand on her hip, as if daring Izzy to contradict her. "You're a book club member now. You're part of the gang. We don't take that lightly, you know. Are you busy tonight?"

"I don't have specific plans but—"

"Then you must come. We hardly even got to talk last night. We can honour Kate. Raise a glass in her memory. Say you'll come."

For someone with no family, no close friends any-more, it felt good to be included. Going to Dee's house also meant she wouldn't spend the evening alone.

"Okay," Izzy said. "I'll come for a little while."

Melanie beamed. "Excellent."

"Thanks for inviting me. I'm lucky to have met you and the others. Everyone has been so welcoming. Especially you and Louise."

"Louise has nothing better to do," Melanie said with a laugh. "She ought to make you feel welcome."

Izzy remembered that Louise wasn't working at the moment.

"Has she been on a career break for long?"

"Career break?" Melanie sniggered. "Is that what she told you? I guess that's one way of putting it. An involuntary, permanent career break."

"She was fired?"

Melanie nodded. "She slept with her boss."

"No way."

"Robert found out, went there, and had a huge fight with the guy. It was all very dramatic. Windows smashed, computers broken, egos wounded. Louise and her boss were both fired."

"Wow."

It was hard to believe.

"Now," Melanie said. "What are we going to do about that hair?"

Izzy gazed at her hair in the mirror. She hated the way it hung around her face. It had been like that for years and she'd never been adventurous enough to change it.

She said, "Something drastic."

Chapter 36

A uniformed officer named Coleman, from Dun Laoghaire Garda Station, drove Jimmy the barman home from the pier. Coleman was a big, pink-faced man in his fifties, and his skin seemed to give off a salty smell like boiled ham.

During the drive, Jimmy felt sicker than he would have expected. Hardened guy like him, bartending for a decade, seeing all kinds of shit, he thought he'd be able to handle seeing a dead body.

Turned out, he wasn't.

Coleman seemed to sense that, when he took Jimmy's statement at the East Pier. Hence the ride home.

Jimmy wanted to roll down the window, but it wasn't his car, so he contented himself with holding his breath, and trying to forget what he'd seen.

Working at the pub had turned Jimmy off alcohol. On mornings, while his customers nursed hangovers, Jimmy liked to walk the pier.

This morning, he'd gone to the side of the East Pier, where he could look out over the sea, towards the

Martello Tower to the south. The sea had been calm, much calmer than the previous day. He'd stepped onto the rocks at the water's edge. Once he found his balance, he took a minute to meditate. It was nothing fancy, just closing his eyes, and taking a few slow breaths. A simple routine, but it calmed him.

When he opened his eyes, he caught sight of a patch of seaweed clinging to the rocks near his feet. After a moment, he realised it wasn't seaweed.

It was hair.

A woman's body floated in the water, face down.

Embarrassingly enough, Jimmy had gone to bits after that. Hadn't even been able to call an ambulance. Another passer-by did that – an old man who recognised the dead woman as Kate Long.

Paramedics and cops were soon swarming the area, and Jimmy was ushered to an ambulance where he recovered from the shock.

Kate used to come into the pub once in a while. She was a stunner. Nice lady too. Did a bit of acting. Once she'd been featured in the local newspaper.

Jimmy stared out the window of Coleman's car, watching the streets pass by, but not really seeing anything.

The shock, which had prevented him speaking much, was beginning to wear off. But the image of Kate Long, floating face down, was burnt into his retinas.

Jimmy rented a room in a house with four other guys, over on De Vesci Terrace. The car passed Melanie and Tom Flynn's place and eased to a stop outside

Jimmy's door. His housemates would be at work, and Jimmy had a day off today, so he would be alone.

"You want to come in for a cup of tea?"

"No, I better be going," Coleman said.

"Okay, yeah."

Jimmy didn't move at once.

Coleman kept looking at him. After a moment, he unfastened his seat belt. "Ah, sure, why not?"

*

After getting up late, Robert had tea and toast, with lots of butter and lots of marmalade. Then it was time for Baxter's walk. He clipped Baxter's leash onto his collar, then searched for his jacket while the dog waited impatiently.

Robert called up the stairs, "Louise? Where's my green jacket?"

"What green jacket?"

From her tone, Robert concluded that her mood hadn't improved so far today.

"The one with the yellow stripes."

"Did you look on the coat rack?"

"Of course, I did. And it's not in the wardrobe either."

"I don't know what to tell you then. Are elves stealing your clothes?"

Robert scowled. Perhaps he really was going senile. The jacket should have been right there on the rack, but there was no sign of the damn thing. Baxter began to whine.

"Alright, alright," Robert said, picking out another jacket. He led the dog outside.

They walked down the road towards the sea, going onto Queen's Road. It was a slight deviation from their familiar route, and Baxter resisted, trying to pull Robert towards the library.

"In a minute, boy."

Louise said that Kate had been found dead in the water next to the East Pier. As they approached, Robert saw that the pier was open but an area to the side was blocked off by tape.

"What a shame," Robert said to himself. He shook his head sadly. "She never did amount to anything."

He stood looking at the scene for a minute before letting Baxter pull him back to the usual route. On Crofton Road, they passed Tess and Gareth's house and continued on to De Vesci Terrace, a lovely road with a row of elegant houses. Of course, a lot of them were subdivided into less than grand apartments, and some of the houses needed a bit of work done.

As they approached Melanie and Tom's house, which was one that needed a lot of work, Robert let Baxter off the leash.

"Go on, boy. Do your business."

Baxter darted through Melanie's gate. Robert kept his distance. That was best so that he could claim plausible deniability if Melanie or Tom happened to be home. After half a minute, he moved a little closer to make sure Baxter was doing the job.

"Good boy. Come on now."

Baxter came tearing out of the garden, like a killer fleeing a crime scene.

Robert put the leash on him, and they continued walking, down the terrace past Jimmy the barman's place. When Robert glanced at the house, he saw Jimmy and a Garda standing inside the front window, looking back at him.

Chapter 37

Izzy felt like a new person when she emerged from the salon. She'd been there for nearly two hours. Melanie had shampooed, combed, and scissor-cut Izzy's hair, so that it hung straight.

The sides were long enough to touch her chin and the back was short enough that the pale skin of her neck was visible. Izzy had decided against getting any colouring done.

She walked down the street, a bounce in her step. For a little time, she'd almost forgotten about her troubles, and that felt wonderful.

When she reached the Chinese shop, she pushed the door but found it locked. Surprised, Izzy rapped her knuckles on the door.

She put her face to the glass, noticing that the lights inside the shop were off and she could see no one inside.

Disappointed and confused, she was about to leave when Dylan appeared from the back of the shop. His face was uncharacteristically serious as he opened the door.

He stared at her for a moment. "Sorry. Hardly recognised you."

"I just had my hair done. What's going on?"

He called over his shoulder before turning his attention to Izzy again.

"Come in."

Izzy did, and Dylan shut the door. Mrs. Zhao appeared. Unlike yesterday, she was dressed stylishly in a navy silk top, black trousers and shiny high-heeled shoes. With the make-up and jewellery, she looked like another person. Mrs. Zhao barked at her son. Although Izzy didn't know Chinese, she recognised a scolding when she heard one.

"Is something wrong?"

"I gave you the wrong day for your appointment," Dylan said. "Today is Spring Festival."

"What's Spring Festival?"

That earned an eye-roll from Dylan. "Chinese New Year. When I made your appointment, I forgot we'd be closed today. I don't really celebrate this stuff. I mean, I didn't when I had my own place, but now..."

"Your mom looks annoyed."

Mrs. Zhao came over and locked her eyes on Izzy.

"My son is careless! But it is good for you to have *tui na* today. Come with me."

"I don't want to interrupt." Izzy tried to back away, but Mrs. Zhao gripped her arm.

"It would be inauspicious to turn you away."

Dylan whispered, "It's easier not to fight."

That struck Izzy as true. She allowed herself to be

led down the corridor to a sterile-looking treatment room with anatomical charts on the wall. A massage table lined with disposable paper stood in the centre of the room.

Mrs. Zhao closed the door, then put an apron on over her fancy clothes. Izzy's guilt intensified. But there was no arguing with Mrs. Zhao, who directed Izzy to take off her top and lie down on the table on her front. Mrs. Zhao busied herself with some plastic contraptions at the side of the room. It was incredibly uncomfortable to undress in the presence of a stranger, revealing her scrawny body. Her weight had been well below a hundred pounds for weeks, much to Adam's irritation.

She lay down.

After a moment, Mrs. Zhao's firm hands began to massage her back and shoulders. It wasn't a relaxing massage. More like a mild assault, with pushing, pulling, squeezing and kneading. It progressed to intense joint manipulation so painful that Izzy had to force herself not to scream.

After half an hour, the massage ended. She felt like she'd been thrown around inside a washing machine.

"Will I be getting acupuncture?"

"Not today." Mrs. Zhao went to the side of the room and came back with a large bag. She pulled out a clear plastic object which resembled the head of a plunger. "Today we do cupping."

Mrs. Zhao pressed the first cup against one of the sorest parts of Izzy's right shoulder. She twisted the cup, sucking the air out of it and creating a vacuum against Izzy's skin. The pain was excruciating.

Izzy was just wondering if she could bear it when Mrs. Zhao applied a second cup to her back. Again, the cup was tightened until it hurt.

The process went on until Izzy's back was covered in a dozen cups of various sizes. At that stage, Mrs. Zhao disappeared out the door without a word.

The pain grew more intense as Izzy lay there, like the life was being squeezed out of her. When she thought she couldn't take any more, Mrs. Zhao came back.

Sliding her finger between the first cup and Izzy's skin, she broke the vacuum. Relief washed over Izzy as the cup loosened.

One by one, each cup was removed. Whatever the pain of the massage had been, the pain of the cupping exceeded it. When they were all off, Izzy sat up and put on her top as Mrs. Zhao replaced the cups in their bag.

"Come," Mrs. Zhao said, opening the door and leading Izzy out. She turned to the right, away from the exit. "One more thing."

One more thing?

The words filled Izzy with fresh anxiety, but she followed the older lady as she made her way up a set of stairs.

Izzy swallowed as they reached the top.

Chapter 38

Stephanie Long felt dizzy as she parked next to the kerb on Griffith Avenue in North Dublin. Beyond a strip of grass, some leafy trees, and a low wall, was Dublin City Mortuary, a neat red-brick building that used to be a Garda Station.

Stephanie got out of the car and walked up to the door, where she was met by the State Pathologist, Dr. Fields. They'd spoken on the phone an hour ago, and she had seen Fields on the news often enough to recognise her.

Her job was to investigate any unexplained or suspicious deaths, so she was often photographed arriving at crime scenes.

In person, Fields was very short and very blonde, with luxurious curls that almost touched her hips. Despite wearing a white doctor's coat, she reminded Stephanie of a young Dolly Parton.

"Thank you for coming, Mr. Long. I understand that this is a difficult time for you. The coroner has directed that a post-mortem examination be carried out in this case. However, what I need your assistance with is identifying the body."

"I understand," Stephanie said.

"Please follow me."

Stephanie felt worse with every step, as she was led down bland corridors. Kate was missing, and a woman had been found in the sea. Obviously, someone had put the two things together.

"Never should have phoned her," Stephanie muttered to herself.

"Pardon?" Dr. Fields looked over her shoulder.

"Nothing. Just clearing my throat."

The officers who came to Stephanie's office had heard Kate was missing – probably thanks to Dee – and they had asked a lot of questions.

When was the last time Stephanie saw Kate? Did they have a fight? Was Kate drunk? Did she have family?

Finally, they'd come clean. A woman's body had been found, and they needed to know if it was Kate. The body had been taken to the mortuary and the State Pathologist would be in touch. They'd appreciate Stephanie's assistance.

Kate couldn't be dead. She simply couldn't. This must be some kind of terrible coincidence.

Through a door with a circular window cut out of it, Stephanie saw the sight she'd been dreading: a large room with stainless steel tables fitted with drainage channels. Tables where bodies were cut open. The sharp smell of chemical disinfectant filled the air.

She was going to have to look at the dead woman. She hoped to God it wasn't Kate.

To Stephanie's surprise, Dr. Fields walked straight past the room with the metal tables and brought Stephanie instead to a neat little office with two chairs and a computer.

"Please, take a seat."

Stephanie did. She gripped the sides of her chair like her life depended on it as Dr. Fields picked up a glossy photograph.

She didn't show it to Stephanie yet.

"Does your wife have any identifying features, Mr. Long?"

"Yes... she has, um... a tattoo of a robin on her backside."

Kate had thought it was cute. She'd been disappointed when Stephanie turned out not to be a fan.

Dr. Fields spoke gently. "The body recovered from the water has a tattoo of a robin on the left buttock."

Stephanie swallowed. "Okay."

"I'd like to show you a photograph. Is that okay?"

Stephanie nodded.

It was hardly even necessary to look. How many people had a robin on their ass? Dr. Fields passed over the photo. It was a close-up of a little bird, beak open in song, red breast vividly coloured.

"Does that look like your wife's tattoo, Mr. Long?"

Stephanie swallowed a lump in her throat. "Yes. That's her. That's Kate."

Tears streamed down her face. She handed the

photo back, then wiped her nose with the back of her hand.

Dr. Fields held out a box of tissues. With trembling hands. Stephanie grabbed a handful and pressed them to her face.

"Did Kate drown herself?"

"We don't know yet," Dr. Fields said. "I'll begin the post-mortem this afternoon. Hopefully that will shed some light on it."

"I need to know what happened."

"I know how important it must be for you to get closure, and I promise I'll do my best to find out what happened. Thanks again for your help, Mr. Long. You have my sincere condolences."

There was a long pause.

"That's it?" Stephanie said. "You don't need me to look at her?"

"No," the pathologist said. "A witness at the scene identified your wife, and you've confirmed that. It's not necessary for you to look at the body."

They obviously didn't want to show it to anyone. How bad did Kate look? Stephanie blew her nose and stared into space.

After a while, Fields said, "There's no hurry, but I can show you out when you're ready."

"I'm ready now."

They retraced their steps, arriving back at the entrance, where Dr. Fields offered her hand. That hand would soon be exploring Kate's body, probing every inch of its surface, cutting it open. Stephanie gripped that hand, felt its steadiness, its firm grip.

She mumbled goodbye and hurried back to where her car was parked. Once she was in the car, coldness swept over her.

Kate was gone.

*

Adam peered in the window of the Chinese place. There was no sign of Izzy inside. No sign of anyone. The lights were off, the door locked. Had it actually been Izzy he saw enter the building?

After she sped away in a taxi, Adam went to Elaine's house. He assumed that was where Izzy would go, but there was no sign of her. He'd stood on the doorstep and phoned her number again and again.

Nothing. No answer. If she was inside, she was ignoring him.

He had a big speech – an apology, of sorts –planned out in his head, and she hadn't given him a chance to say it.

Her behaviour was so unfair.

It made him angry.

A nosy neighbour came over to him. She started giving Adam grief for hounding Izzy. Like their relationship was any of her business. Adam didn't have time to deal with the neighbour now, but he'd sort her out later.

He'd show her not to meddle in his business.

He had headed back to the main street and spent a long time walking up and down, ducking in and out of the little shops, hoping he'd run into Izzy again. He knew she wasn't working today, so where could she be?

There was no sign of her in the supermarket. When he came out and was walking back up the street, wondering what to do, he saw a woman duck into a shop.

Unlike Izzy, she had short, straight hair, but there was something about the jut of her chin that caught his eye. And her clothes looked like Izzy's.

Had she changed her hair?

She was far away, so Adam wasn't sure it was her, but he hurried towards the door she'd gone into and found it was a Chinese medicine place.

Had it been Izzy? If so, why? And why was the door locked? The place didn't even seem to be open. Adam knocked on the glass but got no answer. He wondered if there was another way in. A back entrance maybe?

He decided to check.

Chapter 39

Izzy assumed that Mrs. Zhao was taking her to another therapy room when she led her upstairs. Instead, Izzy found herself in a dining room with a large table in the centre. The smell of fried fish came from the doorway to a kitchen.

Dylan stood at the dining room table with a young Chinese woman. The chairs had been cleared to one side and the area was clearly being used for food preparation.

About a dozen other Chinese men and women were scattered around, some in the kitchen and some chatting by the window which looked out over the street.

Mrs. Zhao turned to Izzy. "You need to eat proper food to build your strength."

"I don't want to interrupt your celebration," Izzy said. "I should go."

"Eat first," Mrs. Zhao said. "There is a saying: 'he who takes medicine, but neglects diet, wastes the skills of the physician'."

While Izzy turned that over in her mind, Mrs. Zhao barked at Dylan in Chinese.

He came over. "You can work for your food."

"What do I do?"

"Wash your hands. Then report to the dumpling area."

Izzy didn't like his bossy tone, and she still felt like she ought to leave. However, Mrs. Zhao had disappeared somewhere, so Izzy went to the kitchen and cleaned her hands at the sink. Then she returned to the dining room and joined Dylan at the table. He pushed a large bowl towards her. Minced meat and spring onion were mixed together inside it.

"Here's the all-important pork filling. Now watch carefully."

Dylan took a sheet of dough from a packet and set it down on the wooden board in front of him. He spooned a ball of filling from the bowl and put it onto the centre of the dumpling case.

He lifted two sides of the dumpling case, pinched the dough together in the middle, folded up the sides and pinched them together, sealing the filling within. Then he placed the finished dumpling on a baking tray covered in parchment.

"Want to try?"

As Izzy attempted her first ever dumpling, she became aware that a pretty girl next to her was watching. She was about the same age as Izzy, but had smooth, pale skin and glossy black hair that Izzy would have died for. Izzy wondered if she was Dylan's girlfriend.

The first dumpling contained too much filling, so Izzy couldn't seal it. Minced pork ended up oozing out. Dylan and the girl, who introduced herself as Amy, laughed, but not unkindly.

"You shouldn't be so greedy," Dylan said.

Izzy's second dumpling contained too little filling, but her third and fourth were better, and soon she was a functioning part of the dumpling assembly line.

"I bet you'd prefer a burger," Dylan said.

"No, I see enough burgers at the diner where I work. I want to try something different and delicious."

"You're in the right place," the girl named Amy said in a Dublin accent, admiring the dumplings Izzy was now producing. "Deliciousness guaranteed."

Soon dozens of dumplings were ready on baking trays, and another member of the family began taking the trays into the kitchen.

Izzy made herself useful in the kitchen, washing up some of the dirty dishes that were piling up. When she returned to the dining room, Amy was clearing the table and Dylan was spraying it with disinfectant.

"You all live here?" Izzy asked as they set the table.

"Me, my mom and dad," Dylan said. He glanced across the room to where his parents were standing with another couple.

"I live down the road," Amy said. "With my parents, my sister and our grandmother."

Now that she looked closer, Izzy could see the resemblance between Dylan's father and the man he was talking to.

They must be brothers, she thought.

Izzy looked from Amy to Dylan. "You two are cousins?"

"Sadly," Amy replied.

"Shut up," Dylan said.

She punched his arm. "I love your hair, Izzy."

"I just got it done. My friend Melanie did it."

Amy laughed. "I thought it looked like her work. She's my boss. I'd normally be at work now, but I took a day off."

Izzy was starting to see how tight and interconnected Dun Laoghaire was. Everyone seemed to know, or be related to, everyone else.

Just then, the doorbell rang. Mrs. Zhao disappeared downstairs. She returned a minute later with a young woman who might have been Amy's sister. She and Mrs. Zhao helped an old lady into the room. Frail as she looked, she had made it up a lot of stairs, which impressed Izzy.

"Nǎinai is here," Dylan said.

Izzy heard excitement in his voice.

Amy laughed. "He loves his granny."

"Be quiet," Dylan said. He turned to Izzy, his face brightening. "I'll introduce you to her later."

"Time to sit down, everyone!" someone called.

Immediately everyone seated themselves around the table. Dishes began to come from the kitchen. Whole fish, soup, spring rolls, and dishes that Izzy couldn't identify, like a saucy brown item.

"What's that?" she asked Dylan.

"Pig's tongue and oysters covered in gravy. You want to try?"

"Oh... no, I'm okay."

"You're not a vegetarian, are you?"

Izzy said, "I like meat. I just don't like to be reminded that it comes from animals."

"How about whole fish?"

Izzy shook her head. "I don't like to see the fins, the eyes, the mouth..."

"You have to have the full fish at new year. It symbolises wholeness, and a good beginning and end."

Amy said, "Everything we're eating is symbolic."

Izzy was about to reply when the sound of breaking glass pierced the air.

Chapter 40

Adam scrambled around the back of the wooden shed, out of sight. He pressed his back to the wall and froze. Had he been seen?

He had jumped the wall into the garden at the back of the Chinese shop. It was an overgrown wasteland, where scrubby weeds poked up through cracked paving stones.

At once, he had caught sight of Izzy through the upstairs window. It was definitely her, despite the horrible new haircut. She was standing with an Asian guy. Adam couldn't figure out what the hell they were doing.

He crept around the bush and moved closer to the house. Not looking where he was going, he put his foot through a pane of glass that was leaning against the shed. The glass shattered with a tremendous crash and Adam dived out of sight.

He wasn't scared of whoever was in the building. He wasn't scared of anyone. But he wanted to know what was going on. He needed more information.

Cautiously, Adam peered around the side of the

shed. He ducked quickly back out of sight. The Asian guy was standing in the window, looking out. A second, older man, joined him.

Adam had to find out what she was up to.

Then he'd take her back.

And if anyone else wanted to get in the way, that was their bad luck.

*

Gareth sat in his car, staring at the stock chart on his phone. The screen was smeared with sweat. He knew that a classroom of confused teenagers, sleepy after the lunch break, were waiting for him at the school, but Gareth didn't care.

The only thing on his mind was that he had messed up big time.

His sure-fire investment was going belly-up, and Chisel Cooney was going to kill him if he didn't find the money from somewhere.

Gareth logged into his trading app and placed an order to sell his shares at $0.023 or above. It was a terrible price but what could he do? The market was about to open, and he had to get out of his position.

He brought up the chart again.

Suddenly the NASDAQ was open and SSI's share price began moving. The number flashed red. Traders were dumping shares.

Holy shit, the price was already down to €0.021 cents. Gareth stared at the number in disbelief.

"Get above two point three, you absolute bastard!"

The number had to rise, or his order would never be

fulfilled. The price kept flashing red. More and more people were selling shares, driving the price down, which made more people sell, which drove the price down more.

$0.020.

Gareth decided to sell before he lost even more. He'd thought the pre-market trading was bad, but this was a million times worse.

His money, Tess's money, Chisel Cooney's money. All of it was vanishing by the second.

He scrambled to log into his trading account and set a new order. Sell above $0.019.

Feverish sweat was running down Gareth's sides like rivers. He could smell his own panic in the tight confines of the car.

As soon as he placed the order, he checked the price again. €0.018. Now €0.017. Gareth logged in again and placed a third order to sell *at market*, which meant *dump the fucking thing as soon as you can at whatever price you can get.*

After flashing red a few more times, the price paused on €0.013. Gareth's heart drummed in his chest.

The price dived even lower.

€0.012.

€0.010.

How could the company lose so much value so quickly? The earnings results had been *great.*

Gareth's broker still hadn't managed to dump his shares.

Abruptly the stock chart froze.

Chapter 41

At the sound of glass breaking, Dylan walked to the window. His father joined him and together they peered out.

Izzy stayed at the table for a moment, her pulse racing, nightmare scenarios shooting through her head.

Had Adam tracked her down again? Izzy had to know.

She made her way to the window and looked out on the small garden. She saw a couple of bins, a timber shed, and a paved garden overgrown with weeds, with one large bush in the middle.

Dylan said, "Look. The old pane of glass fell over."

His father nodded. "Perhaps the breeze knocked it over. We can check later. The food is getting cold."

Dylan shrugged before going back to his seat. Izzy and Mr. Zhao continued to look out for a few more moments.

She couldn't tell Mr. Zhao what she knew, what she feared. There was no point ruining Spring Festival. Instead, she followed Dylan. As he approached the table, he looked over his shoulder at her. A nod of the head indicated that he wanted to introduce Izzy to his grandmother.

He bent over and said, "Năinai? Please meet my, uh, friend, Izzy."

"It's lovely to meet you," Izzy said.

The old lady looked sleepy and somewhat dour until she turned her alert eyes on Izzy. Then she broke into a toothy smile.

"What pretty friends Dylan has. *Tài piàoliang! Tā shì nǐ de nǚ péngyǒu ma?*"

"*Tā shì wǒ de péngyǒu,*" Dylan said.

Amy nudged Izzy. "He's insisting you're only a friend. I think he's blushing. Isn't he? Even his ears are turning pink."

Dylan shot daggers at Amy but said nothing. Izzy couldn't help laughing.

She said, "Are you ready to eat?"

"Oh, yes," the old woman said. "I'm always ready to eat. When I was a child in Shanghai, my family had a cook. I was the bane of his life, always asking him to prepare snacks for me. But that was a long time ago. We have no servants anymore."

"We used to be well off," Dylan said with regret.

Mrs. Zhao called on everyone to sit down as the last of the dishes was placed on the table. Izzy sat down with Amy on one side and Dylan on the other.

"Did you see anything strange out there?" Amy said.

"No. Why?"

"Just wondering. My place was burgled last year.

I've never felt one hundred percent happy there ever since."

"Did they take much?"

"No. There wasn't much to take. But they destroyed the place."

Izzy shuddered. Destroying something they couldn't have? That sounded like someone she knew.

"Let's begin," Mr. Zhao said.

Izzy struggled to pick up a dumpling from the plate in front of her with her chopsticks, but it kept slipping from her grasp.

"Do it like this," Dylan said, and stabbed the dumpling with one chopstick. He put the whole thing straight into his mouth.

"Hey, that was mine!"

"Too slow."

Izzy copied his style, skewering the dumpling and bringing it to her mouth. After being boiled, it had been fried, and the outside had a crispy texture, which Izzy liked.

She poured a little sauce from a bowl onto her plate and dipped the remains of the dumpling in it. The sauce contained the sharp bite of vinegar and the bright taste of fresh coriander.

After the dumpling, she moved onto the other dishes. There was so much variety, and Izzy wasn't sure when she'd have a chance to taste these things again. She wasn't even sure what some of the dishes were.

After the main courses, there was fruit and tea.

Everyone sat in conversation. By then, Izzy was drowsy and full.

She was about to ask Dylan to pass the pot of tea from his side of the table when he turned and spoke to his granny in Chinese.

Izzy said to Amy, "He really loves her. It's so cute."

"She's not well. We have to enjoy the time we have with her."

"Really? She looks strong."

"She's a trooper," Amy said with a nod.

Izzy watched Dylan chatting with his granny. He was lucky to have a family. Izzy was completely alone.

Chapter 42

Traffic heading into the city was slow. The sun was low in the sky. In his little Citroen, Gareth Gillen shielded his eyes from the glare as he looked around. He was not even past St. Vincent's Hospital yet, and the cars ahead were not moving. It would take forever to reach Tess's office.

I'm going to die here, Gareth thought.

A heart attack at the wheel, at one of these stop lights.

Might be better than the alternative, though.

Gareth shuddered as he remembered Chisel Cooney's face. What would that man do if Gareth couldn't pay? Gareth had never seriously considered the question until now. Earlier, he'd thought it would be easy. He'd buy shares in SSI, wait for it to go up, then sell and repay his creditors and pocket the profits.

Easy.

But it hadn't worked out like that.

He checked his phone but there was nothing new

on the stock market, since the announcement he'd already read:

New York. February 20th.

Trading on the NASDAQ remains suspended this morning, after a 'flash crash', which saw market indices plummet 18% in a matter of minutes. The dip triggered a so-called 'circuit breaker' designed to halt trading in circumstances of extreme market volatility...

Gareth had read various articles in the financial press, but they all said the same thing.

He'd been frantically trying to sell his shares in SSI, when a message appeared on his trading app, saying that trading on the NASDAQ had been temporarily halted.

SSI had been tanking, but it turned out that so had many other companies' shares. Apple, Tesla, you name it.

Gareth didn't care about the cause of the crash. He was just furious at the timing. Why did it have to happen on the one day when he wanted – no, when his life *depended on his ability* –to sell?

His money was in limbo.

The orders he'd placed had not been executed and he had no idea if they would be. And he had no idea what SSI shares would be worth when trading resumed. Whenever that happened.

Gareth needed to think. That was why he had gone home and packed two bags with some of his and Tess's clothes. They needed to get away somewhere and hide out for the weekend so Gareth could figure out what to do.

The light ahead turned green.

Gareth waited impatiently for the cars in front to move. The first one was slow off the mark. By the time the car in front of Gareth's had finally lurched a few metres forward, the lights were red again.

Gareth toyed with the idea of texting Tess, but he couldn't figure out what to say. Better to just turn up at her office.

On the passenger seat next to him, Gareth's phone rang. The number on the screen belonged to the principal's office. Gareth didn't answer. He couldn't explain to Maggie Connell why he'd walked out of the school.

Tess had texted him earlier, while he was sitting in the car outside the school, trying to sell his shares.

Kate Long is dead. Did you hear?

He pictured Kate sitting on his couch last night. Gareth remembered the feel of her foot in his lap and the coy way she'd suggested that he make them drinks.

"Okay," he'd said.

He'd fixed her a Martini and sat next to her on the couch. She was flirty, a bit too much so, which made Gareth uncomfortable. When she finished her drink, he told her again that he had some papers to mark.

She hadn't liked that.

Kate had said, "Remember the way we used to fool around?"

"That was a long time ago," Gareth said.

"Did you ever tell Tess about it?"

"As I recall, we never actually fooled around. We went on one date, and that was about a million years ago."

Kate flinched.

"Didn't you enjoy it?"

Gareth had shrugged and wondered why she was talking about ancient history.

"It was okay. As I recall, we walked around the shopping centre for about an hour, and you smoked three cigarettes at the same time. You seemed bored."

Kate didn't like his recollection of their one date very much.

"Maybe I'll tell Tess we used to be an item," she'd said as she got to her feet.

"We were never an item," Gareth said. "It was just that one date."

At the time, he'd been crazy about Kate, but it had been clear that she had no interest in him. Now she was throwing herself at him and he felt nothing at all. No excitement. No arousal. It was like he'd told Robert in the pub last night. Was that down to stress? Gareth didn't know.

"Still," Kate had said. "I think Tess might be interested. As her friend, I ought to have told her long ago. Better late than never, I guess."

Kate stormed out of the house then, leaving Gareth feeling angry and worried.

And now Kate was dead.

The traffic ahead still looked like a nightmare so Gareth turned down a side street, hoping it would be quieter than the main road. Thankfully it was.

Finally, some luck. Only a tiny scrap, but that was *something*.

He hit the accelerator, relief washing over him now that he was finally moving at a decent pace, until blinding headlights from behind lit up the interior of the Citroen. Gareth checked the mirror, saw a dark SUV riding his tail.

He watched as the SUV accelerated around as if it wanted to overtake him. It didn't pull ahead, though.

Rather, it came alongside and then held that position.

Gareth glanced over, trying to catch a glimpse of the driver. The SUV's tinted windows revealed nothing.

"Shit," he muttered.

A moment later, the SUV lurched sideways, smashing into his car.

Chapter 43

After the wonderful meal had settled in her stomach, Izzy joined Dylan and Amy in the kitchen to help clean up while the older folk continued talking at the table. She figured washing the dishes was the least she could do, and the two cousins were good company, never missing the slightest opportunity to make fun of each other.

The house grew dark while they were cleaning. When Dylan flicked the lights on, the harsh glow of a naked bulb emphasised his strong cheekbones and lean face. He could have been a model. Realising she was staring at him like a lovesick teenager, Izzy averted her gaze.

Izzy was amazed to think of all the people she had met since she arrived in Dun Laoghaire, and how kind everyone had been to her. It was so different to the recent months.

Living with Adam had been wonderful at the start. So, when he'd proposed, in front of all his friends and all her friends in a bar one night, she had barely thought about her answer.

"Yes," she said, with everyone's eyes on her.

But Adam became increasingly resentful and moody. Every interaction she had with another human being became a reason for him to get jealous. She began tiptoeing around him, taking care not to ruin his mood. In that way, her social life had dried up and she had almost stopped talking to Elaine.

Dylan, with his no-nonsense attitude, would have laughed at her if he had known.

"I better go," Izzy said once she finished washing.

Dylan was wiping the kitchen surfaces with a damp cloth, trying to remove the grease. Amy was drying the last of the dishes and putting them away in the cupboard.

Izzy dried her wizened hands on a towel. She didn't want to outstay her welcome. She decided to go for a walk before the book club meeting.

"Are you sure?" Amy said. "You're welcome to stay."

Izzy nodded. "But thank you."

Amy surprised her with a hug. After that, Izzy went back to the sitting room and thanked Mr. and Mrs. Zhao for dinner, and said goodbye to Dylan's grandmother, before heading for the door.

Mrs. Zhao and Dylan exchanged a few words in Chinese. Then Dylan grabbed his jacket.

"I've been ordered to walk you home."

Amy laughed.

"This is getting to be a routine," Izzy said.

Dylan shrugged. "*You* try arguing with my mom."

"No thanks."

They stepped out into the dimming street. Street lights glowed pink as they came on. Only a small patch of pale blue was left in the sky.

"I want to walk a little," Izzy said.

Dylan locked the door of the shop behind him. "Sure. Which way?"

"I haven't walked the pier yet."

"Which one? The West Pier isn't well lit at night. And the ground is uneven."

"I guess it's the East Pier then."

They walked side by side, down the street to the church on the corner, where they turned onto Marine Road, and faced the sea.

Dylan told her about the MBA he was doing, and how he was thinking of becoming a consultant after he graduated. Maybe at Deloitte. Izzy tried to listen, but she was distracted as they passed County Hall, where Elaine had spent so many years.

"I'm sorry about your friend," Dylan said, as they reached the pier. He came to a halt in front of a pile of flowers, a photo of Kate smiling up from the middle of them.

A moment earlier, Dylan had been speaking about the statistics module in his Master's, so the change of pace caught Izzy by surprise.

"Me too," she said. "And I'm sorry your grand-mother is unwell. Amy told me."

"She's just old," Dylan said. "Her health isn't great. But she's tough. Growing up in Shanghai in the '40s. The Japanese occupation, before the Americans arrived... She's seen a lot." He smiled. "She wanted to go and live in the U.S.A. but ended up here."

They were silent for a moment.

"Upper or lower?" Dylan said.

"Huh?"

He pointed towards the pier, which was split into two parallel paths, one higher than the other.

"Upper or lower?"

"Upper," Izzy said.

It was cold and fully dark now, but overhead lights illuminated circles on the ground. Izzy wasn't surprised that the place was deserted. A lighthouse glowed at the end of the pier.

"We can just walk a little," she said. "We don't have to go to the end."

"Okay." They were silent for a moment. Dylan blurted, "My mom didn't really ask me to walk you home."

"So why did you come?"

He shrugged. "I didn't want you getting lost."

Izzy stifled a smile. Dylan was cute when he blushed. She could hear the black water lapping against stone, the creak of boats tied up on the marina, and the whistle of the breeze in the boats' sails. They walked half the length of the pier, to the corner of the L-shaped structure, before Izzy stopped.

"Let's go back," she said.

"Fine by me."

They turned around. Izzy was about to walk back

towards land when a figure stepped into the light a short distance away.

Adam.

Chapter 44

Melanie walked home from the salon. She was tired from being on her feet all day, and starving, very much in need of some carbs. Pasta, bread, potatoes, rice – they all sounded pretty damn good. Though she knew she ought to cut that stuff out if she was going to lose a few pounds before summer, like she'd planned, it was hard to live on rabbit food.

The cold evening made her even hungrier.

She'd started the day well, with fruit and yoghurt for breakfast. Then at lunchtime, she'd given in and had a grilled pork sandwich at the Argentinian café.

At that point, it seemed to her like a little dessert wasn't going to make much difference, so she'd added a few *alfajores* to her cappuccino order. Delicious little cookies with a creamy caramel-like filling.

And now? There hardly seemed much point being virtuous. She might as well have a pizza and begin the diet tomorrow. As she neared home, Melanie smiled, glad that the issue had been resolved.

She thought about what she should post to her social media. Pictures of her and Kate? A poem to honour her friend? She could ask the others tonight, at the book club meeting, though she would have liked to stay home and read.

Or better yet, get Tom to look at the cool apartment she'd found on the north side of the city. She'd also found a unit that used to be a restaurant, but it could easily be refitted to a hair salon.

Melanie turned into her driveway and walked up the strip of concrete between Tom's car and the grass. She put her hand in her pocket to get her keys, but they snagged on a loose thread inside the pocket.

Melanie had been meaning to do something about that thread forever, but she always forgot. She gave the keys a tug, felt the thread snap. The keys went flying through the air, landing somewhere in the grass.

"Damn it."

She stepped onto the lawn, squinting as she tried to find any sign of her keys. She couldn't see a thing. She took another step, bent over and peered at the ground.

Tom was already home, so, if she had to, she could just knock on the door, and he could let her in. She was about to do just that when she saw something a couple of paces away.

She recognised the shape of the small rectangle of plastic. It was her loyalty card for the supermarket, which she kept on her keyring. Whatever angle it was at, the card caught the reflection of a street light down the road.

Melanie went over and scooped up the keys. Her

hands sank into something wet. The keys were slimy in her hands.

Bringing her hand closer to her face, she caught the smell.

Melanie gagged as she realised that the keys, her hand and the sleeve of her jacket were all smeared with shit.

Baxter's shit.

Chapter 45

Adam's tangled hair was wilder than normal, his gaunt face covered in wispy black stubble. He wore a puffy green jacket over a white T-shirt.

He stepped forward, moving out of the pool of light he'd been standing under. Now he was silhouetted against the light behind. A dark form, as dark as the water around the pier. Izzy's pulse began to race.

Sensing a shift in the atmosphere, Dylan followed Izzy's gaze to where Adam stood.

"That's my ex," Izzy whispered.

"Okay," Dylan said.

"I... I left him yesterday. He's not happy about it." An understatement, but Izzy didn't have time for long explanations. "He's the reason my car window is busted."

"Got it," Dylan said.

They stood still while Adam moved towards them. His pace was slow, his face hidden by darkness.

Dylan was taller and thinner. Adam was more muscular. Izzy had the unnerving thought that, if it ever came to a fight, Adam would win.

A cold breeze blew across the pier.

The three of them were the only ones in sight. Most folk probably didn't come out here at night. They were probably too sensible. Izzy imagined it was the kind of place where troublemakers might gather.

A few more steps brought Adam into the nearest pool of light. He was about ten feet away from them, standing right in the middle of the path.

They could go down to the pier's lower level, but there were no steps nearby. They'd have to backtrack. And that would take them farther from land.

"What happened to your hair?" Adam said.

Anger surged within Izzy's chest.

"None of your business. What do you want?"

"That's some greeting for your fiancé." Adam came to a stop. Plunged his hands deep into his pockets.

She said, "We're finished. It's over."

"Don't say that, Izzy. I can't live without you."

For a moment, she saw despair in his eyes, and had to resist the urge to comfort him.

Instead, she said, "Believe me. It's over."

"I don't accept that."

"I'm not asking."

He raised his voice. "You're telling me I don't have a say?"

"I don't need your permission, Adam. It takes two people to make a relationship."

Silence seemed to stretch into an eternity. Adam was the first to break it.

"Come home with me now."

"Back off," Dylan shouted. "Don't make me kick your ass."

Adam seemed to notice him for the first time. He looked Dylan up and down and laughed.

"Who are you?"

Dylan brought up his fists in front of him. "I'm the guy that's going to lay you flat on the ground."

"Are you, aye?" Adam turned his attention back to Izzy. "Where did you find Jackie Chan here?"

"Getting racial." Dylan nodded. "That's a real classy move, asshole."

Adam didn't seem to hear. He stared at Izzy. "You haven't given me a chance to talk to you. That's all I'm asking for. Talk to me. I *love* you."

It wasn't true.

She'd been certain of that since Valentine's Day, when Adam took her to a fancy restaurant. He insisted that she try the sirloin steak, even though she had no interest in it. She wanted the monkfish, which sounded delicious. He'd got into a foul mood over that one little point.

Eventually, Izzy had given in and eaten the steak, but Adam's mood didn't improve, and they spent literally hours arguing about it.

Izzy was still confused the next day at work, which was why she'd mentioned it to Hannah. The other waitress didn't seem surprised.

"I wasn't going to say anything," Hannah had said, "because you never listen to *anything* I say about Adam—"

"That's not true."

"—but I've got one word for you. *Control.*"

"What the hell is that supposed to mean?"

"Think about it. He's controlling you."

Over break time, Izzy searched online for articles about controlling relationships, trying to prove Hannah wrong. Izzy and Adam's relationship wasn't like that. They were in love.

Her outrage had faded when she stumbled across the phrase *coercive control.* The more she read about it, the more she realised how aptly it described her situation. The subtle manipulations, the deft isolation of the victim from their friends and family. Izzy felt like she was reading about her own life.

That was when she knew she had to leave Adam. Thanks to Elaine's house, escape was still possible.

She had no intention of going back to Adam.

"Let's go," Izzy whispered to Dylan.

He nodded. Looping his arm in hers, he began walking towards Adam. Adam's eyes blazed as he zeroed in on their touching arms.

"So you're moving on? Is that it?" Adam said. His loud voice rang out over the water. "With your new boyfriend?"

"I want to be alone."

"That's not what it looks like. It looks like you found a boyfriend as soon as you disappeared from my life." Even in the darkness, Izzy noticed Adam's face turn red. "You don't care about me at all, do you? You want to make a fool of me."

Izzy said nothing.

They were five feet away from him. They moved closer to the wall at the pier's side, keeping as much distance from him as they could.

"Izzy, stop!"

She didn't slow her pace. Not till Adam pulled a switchblade from his pocket.

"I said *stop*."

Adam held the knife up. He pressed the button and the blade shot out. A surge of panic hit Izzy.

"What's your problem?" Dylan said.

"This has nothing to do with you. Go and leave us alone."

"I'm standing here with a knife in my face, aren't I? Sounds like it has something to do with me."

"You're a cheeky wee cunt, aren't you? Izzy and I need to talk. Leave us alone."

Dylan stood his ground. "Make me."

"Enough." Izzy couldn't take anymore. "Do you want to hurt me, Adam?"

"Of course not."

"Then get out of my way."

She tightened her grip on Dylan's arm and started walking again. Moving around Adam. She held her breath as she came alongside him.

Adam tore off his jacket. He let it fall at his feet and stood there in his T-shirt, goosebumps mottling his bare arms.

The blade was still in his hand.

He said, "Do I have to show you I'm serious?"

Before Izzy could do anything, he drew the switchblade across his arm, carving an *I* just below the elbow. Izzy's eyes widened.

"Stop it."

Ignoring her, Adam cut a horizontal line next to the first cut. Then a diagonal line. Then another vertical line.

Z.

Blood streamed down his arm.

Dylan stared in disgust. "You're sick," he said.

Adam ignored him. "I love you, Izzy."

She watched in mute horror as he carved a second *Z* into his arm. As he did the *Y*, Izzy pulled Dylan away. She thought she was going to be sick.

"I can't live without you. I'll kill myself."

She ignored him and kept walking. Her legs were like jelly. Her heart was racing. But she kept going.

After a few paces, she looked over her shoulder to see if Adam was following them. He wasn't. He was standing in the same place, Izzy's name carved deep into his arm, his blood dripping onto the ground.

Chapter 46

When Stephanie got home from the morgue, she knew she had to phone Kate's parents to tell them their daughter was dead. Stephanie was slumped in her favourite armchair with a cup of tea. She'd already drank half it without noticing. She'd been in a daze all day.

Kate was gone.

It seemed impossible. Her things were all around. A hairband sat on the table next to Stephanie's cup. So did a tube of lipstick, a packet of gum, and some head-shots Kate had got taken by a portrait photographer last month.

Stephanie steeled herself before picking up the phone and dialling the number for Mina, Kate's mother.

As it rang, Stephanie tried to remember the last time she had phoned her. She'd done it maybe once or twice, but definitely not more, and never without a good reason.

Mina answered. Stephanie heard music in the

background, and laughter. It sounded like she was in the middle of a party.

"Hello?"

"Hi Mina." It always felt weird using her first name, but the woman was her mother-in-law.

"Who is this?"

"It's Stephanie." No. Better to give her one shock at a time. "Stephen. It's Stephen."

"Stephen? Is everything alright?"

There was a lot of background noise.

"Are you at home, Mina?"

"What?"

"*Are you at home?*"

"On Friday evening? Of course not."

Mina was a lot like her daughter. Both of them thought weekdays were for surviving and weekends were for living. Being in her fifties hadn't slowed Mina down.

"I have some bad news. Perhaps you could go somewhere quiet?"

"What is it?"

"Are you with James? Is James there?"

Stephanie pictured Kate's bellicose father.

"He's gone to buy another round. We're in a bar. What is it you want? The band is about to start playing."

"Could you leave?"

"For god's sake, Stephen. What happened? Spit it out."

Stephanie cleared her throat. "Like I said, I have

some bad news. You might want to sit down before you hear this."

"Has something happened to Kate?"

"She's... there's been an—"

"What? What happened? Where's my daughter?"

"She's - I'm sorry, Mina. I'm sorry but—"

"What happened?"

"Kate's dead."

A long pause.

"What did you say?"

"Kate is *dead*."

"What? No... You're lying." When she spoke again, Mina's voice had gone low and mournful. "What did you do to my girl?"

"Nothing!"

"I never liked you."

"Look, I know it's hard to hear this—"

Mina wailed. "You killed my baby girl."

"I didn't. I swear."

"She told me you were up to something."

"What?"

"She said you were distracted all the time. You're going to rot in jail. So help me god, I'll make sure of it, you little creep."

Stephanie ended the call. She leaned back in the couch and sighed.

Great.

That was one job done.

Chapter 47

Izzy's pulse was still racing when she and Dylan turned onto her street. The image of Adam carving her name into his arm was etched onto her brain. It would stay with her for a long time.

Blood dripping down his pale skin. The green jacket bundled at his feet. The terror that he wasn't going to let them pass, that he'd hold them prisoner on the pier.

That he'd kill them.

Izzy wasn't ready to talk yet, so when Dylan began to speak, she stopped him.

"Just... just give me a minute."

They walked in silence. Past the Murphy house, up to Elaine's. Izzy unlocked the door.

"Want to come in?" she said.

"Okay."

Dylan followed her into the hall.

"I need a hot drink," Izzy said. "How about you?"

She walked down the hall to the kitchen, flicking on lights as she went. The room still smelled like medicine.

"Got any coffee?" Dylan said.

Izzy busied herself filling the kettle, turning it on, and spooning ground coffee into Elaine's French press.

Dylan sat down at the kitchen table.

"Can I talk now?"

Izzy poured the coffee into cups and brought them with her to the table, where she sat opposite Dylan.

"Go ahead."

"Do we need to call someone? An ambulance? A doctor? A psychiatrist?"

Izzy had asked herself the same questions already. "No. Adam's trying to control me. He wants me to react."

"You only left him yesterday?"

Izzy nodded. It felt like a year ago. She told Dylan briefly how she'd packed her bags and fled while Adam was at work.

"Holy shit," Dylan said. "You had to sneak out? Like you were breaking out of jail?"

She nodded, said nothing.

"Was he violent? Did he ever hurt you?"

"No. Not physically."

"But he might?"

"I don't know," Izzy said. "I didn't think so, but..."

"Your car."

"My car." Izzy nodded. She thought for a moment. Trying to decide whether to say what was at the back of her mind.

"What else?" Dylan said, obviously sensing that there was more. Something left unspoken.

There was.

The girl with the bulging eyes, and dark rings underneath. The girl with the thin lips, and narrow eyebrows, with hair scraped back in a severe ponytail. A stud on one ear.

"There was Ruth."

"Who's that?"

Izzy told him.

Adam had mentioned his 'crazy ex-girlfriend' on his first date with Izzy. Ruth was her name, and Adam had been in a relationship with her when he lived back in Scotland.

Izzy had been sympathetic as Adam described Ruth's behaviour, how she'd flirted with other guys to drive Adam wild, how she'd spread lies about him when she didn't get her way. She sounded like a nasty piece of work.

"But that's all in the past," Adam had said. "I'm more interested in the future."

He broke out in a smile and gave Izzy a cheesy wink, which made her laugh.

Was that really only a few months ago? Things had moved quickly after that. Izzy and Adam had become almost inseparable. They'd moved in together. He'd proposed. Elaine had died. And then Izzy became more and more isolated, as Adam got increasingly jealous and controlling. Disappearing for hours at a time, saying he was working. Izzy wondered if that was the truth.

Izzy looked across the table at Dylan. "He never really said how things ended with Ruth."

The more she had asked, the more evasive Adam got. Eventually, Izzy had Googled her. Adam had made the woman sound so nasty that Izzy was scared she would come to Dublin and try to win Adam back. Izzy wanted to know if Ruth still loved him.

But that wasn't what she had found.

Not even close.

"So how did things end?" Dylan asked.

Izzy took a sip of coffee. She could feel Dylan's eyes on her, but she took her time before continuing, because the next bit was hard to say. It was hard to even believe.

Her online sleuthing had taken her down a rabbit hole of news articles, all featuring the same photo of Ruth. The one that haunted Izzy's mind.

"How did things end?" Dylan repeated.

A note of impatience had crept into his voice.

Izzy swallowed.

She said, "Ruth was murdered."

Chapter 48

When the black SUV rammed him, Gareth's car swerved onto the footpath. He stomped on the brake, bringing the car to a stop inches from a beech tree growing out of the pavement. The seat belt snapped tight against his chest.

He sat there, breathing hard. His brain was trying to catch up with the fact that he'd been forced off the road.

He could have been killed.

Luckily there had been no pedestrians on the path. If there had been, he would have gone straight through them like bowling pins.

The SUV came to a halt on the road a short distance from Gareth's Citroen.

The vehicle was ominously still, its rear lights glowing blood-red.

Gareth unfastened his seat belt. He couldn't take his eyes off the SUV.

Normally he would have gone over there, shouting and screaming, demanding to know what the driver thought they were doing.

Today wasn't a normal day.

Not when you owed a loan shark €100,000 and it was due in a matter of hours.

A few cars passed by, moving around the stopped SUV and shooting glances at Gareth's car, up on the footpath. The SUV's driver ignored the beeping horns.

The front passenger window of the SUV rolled down. From where he sat, Gareth still couldn't see who was in the vehicle.

He waited breathlessly for someone to do something. For a face to appear in the open window, for the car door to open.

Nothing... until someone flung a cigarette butt out the window. The glowing butt hit the road and sent sparks flying through the air.

Then the SUV accelerated hard, tearing down the road and out of sight.

Gareth swore under his breath, then wiped his sweaty face with his hand. He wasn't sure how much more excitement he could take.

He reversed gently, his neck snapping back as the rear wheels dropped down onto the road.

Before he could pull away, his phone beeped with an incoming message. It was a photo, sent from an unfamiliar number, and it showed Tess emerging from her office. A time stamp showed that this had happened only a minute ago.

An icy feeling surged through Gareth's whole body.

Someone was watching them both.

Gareth dialled Tess's number. She picked up after two rings, her voice betraying her surprise.

"Gareth?"

"Hey. How are things?"

"Fine," Tess said.

"Are you okay?"

"Why wouldn't I be?"

"Where are you?" Gareth said.

"Walking to my car."

"When you get in, lock the doors. And be careful driving home."

"Why? What's wrong?"

"Nothing." He knew she could see right through him. Tess was no fool. That was for sure. And even to his own ears, he sounded suspicious.

"Tell me, Gareth. You're scaring me."

Cooney wasn't going to harm Tess. Not yet, anyway. He was reminding Gareth to pay. That was all.

"Are you going home?" he asked.

"I'm going to Dee's house."

"Okay." That was probably a good thing, Gareth figured. "I'll talk to you later."

"Wait a minute. You can't just say we'll talk later. What's happening?"

"Just don't talk to anyone and be careful driving."

"Gareth—"

He ended the call, then glanced at the back seat where he'd left the bags he'd packed for him and Tess. Useless. Cooney wasn't letting them go anywhere.

Chapter 49

Izzy watched Dylan as she told him about Ruth. There was astonishment in his eyes. Elaine had already been dead by the time Izzy found out this stuff, so this was the first time she had told anyone.

Dylan said, "Adam killed his ex?"

"I didn't say that."

"He's obviously a lunatic. He sliced himself up just to get your attention. So what happened? Was he a suspect for his girlfriend's murder?"

"Yes." Izzy sighed. "He was the main suspect. He stood trial."

"Incredible." Dylan gave a shake of the head. "And he never told you any of this?"

"No. I had to dig it all up myself." She finished her coffee and took a moment to compose herself. "When I found out, I asked Adam about it. He went ballistic and said the police wanted someone – anyone – to go down for the crime. Said they tried to frame him. At the time, I believed him. I thought it was impossible that he'd hurt someone. Now I'm not so sure."

"How did Ruth die?"

"She was stabbed to death in the apartment they shared. Adam's alibi was that he was fishing with a friend. The friend backed him up, but the jury wasn't sure he was a credible witness."

"The guy lied to protect Adam?"

Izzy shrugged. "That seems to have been what people suspected."

"Should we tell someone?" Dylan said.

"About Ruth's murder? It's not a secret. Adam has already had his day in court."

"But tonight, the pier."

"He only hurt himself."

But Izzy had thought he was going to hurt her too. The fact was that she didn't know him as well as she'd thought.

"Do you want me to stay?" Dylan said.

Izzy liked the idea of having Dylan with her, but she wanted to let him get back to his family. And anyway, she'd agreed to meet the book club gang later.

"Go, Dylan. I'll be fine."

"You sure?"

Izzy nodded.

Dylan took out his phone. "I'll give you my number. Call me anytime. If Adam comes to your door, or you feel nervous or... or anything."

He took her number too. Then Izzy walked him to the door.

Dylan said, "I think I'll check the pier and see if he's still there."

"You don't need to do that."

"I just want to look. I'm curious."

"If you see him, leave him alone."

"I will. You take care too." He flashed her a reassuring smile.

Izzy watched him walk down the road towards the sea. Once he'd disappeared from view, she closed the door and made her way back to the kitchen.

She washed the coffee pot and the mugs, then made her way to the sitting room, exhausted and upset after everything that had happened.

She took out Elaine's diary and lay down on the couch with it, covering her legs with a blanket.

November 12th

I had the most upsetting conversation with Izzy. As if agreeing to marry the Scotsman were not bad enough, now she's decided to move into his apartment with him at the end of the month.

I pointed out as gently as possible that she doesn't even know the fellow. That did not go down well.

My niece accused me of not wanting her to be happy. Honestly, nothing could be further from the truth. More than anything else, I want to protect her. Despite what she may think, I've met charmers in my time. I think she needs to tread carefully.

Izzy's phone beeped with a text message from Dylan.

No sign of Adam.

Izzy typed, *OK thanks*, and hit the send button.

She turned her attention back to the diary. Izzy remembered the conversation Elaine was talking about.

Elaine hadn't sounded upset, but her voice had become clipped the longer the conversation went on.

And Izzy had been angry.

"You want everyone to be a lonely spinster like you," she had said.

She blushed at the memory. What an appalling thing to say.

November 13th

Adam came to the house this evening. He was all smiles on the doorstep, but I was reluctant to let him in. It was late and I didn't want to talk. However, he said that Izzy had sent him to make peace, so I thought I better hear him out.

I made tea and we sat in the front room. He gave me a sob story about how he has always been mistreated, had bad luck etc. It turned into a bit of a rant and I started to wonder how I could get rid of him.

I wonder if Izzy even knew he was here.

I told him how I felt. I said he and Izzy should get to know each other better before they think of getting married or living together. The whole thing is so rushed.

He talked around the point, never really giving me a proper answer, but saying that they love each other very much.

When I didn't change my tune, he flipped like a switch. He said I shouldn't try to turn Izzy against him.

He took his cup of tea (he had not drunk a drop of it) and poured the whole thing on the floor. The way he did it was so slow and deliberate. I was too shocked to complain.

Adam stormed out of the house then.

I rang Izzy but she did not answer. I might try again tomorrow, or else I might see if I can meet her for a coffee.

I spoke to Father Peter about it on the phone. He suggested that perhaps I should give Izzy a little more space. Honestly, he's useless sometimes. I can't give Izzy more space. I dare not blink in case she hurries up the aisle to become Mrs. McGregor.

November 18th

The man in the hoodie was outside the office again today. I haven't seen him for a while, and I was be-ginning to chalk the whole thing up to an overactive imagination.

I think he saw me looking. He pulled his hand across his throat in a gesture that chilled my blood.

A threat?

The doorbell rang, startling Izzy.

The sound was terrifying in the silent house, espe-cially given what she'd just been reading. She'd been holding her breath as she read about Adam's visit, not to mention the stalker reappearing.

Izzy moved to the window. She pulled back the curtain to see Louise on the doorstep. Louise gave a cheerful wave. Even from here, Izzy could see that she was again beautifully made up, smartly dressed, and festooned with chunky jewellery.

Izzy waved back. She grabbed her jacket and made her way to the door. Ready for the second meeting of the book club.

Chapter 50

When Melanie saw Louise and Izzy coming down the footpath towards her, she ducked into a dimly lit garden. She waited in the shadows until they had passed by before re-emerging. She'd catch up with them soon, but there was something she had to take care of first.

Melanie had washed her hands a hundred times, but she still felt like they were dirty. Smelly and greasy and disgusting from Baxter's filth. And so were her keys, though she'd washed them too, and disinfected them with antibacterial spray.

Tom had heard her yells coming from the garden, and let her in. Standing in the hallway Melanie had been so mad, she'd hardly been able to get the words out to explain, but Tom had caught her drift soon enough.

He got mad too when he heard about Baxter befouling their garden again.

"I'm going over there to kick Robert's ass," Tom said.

That kind of remark used to impress Melanie. In the past, she would have put a restraining hand on

Tom's chest, begged him not to get physical, and said, in a stern voice, "He's not worth it."

But she knew by now that there was no need. Tom didn't kick asses. He was more of a keyboard warrior.

"I've got a better idea," Melanie had said, sparing them both an empty display of bravado.

As soon as she got cleaned up, she'd grabbed the mini fire extinguisher she and Tom kept in the kitchen and lugged it to Louise and Robert's road.

She made her way up the steps to their house, hit the doorbell and raised the extinguisher. She pulled the pin to unlock it.

Baxter's barking came from the other side of the door.

"Dumb mutt," Melanie said.

She heard a muffled cough, then footsteps as Robert came down the hall. He muttered to the dog in his usual idiotic way.

"Who is it, boy? Who is it?"

Open the door and find out, asshole.

After an age, the door opened. Robert wasn't even looking her way. He was holding Baxter by the collar, whispering something in the dog's ear.

What a dope.

"Robert?"

He looked up. "Mela—?"

Aiming the extinguisher at him, she shot foam all over his face.

With a yelp, he staggered back. Baxter backed away too. A lot of use he was as a guard dog.

Melanie kept spraying until the extinguisher was empty. Meanwhile, Robert was shouting and trying to shield himself from the blast.

When the foam ran out, Robert wiped foam off his beard, and stared with bewilderment at his soaked shirt and pants.

"What the hell are you doing? Are you crazy?"

"You'll see crazy if you ever let that dog shit on my grass again."

She threw the empty extinguisher at Robert's head.

*

"*Murderer!*"

The shouts from the street continued as Stephanie grabbed a carton of milk from the fridge and brought it to the bedroom. It was the same milk she'd used earlier to make cocoa. It had already been expired then, so it had to be worse now. She stepped through the open door to the balcony and looked down.

Kate's parents stood on the street below. They'd arrived twenty minutes after Stephanie phoned them. Fresh from the pub where they'd been partying till they got the news.

Perhaps it hadn't been a great time to tell them Kate was dead. They both appeared to be drunk and in a bad mood.

Kate's father, James, waved his fist angrily. His wife, Mina, cupped her hands around her mouth to focus her voice.

"*Killer. Murderer. What did you do to our little girl?*"

Stephanie had tried reasoning with them, had tried

telling them that it was an accident. But for some reason, they were convinced that Stephanie had driven Kate to suicide.

"I always knew you were a creep," James shouted. "I told Kate not to marry you. My little girl."

A crowd was gathering on either end of the road, a safe distance away.

"This is your last warning, you maniacs," Stephanie shouted down. "Go home and sleep it off."

"Screw you."

Stephanie shook her head. "Fine."

She took the cap off the carton and poured the expired milk over the side of the balcony, swinging it in an arc so that it hit Kate's parents. James gasped. Mina froze with her arms out in front of her as chunks of congealed milk stuck to her hair.

"How dare you?" Mina screamed, her voice rising an octave. "I'm going to wring your neck if you don't come down here."

"I don't think so."

Stephanie was about to go inside when she saw a new arrival. It looked like Paula Phillips, Dee Phillips's mother. Of course, that gossipmonger would turn up whenever something bad was going down.

Paula walked up to James and Mina. She pointed at Stephanie while she spoke to them. The conversation continued for about a minute.

Stephanie continued to watch, feeling increasingly uneasy. Something told her that this was not a good development.

A moment later, Mina looked up at Stephanie with an almost comical expression of shock and screamed, "You're a *tranny*? My girl killed herself because you're a no-good tranny?"

Jeers came from one of the onlookers.

Kate's father put his hands on his head like he was trying to stop it from exploding. His wife continued shouting, and Paula Philips shook her head, like she was very disappointed.

Stephanie darted into her bedroom and slammed the sliding door so hard it nearly shot off the rail.

She threw herself down on the bed and cried.

Chapter 51

Izzy and Louise walked down The Metals. The care Louise took in her appearance made Izzy feel like a slob. She hadn't a stick of jewellery on, and her clothes were singularly unimpressive. But her new haircut had given her a small boost, and Louise had complimented her on it.

The lane was deserted, and silent except for the rumble of a train below them. After a minute, the lane opened up into a broad junction. They crossed it and passed the entrance to the People's Park. Through its locked gates, Izzy admired the elegant layout of the park, with its fountains and bandstand.

"Nice, isn't it?" Louise said. "The park was laid out by J.L. Robinson, who also designed the town hall."

TOWN HALL was still engraved on one side of the building, but these days Elaine's old workplace was called County Hall, and modern offices had extended the beautiful old structure.

She said, "Dun Laoghaire must be an interesting place, from an architectural point of view. Even to my untrained eye, there seems to be a lot to admire."

"Oh, yes." Louise's eyes lit up. "It's quite a hodge-podge, from the Victorian terraced houses to neoclassical buildings like the original train station (now a restaurant), to various eyesores from the 1970s."

"You sound like you'd like to redesign bits of it?"

"If I had the chance, certainly."

Izzy almost asked Louise about her 'career break', but decided it was none of her business.

Louise said, "As you'll no doubt have noticed, the town is built on a hill. It's a boon because even houses some distance from the sea can enjoy a sea view. Older buildings near the shore, like the train station and the yacht club, were designed as one-storey structures so as not to block the view. Unfortunately, modern builders have been less considerate. Anyway, here we are."

They were halfway up a narrow, terraced street. Louise turned into a driveway. She stabbed the doorbell with her index finger.

The door opened at once.

Light spilled out of the hallway, where a grey-haired lady wearing glasses and a cardigan was taking off a coat.

"Hello. I'm just in the door myself," she said. "Come in. It's so good to see you again, Izzy. How are you?"

The woman threw her jacket over the banister at the bottom of the stairs.

"Hello... Paula," Izzy said, after a moment searching her memory for the woman's name. "Good to see you too."

"Come in."

Izzy stepped into the narrow hallway. Old photos lined the walls on both sides. A staircase lay to one side, its steps covered in threadbare carpet.

"Hello ladies," Dee said, appearing from a doorway at the side of the hall. She looked at her mother. "Oh, you're back too?"

"Wait till I tell you what I saw a minute ago."

Dee's eyes lit up. "Come in, come in, everyone. You can tell us everything inside. Go through that door."

Izzy stepped past her and entered a tiny sitting room. It was empty but the television in one corner was on. It blared at a deafening volume.

"Sit down," Paula said.

Izzy knew that Paula couldn't have been older than sixty-five, as she had worked with Elaine, but she looked older. There was something old-fashioned about her face and her clothes.

Izzy stepped around a coffee table piled high with tabloid newspapers and glossy women's magazines. She sat down on a stained armchair in the corner, next to a radiator that was struggling to warm the room.

"I love your hair," Dee said, muting the TV.

"Thank you. Melanie did it."

Louise sat on the couch next to Izzy's chair. They were so close their legs were almost touching.

"What's the big news?" Louise said. "You said you learned something?"

"All in due course," Dee said with a wink. "Let's wait for the others to arrive."

Paula came and lowered herself into a chair. "Poor Kate," she said. "What a shame! Struck down in the prime of her life."

"It's terrible," Louise agreed. "I wish Robert hadn't done what he did. Well, anyway, it doesn't matter now."

Paula's voice grew excited. "Kate's parents are outside her apartment, shouting at Stephen. He won't let them inside. He's throwing liquids down at them from the balcony! Talk about shameful. There are a hundred people standing around looking at him. I wouldn't be surprised if there's trouble later."

"It's Stephanie now, isn't it?" Louise said.

Paula snorted. "That's the problem. No wonder poor Kate couldn't take it anymore and had to end things. If her death was suicide, of course. It could be something more sinister."

Izzy was confused. "Why are Kate's parents shouting at Stephanie?"

"It's usually the husband," Dee said with a knowing look.

Izzy heard the purr of a car's engine. She was about to ask what Dee meant when the doorbell rang.

Dee went out to the hall, followed by Paula.

"I don't know which one is nosier," Louise whispered.

The comment was so unexpected, especially coming from Louise, that Izzy laughed. She watched Louise pull an antibacterial wipe from her jacket and clean her hands with it.

"Want one?" she said.

"Um, no thanks. I'm okay. So, Dee lives here with her mother?"

Louise hid the wipes away. "Yes. She's a bit of a cheapskate. She'd never pay for her own place."

A moment later, Dee and Paula returned with Tess. The lawyer looked awful. Her limp red hair hung like weeds from her head, and her face was haggard and sickly pale. An intense glow came from her eyes, however.

She sat down.

"Are you alright?" Louise said. "You look tired."

The doorbell rang again before Tess could answer. This time it was Melanie. Her face was flushed, and she grinned cheerfully.

"Hello, ladies!"

Soon everyone was seated.

Izzy pointed at Melanie's sleeve, which was covered in white foam. "You have something on your jacket."

Still grinning, Melanie brushed it away.

"Now, what did you mean, it's usually the husband?" Louise said, turning to Dee again.

The librarian leaned forward in her seat and pushed up her glasses, which had slid down her small nose. "Well, that's the thing. I've heard that they're not at all sure that Kate's death was an accident. It looks like she was murdered."

"No." Melanie gasped. "Who said that?"

"I can't reveal my sources."

"Did your brother tell you?"

Izzy remembered that Dee's brother was a Garda.

"I heard it through the grapevine – that's all I can say."

"It *couldn't* have been an accident," Paula said. "A healthy girl like Kate? No way would she just fall onto the rocks and die. It doesn't happen. Impossible."

"You think she killed herself?" Tess said.

Dee nodded. "It's possible, but I think it's more likely that Stephen/Stephanie killed her. He told Kate he was a woman, then she freaked out, and suddenly she turned up dead. It's awfully convenient, isn't it? Does that sound like a coincidence to any of you?"

There was a long silence.

"What do you think?" Paula said.

Izzy realised everyone was looking at her. "I don't know. I only met Kate once and I've never met her husband. I can't really speculate."

Paula rolled her eyes. "A very diplomatic answer. You should be a politician. God help her, but Elaine was the same. So tight-lipped. You'd need a crowbar to get an opinion out of her."

"*Mom*," Dee said, but looked amused.

Izzy felt her cheeks become hot. She bit her tongue, though, not wanting to get into an argument. After all, she was a guest in Dee's home.

Louise broke the silence. "If Kate *was* murdered, it could have been someone else who did it. Someone besides Stephanie."

"Who else would want her dead?" Dee said.

"I don't know about motive," Louise said, "but there are dangerous people around, aren't there, Izzy?"

Chapter 52

After checking the pier, Dylan Zhao texted Izzy and set off for home. Though there was no sign of Izzy's ex, Dylan had the unnerving feeling that he was being watched.

Adam's wounds had looked deep enough to need stitches, so maybe the guy had gone to hospital. But then why did Dylan feel like someone was watching him?

He kept looking over his shoulder, trying to catch a glimpse of whoever was pursuing him.

There was no sign of anyone though.

The street was dark and unusually quiet.

He was being paranoid, more shaken by the experience on the pier than he'd let on. He was letting Năi-nai's superstitious streak infect him. For her, everyday misfortunes were apocalyptic omens.

He wondered how Izzy was feeling. He didn't believe in love at first sight, but he did think you could get a vibe from people fairly quickly.

And Dylan liked Izzy's vibe.

Adam was a different story. The guy may have

murdered his ex. He was dangerous. Dylan felt a fever-ish prickle on his skin. He didn't want to lose Izzy, when he'd only met her. Dylan had the feeling that Adam wasn't about to go away quietly.

Jackie Chan, Adam had called him.

A familiar irritation swept over him. As a kid, he'd made himself as Irish as possible, playing Gaelic football and hurling, learning the Irish language flu-ently, celebrating St. Patrick's Day more enthusiasti-cally than his friends. And he'd always insisted that his mother make him Irish-style lunches to bring to school: sandwiches, apples, and packets of crisps.

No matter what he did, though, there was always some idiot who singled him out for looking different.

Reaching home, Dylan opened the shop door and let himself in, then locked it again and headed up-stairs to re-join the party. Everyone was still sitting around the table, talking.

"You were gone a long time," said his mother in Chinese. She had a knowing look in her eye.

Dylan shrugged, and slipped into the seat next to Amy. He grabbed an apple and bit into it.

"How was your stroll on the promenade, Romeo? Did you get a goodnight kiss?"

"Piss off."

Amy glanced at Dylan's mom. They both broke out laughing.

In Chinese, Năinai said, "Take care of that girl. She is a good one."

Dylan nodded but said nothing. He wasn't about to contradict his granny.

His father came up the stairs with a dustpan and brush. He was wearing his jacket, so he had probably been in the garden.

"I guess that spare window pane fell over in the breeze," he said with a baffled shrug.

He went into the kitchen and Dylan heard broken glass fall into the bin.

Chapter 53

In Dee's sitting room, Izzy felt her chest tighten. Louise was gazing at her, a questioning look on her face. The other women leaned forward in their chairs, waiting for Louise to explain.

There are dangerous people around, aren't there, Izzy?

"I'm not sure I follow," Izzy said.

"I don't want to air your dirty laundry in public, and I wouldn't mention it if I wasn't worried about you, but we both know that Adam McGregor is a menace."

Louise gave Izzy's knee a pat. Maybe it was meant to reassure but Izzy found the contact irritating.

"What do you know about Adam?"

"I saw him hanging around outside your house earlier. He rang the bell but there was no answer. I guess you weren't home."

Maybe it had been when Izzy was getting her hair cut.

"What happened?"

"I confronted him," Louise said, puffing her chest

out with pride. "I told him I wasn't happy with the way he was treating you. Said he should leave you alone."

Izzy felt a strange mixture of emotions. Irritation that Louise had meddled with her life, gratitude for her attempt to help, and worry that Louise had put herself in danger by getting involved.

"You shouldn't go near Adam. He's unstable."

"He certainly is," Louise said.

"How did he react?"

"He was rather rude. He told me to mind my own business. And he didn't put it as politely as that."

"I bet," Izzy said. "I ran into Adam earlier this evening. I can tell you, you shouldn't go near him."

Dee and Paula spoke at once, asking Izzy what happened.

"Who is this guy?" Tess said, her words cutting through the other voices.

"My ex-boyfriend. Ex-fiancé actually. I lived with him before I moved here. He's not taking the breakup well. Anyway, to get back to the *original* point, Adam may be unstable but there's no reason he would have hurt Kate," Izzy said. "He's probably more of a danger to himself. Tonight, he carved my name into his arm."

"No," Louise gasped.

The others all seemed equally shocked.

"Where was this?" Dee asked, talking over her mother, who was asking the same thing.

"On the pier."

"The East Pier?" Louise said. "Near where Kate was found?"

Izzy said nothing.

Tess was silent too. She stared into space. Her chest rose and fell rapidly, driven by her shallow breaths.

"What does this madman look like?" Dee said. "I want to know in case I see him."

Louise took out her phone. "I'll show you. I'm just worried about Izzy and the rest of us. I was shocked at the way Adam spoke to me, so I looked him up."

She brought up a photo of Adam and angled her phone so everyone could see. The picture was a black and white portrait from the McGregor Fine Foods website. There was a roguish look in Adam's eye. He wore a white shirt, his messy hair was slightly restrained by gel, and his face freshly shaved. Izzy used to find the photo sexy.

She could recite the caption from memory.

Adam McGregor is an entrepreneur and the founder of McGregor Fine Foods.

"Good looking fellow," Paula said.

"I found more than a photo," Louise said. "Back in Scotland, he was charged with murdering his girlfriend."

Cue more gasps from the ladies.

Izzy swallowed. "He wasn't found guilty."

"He wasn't found *not guilty* either," Louise said in the tone of a patient schoolteacher reminding a child of her mistake.

"What was it then?" Tess snapped. "There's only two possibilities in a trial."

"Not in Scotland," Louise said. "It turns out Scotland

is unique in having three possible verdicts at a trial. Isn't that so, Izzy? It's not just guilty or not guilty. There's another option."

Izzy cleared her throat.

"*Not proven*," she said in a small voice.

"What does that mean?" Tess asked.

Louise said, "It means he did it, and everyone knows that he did it, but they can't prove it."

Izzy felt like this evening's meeting had got way out of control.

"It doesn't mean that," Izzy said. "It means they don't have enough evidence to secure a conviction."

"And not enough to clear him either," Louise said.

Izzy broke out in a fit of coughing before she could reply. Promising to get some tea, Paula left the room.

"I'm sorry for upsetting you," Louise said while Izzy coughed. "I was just so shocked after he yelled at me. As you say, he wasn't found guilty. But I thought that if there's a dangerous man around, everyone should be aware of it."

Izzy felt exposed and she wanted to leave.

Soon Paula was pushing a cup of boiling water into her hands. Izzy drank it down though it burnt her tongue and scorched her throat.

"You left him?" Melanie asked. "Maybe he has a grudge. Not only against you, but us, now that we're your friends. He could have killed Kate to spite you."

Izzy recovered a little. She said, "I don't think so. We don't even know if there's anything suspicious about Kate's death. We shouldn't get carried away."

Dee frowned deeply, so that her brow wrinkled, and her half-moon glasses were pushed out from her face. "If there's a killer on the loose, we need to know. And soon."

"I still think it's Stephen," her mother said.

Melanie scowled. "You mean Stephanie."

Izzy felt a headache coming on. Her back was sore, her throat too. She wanted to get out of there.

She said, "If the death is suspicious, there'll be a full investigation. I'm sure there could be other suspects around here, besides Stephanie or Adam."

"Like who?" Dee said.

"I don't know. But I was reading my aunt's diary earlier, and she mentioned a guy who was hanging around outside her office."

"Your aunt's diary?" Louise said. "You got it back?"

"No. This is another volume," Izzy explained. "The last month of Elaine's life."

"Anything juicy in it?" Paula said. "Does she mention me?"

"I don't know. I haven't read it all."

"Do you have it with you?" Dee said. "Let's see."

"No, it's at home."

"Well, read it and let me know."

Yeah, right.

Izzy decided she'd never trust Dee or Paula with any sensitive information.

Abruptly, Tess got to her feet. "I'm leaving," she said.

Everyone spoke at once, asking her to stay.

Tess shook her head impatiently. "I'm tired. I need to catch up on my sleep."

Izzy sensed that there was more to it than that. However, she also wanted to go. It seemed that Dee had invited everyone to her house to gossip and Izzy didn't want to be part of it.

"I should go too," Izzy said. "I've got work tomorrow."

Within a matter of hours, Izzy would be back at the diner with Mr. R. and Hannah, and Adam would be free to walk in any time he liked.

Chapter 54

Chisel Cooney came early. Gareth wasn't ready, not even a little.

After driving home, his hands shaking the whole way, Gareth had grabbed the two bags, full of his and Tess's hastily packed clothes, and brought them into the house from the car.

He'd left the bags in the hall and gone to his study, where he knocked back a shot of whiskey to calm his nerves. He barely felt the burn as it passed down his throat. The whiskey warmed his belly, though.

That bastard nearly killed me. And he threatened Tess.

A real man would do something about it, something more than panicking.

Gareth caught a glimpse of himself in the mirror. His reflection looked dishevelled and frightened, and he quickly moved away from it.

He played with the empty glass, moving it from one hand to another. Then he stopped and flung the glass at the wall. It shattered into a thousand pieces and filled the air with the smell of whiskey.

Gareth slumped into the chair at his desk and checked his broker's app, praying under his breath for a miracle. One part of his prayer was answered.

The NASDAQ had reopened after the flash crash. *Good.* Most stocks had reverted to pre-crash levels. *Good.* But not SSI.

His stock had tanked even more. And Gareth's broker had executed his order at the worst possible price.

Gareth had lost a fortune. And this was a fortune of borrowed money.

He felt like crying. He'd been living a pretty good life until his desire to get rich quick had got the better of him. Why hadn't he been satisfied with that? Who cared if Tess earned more than him? *She* didn't mind.

There wasn't much time until he needed to bring Chisel Cooney his money. He had to do something.

An idea came to him. Shorting SSI.

The company had shown itself to be a terrible investment, whatever his investment guru had written in her stupid newsletter. It kept going down when it should have gone up.

So what if he bet on the company going down?

Gareth jumped to his feet. This could work. It was a desperate all-or-nothing kind of move, but he didn't have much choice. Though he'd avoided shorting stocks, because of the risks, now might be the time to try it.

Best of all, it was a leveraged bet. If he won, he'd win big. On the other hand, if he lost. No, Gareth couldn't afford to think about losing.

He placed the order, then poured a generous finger of whiskey into a fresh glass, then paced the study. Every few seconds he checked SSI's stock price.

And damn if the bastard didn't start rising.

As soon as Gareth had established his short position, the fucker started climbing to the moon. Up and up and up it shot.

That was when the doorbell chimed. The sound made Gareth's heart skip a beat.

He remained where he was. When the bell chimed again, he walked down the hall as silently as he could, wondering if he could pretend he wasn't home. There was little chance of anyone being fooled. The lights were on, and his car was outside. Maybe Gareth had even been followed home.

He opened the door. Chisel Cooney's goons, the twins, stood on the doorstep. They looked even bigger than the last time. A black SUV was parked across the end of the driveway. Gareth noticed that it was blocking his car.

"Good evening," said a familiar voice. The twins moved aside as Chisel Cooney came up the steps between them. He had his usual golf club in one hand. The other held a cigarette. Cooney took a leisurely pull on his cigarette, then blew a smoke ring into the night air.

"I was just on my way to meet you," Gareth said. "I thought I was meant to come to you. I mean, I didn't think you'd come here. So... so you're here."

Realising he was babbling, Gareth shut his mouth.

"What are those?" Cooney jabbed his cigarette at the two travel bags in the hall.

"Nothing."

Cooney smiled. "You're not thinking of going anywhere, are you?"

"Not now. They're for Sunday, maybe? The wife and I might go away for the night."

"Very nice. You're ready early. Here it is, only Friday night, and you've got your bags packed." He paused. "Are you going to invite us in?"

"Of course," Gareth said. "Come in."

It seemed that Cooney was going to pretend he hadn't nearly killed Gareth and Gareth would pretend not to have been nearly killed. All very civil.

He stepped back, opened the door wider.

Before entering, Cooney turned and called to another man standing by the gate. Gareth hadn't noticed him before. He was a lean bespectacled fellow of about forty, wearing a crisp suit, and carrying a briefcase.

Chisel Cooney raised the golf club and pointed. "This is Lorcan, my solicitor."

"You brought a lawyer?" Gareth couldn't keep the surprise out of his voice.

"He handles certain transactions for me."

Cooney stepped past Gareth into the hall. Then came the twins. They both glared at him like they couldn't wait to get their hands on him. Last was the solicitor, who greeted Gareth by rapidly raising and lowering his eyebrows.

Gareth swallowed, closed the door, and followed the men into his front room.

Cooney sank into the chair by the fireplace, crossing one leg jauntily over the other, and letting the golf club rest against the side of his chair.

The twins stood on either side of him.

Lorcan placed his briefcase on the coffee table. Behind his glasses, the man's sharp eyes ran around the room.

It was weird and extremely unnerving seeing them here. He hoped Tess stayed at Dee's house a while longer.

"Come in," Cooney said. "Sit down. We have much to discuss."

Gareth realised he was still standing in the doorway. He perched on the edge of the chair farthest from the men.

"How's work?" Cooney said.

Probably the last question Gareth expected. How was work? Gareth had walked straight out of the school hours ago without a word to anyone. That wasn't a great sign.

"It's okay," Gareth said.

"I'm glad to hear that. You don't find it stressful, do you?"

"Teaching? No, not really. Normally it's plain sailing."

"I'm glad. My line of work is plain sailing too, most of the time." Cooney took another puff of his cigarette. Tess would have had a heart attack if she knew someone was smoking in her house. "I provide loans. People pay me back. Simple."

"Sure."

Cooney blew another smoke ring. "When people are late, or when they refuse to pay, I have to take action. It's about fairness and respect, right?"

"I suppose, but—"

"One person doesn't pay me back, the next guy will ask himself why *he* should. You know what I mean?"

Fear snaked its way across Gareth's chest, paralysing him.

Cooney said, "I can't let a slight go unpunished. You're late and you're planning to do a runner, and that makes me look bad. Makes me look soft. I can't afford to look soft."

"Please don't hurt me."

"Like I said, I can't let a slight go unpunished. But maybe I don't have to kill you. Do I have to kill you?"

"No, you absolutely don't. You do not have to kill me. Please don't."

"Can you get the money?"

"Take my car," Gareth said. "The keys are on the table."

"Of course, I will," Cooney said. "But that's not nearly enough. You now owe me €100,000. And I bet you owe other people too. You have a sneaky look about you."

"I thought I'd have the cash by now but I don't. I'm sorry. What can I do? I—"

Cooney held up his hand, silencing Gareth.

"I'll take the house. Everything will be done properly, I can assure you. Lorcan will handle the paperwork. It will be a simple transaction, and we will conclude it swiftly."

"But you can't."

Cooney's eyes narrowed. "Why not?"

"Because the house isn't mine," Gareth explained. "It belongs to Tess."

Cooney said, "Then we need to talk to her too."

Chapter 55

Tess got to her feet, brushed down the trousers of her dark suit, and walked out of Dee's front room. Izzy followed her to the hall and stepped outside, glad to leave the house behind. The second book club meeting hadn't been like she'd expected. She hated the way she'd been ambushed by Louise, and she didn't like Dee and Paula's gossiping much better.

If Dee was so quick to gossip about others behind their backs, Izzy was sure she'd do the same to her. And she was sure they'd spread the rumour about Elaine's sleepwalking, making a laughing stock of her.

Tess moved quickly down the path and out onto the street, her arms swinging and her long coat billowing around her thin frame. She reached what must have been her car, a dark saloon parked at the kerb.

"Goodbye," Izzy said, as she turned down the footpath.

Tess paused, a confused look on her face, as if she had forgotten about Izzy.

"Want a lift?"

"Sure. That would be great."

Izzy went around to the other side and got in the front passenger seat. She fastened her seat belt and sniffed the interior. It had that distinctive new-car smell and it looked like it could have come straight out of the factory.

Tess got behind the wheel, shut the door and closed her eyes.

"Are you okay?" Izzy said after a moment.

Tess kept her eyes closed. She put a hand to her forehead, like she was suffering from a migraine.

"Sorry. I'm probably less of a bitch than you think. You're not seeing me at my best."

"It's okay."

"You're not seeing my friends at their best either. Dee is a pain in the arse, but she was worse than usual tonight. Her mother was her usual level of annoying."

They were silent for another moment. Izzy looked out at the dark street. A streetlight, half concealed by trees, cast dramatic shadows across the tarmac.

She wondered what exactly it was that was making the lawyer so edgy. It couldn't have been Kate's death, because Tess had also been like this last night, when Kate was still alive.

"I'm not trying to pry. But if you want someone to talk to, let me know," Izzy said. "I can keep a secret."

Tess opened her eyes, turned them on Izzy.

"Maybe you can," she said. She looked away again and sighed. "But I don't know what tell you. I suspect that my partner is up to something."

"Like what?"

"I don't know, but he's been acting strange lately. I have no idea what he's mixed up in. He's only a damn school teacher. How much trouble can they get into?"

"You could ask him what's on his mind."

"I did," Tess said. "But maybe I'll try again. One way or another, I have to know what's going on." Tess fixed her gaze on Izzy. "I'm thinking you had a rough time with your ex."

"Adam? Yeah, I did. I still am."

"Well, feel free to talk to me about it too. But not tonight," Tess added. "Tonight, I'm going to clear the air with Gareth. I'll make him come clean with me. I can't stand it anymore. Not knowing what he's doing."

"I'm sure you'll feel better afterwards."

They were silent for a moment.

"Huh," Tess said. "That bracelet..."

"What?"

Tess looked absolutely stunned. After a moment, she shook her head as if she couldn't believe it.

"Never mind. It might be nothing."

Tess composed herself, then started the engine and got the car moving.

Her driving was smoother than Izzy had feared. She'd expected jerky, staccato acceleration, much like Tess's manner, but she steered the car smoothly.

Izzy didn't have to give Tess directions. She knew where she was going, and she brought the car to a stop directly outside Izzy's house.

"Thank you, Tess." Izzy glanced around, satisfying

herself that there was no sign of Adam, before she got out of the car. "And good luck with Gareth."

"Good luck with Adam. I hope you've seen the last of him."

Izzy thought not, but she said nothing. She watched Tess do a sharp three-point turn and accelerate back the way they had come.

Then Izzy went inside the house. It was almost as cold inside as it was outside. After Izzy had fixed herself a cup of warm water, she ironed her uniform for work at the diner. It was a green and white dress that went down below her knees, but which Adam always said was too revealing.

Once the ironing was done, she went to the bathroom and had a quick shower.

When drying herself, she glanced in the mirror and was shocked to see a dozen perfectly circular bruises on her back. The marks were a shocking purple – souvenirs of Mrs. Zhao's cupping. Izzy hoped the painful therapy and bitter medicine would be worth suffering.

She changed into her pyjamas, went to the spare bedroom and curled up in bed with Elaine' diary.

December 1st

Izzy hasn't returned my calls for days. I've just had a bit of a weep. Silly, I know. But these things do wear you down.

I woke up with dirt on my feet again and I feel as if I've I caught a chill. I must have been outside during the night. Down to stress, I am sure. I must ask Father

Peter to say a prayer for me. Sometimes it's just nice to know that someone is thinking of you.

I saw Louise's mystery man going into her house today while Robert was out. I wonder if they want to get caught. Perhaps she wants to punish Robert? Honestly, the way she carries on is just shameless.

Louise's mystery man? Amazing!

Izzy flicked through the pages to see how much was left. The passage about Izzy not returning Elaine's calls hit her hard. It was true. To avoid upsetting Adam, she had, by that point, decided to interact less with her aunt.

She'd sold out her own family for him and look where that got her.

The fact that Louise's lover came to Louise's house was a shock. Izzy couldn't believe her neighbour would be so brazen about her affair.

Izzy flicked through the next few pages and came to a stop on the entry for the fifth of December. That was the day Elaine was believed to have died, though her body had not been found until later.

December 5th

The Scotsman came by this afternoon. He said I'm poisoning my niece's mind against him. That would be some achievement given that she's ignored me for a week. In any case, all does not seem well in paradise. I hope she gives serious consideration to breaking the engagement.

The Scotsman told me in no uncertain terms that I should stop calling Izzy 'or else'.

There was a little more in the diary, but Izzy couldn't face it right now. She was already in floods of tears and her heart ached.

She closed the diary and took a long breath.

She remembered that night. Elaine had phoned her late in the evening while Izzy was in the shower. She'd left a voice message, asking Izzy to call her back.

Izzy remembered telling Adam that she'd missed the call. His face had darkened. He'd left the apartment a short time later, without giving Izzy any explanation. He often went out without explaining where he was going or what he was doing.

What if, that night, he went to see Elaine again?

What if he went back to this very house to show Elaine what he meant when he said *or else*?

Chapter 56

When Tess pulled into the driveway, Gareth's car wasn't there, which was weird. Where the hell was it? He should be home. Him going to the pub the previous night had been odd enough.

She leaned back in her seat, closed her eyes, and let out an irritated sigh.

"Fucking hell. What now?"

Her old fear returned, the one that kept coming back to her. The idea that Gareth was with another woman. Someone sexier and more fun than Tess.

Someone like Kate.

What had happened between Gareth and Kate last night? And why was she dead now? Tess had the ominous suspicion that Gareth was in trouble, and somehow it was connected to Kate's death.

She got out of the car and climbed the steps to the house. A passing train rumbled behind her while a powerful gust of wind rattled the ropes of boats' sails in the harbour.

She let herself into the house.

All was quiet until Tess heard a groan.

Holding her breath, she moved towards the door to the sitting room. She peered inside but saw no one. The air smelled like tobacco and whiskey. Tess stepped inside and saw that the door to Gareth's study was open.

"Tethhh?"

"Gareth?"

"Tethhh?"

"When the fuck did you start lisping?"

She crossed the room and froze when she saw Gareth. He was sitting on the chair behind his desk, tied to it with thick rope.

His face was a mask of blood, like a tin of red paint had been emptied on his head. His eyelids were swollen shut.

Tess stepped closer.

A strange coldness swept over her. Her instinct had been right. He really was up to no good, mixed up in some bad trouble.

"What happened? Who did this to you?"

Gareth spat blood and a couple of teeth onto the desk in front of him. He made an effort to enunciate more clearly.

"Thank God you're here. Untie me."

"Tell me first," Tess said.

"What?"

"Tell me what's going on."

"I'm in pain."

"Then talk fast. I knew you were keeping a secret from me. Is this about Kate? Did you kill her?"

Gareth's swollen eyes widened as much as they could. "What? No. Of course not."

"What's this about then?"

"I-I borrowed some money." He shook his head. "I couldn't pay it back."

"Borrowed it from where?"

"First from the bank. Plus the credit card. Then a loan shark."

"Amazing." Tess allowed herself a derisive snort. Gareth was almost too stupid to believe. "What happened?"

"I lost it on the stock market."

"Genius. Why did you do this? We have money."

"You do," Gareth said.

"Now you're in debt. How much do you owe?"

"Too much."

Tess joined the dots.

"That loan shark was here. And he took your car." She sighed. "You could have spoken to me. I have cash in my current account."

"Not anymore... I had to borrow that too."

"What? How?" She was suddenly angry.

"I know your PIN."

Tess had always been driven to succeed, to make her parents proud. She had a fat salary and a nice pension, but she didn't check her bank balance very often. Money itself wasn't what motivated her. It seemed, though, that she'd have kept a closer eye on her savings.

Gareth said, "They're going to kill me if I can't pay them back."

"Good luck with that."

"I'm sorry. I need your help."

Tess had never seen her boyfriend look so pathetic, and yet she felt no sympathy for him.

"How can I help? You already stole my savings."

"They want the house."

"The house?" Tess laughed. "Your loan shark wants my house?"

"Yes."

"Well, he can go fuck himself."

She breathed easier now that she had some idea what was going on. A tremendous sense of relief washed over her.

Perhaps sensing this shift, Gareth's eyes widened even more, straining against the bruising.

"Tess, please—"

"It's my house. I'm not giving it away."

"They'll kill me."

"You've kept me out of this so far. Why should I get involved now?"

"I don't believe this."

"Who's the loan shark?"

"His name is Billy Cooney."

"That sounds vaguely familiar," Tess said. "Melanie's cousin?"

"Yes. Do you think Melanie can help?"

"Of course not. She wants nothing to do with him. They don't speak."

Gareth said, "Please untie me."

She leaned against the wall and gazed at him. It was a shame she'd wasted so much time on him. He'd managed to mess up even the steady life of a school teacher. And he wanted to drag her down too.

"Listen carefully," she said. "I want you out of here tonight."

"I need the money immediately."

"That isn't going to happen, Gareth."

"But—"

"Shut your mouth and listen. I'll untie you. Then you can pack your things. While you're packing, I'm going to visit the Garda Station and report everything you've told me."

"You can't do that!"

"I can and I will. Perhaps I have another crime to report too. I think I know who murdered Kate."

Gareth's eyes widened. "She was murdered?"

"Never mind, Gareth. It's none of your business. I thought you did it but I was wrong. Maybe my other idea is wrong too. Anyway, while I'm gone you'll have a little time to grab your things. Perhaps some officers will escort me home to dust the house for fingerprints and gather other evidence. If you're still here, they'll want to speak with you."

"You're kicking me out?"

"You're very welcome to explain yourself to them. They'll probably be understanding, given that you're a teacher, a pillar of the community."

Tears rolled down Gareth's cheeks. "Tess."

"Do you understand me?" Tess asked.

After a moment, he nodded.

Tess untied the rope. Just then her phone beeped. She pulled it out, checked the screen and saw that she had received a message. An impossible message.

It was from Kate.

Chapter 57

According to the clock radio next to Izzy's bed, it was 22:53 when she woke to the sound of a noise downstairs. She froze, suddenly alert.

She felt like she had only just fallen asleep, though she had been in bed for an hour and a half, tossing and turning and thinking about Elaine's diary.

Before going to bed, she had resolved to go to the Garda Station in the morning and tell them her suspicions that Elaine had been worried about Adam, that he had threatened her on the day that she had been found dead.

This all flashed through her mind in an instant.

Cold, blue moonlight spilled into the room from a gap between the curtains. The bedroom door stood open, as she had left it. She listened for the sound which had woken her.

Izzy squeezed her duvet between her fingers and listened. Blood pounded in her ears. She heard nothing else. Had she imagined the noises?

Had she been dreaming? No. It came again. The sound of footsteps. Someone was downstairs.

Had Adam broken into the house? Would he climb the stairs, his boots causing the wood to creak beneath him?

His rage would be terrible.

He'd hurt her. She knew he would.

He'd have his switchblade with him. The one he used to carve her name into his arm. Maybe he'd use it on her this time. Maybe he'd write *ADAM* on *her* arm.

The noises were faint, but Izzy knew someone was downstairs.

Just underneath her.

Then came the most terrifying sound Izzy had ever heard. A demented scream that turned her blood to ice.

"Holy shit," Izzy shouted. She turned on the bedside lamp and scrambled out of the bed.

A crash. Someone moving. Faster footsteps.

Izzy broke out coughing. Doing her best to ignore it, she grabbed the nearest object she could conceivably use as a weapon, which was a twelve-inch figurine of a ballet dancer. Pretty useless. But she took it anyway, together with her phone, and ran out to the top of the stairs.

"I'm calling for help," she shouted.

She waited for a response. Waited for Adam to speak.

I've come to take you home.

But all was silent now.

Izzy descended the stairs slowly. In the hall, she saw that the front door was ajar. She wondered if an intruder left it open or if she had not closed it properly.

She stepped outside. The movement startled a fox standing in the grass. It ran out the garden gate, its fluffy tail trailing behind it. Izzy saw nothing else. There was no one around.

The fox must have made the terrifying sound she heard. But what about the footsteps? Was that the fox too or had someone been in the house?

Was someone *still* in the house?

As she stood thinking, she became aware of the smell of smoke on the night air. Something was burning.

She went back inside, walked through the whole house, checking that no one was hiding. She found nothing, nobody, and she set the ceramic ballerina down on the kitchen table.

Izzy didn't think she'd be able to relax until she knew what was burning, and if the authorities had been called.

She slipped on her shoes and put a coat on over her pyjamas. Then she grabbed her keys and went outside.

Izzy tried to get a sense of where the smoke was coming from. Her first thought was the pier. Maybe Adam was up to something there?

It wasn't from that direction, though. She noticed that smoke was coming from the direction of the main street, rising over rooftops in belligerent billows.

She walked towards it, looking all around her as

she went. At any moment she might catch sight of Adam's van.

Or Adam himself, with blood running down his arm, eyes blazing, hands reaching out to grab her—

A siren wailed in the distance and that comforted Izzy a little. She knew how much Adam hated the police.

She broke into a run when she came to the main street and saw smoke coming from the Chinese shop.

Flames billowed out the front window. Izzy couldn't believe it. Three figures were huddled together in the middle of the empty road.

"Dylan?" she called.

It was him alright. He turned at Izzy's shout. He was wearing a T-shirt and pyjama bottoms. His parents stood beside him, staring stoically at the burning building.

The front windows of the shop were broken. Wicked flames licked through the holes.

Izzy felt the heat as she jogged over to the family.

Dylan said, "What are you doing here?"

"I smelled the smoke. What happened?"

Dylan shook his head. His face was set in a hard expression. "Someone set the house on fire."

Izzy's heart sank. It was as she'd feared. "Thank God you're all okay."

"My parents were in bed, but I was awake. I heard a window breaking."

"A Molotov cocktail?"

"Something like that." Dylan had to shout over the

rising sound of the siren. "That's probably why the fire spread so fast. We only just managed to get outside."

Izzy saw that the upstairs was ablaze too. A few hours earlier, she'd been eating dumplings there. Now it was an inferno.

Flashing blue lights lit up the far end of the street as a Dublin Fire Brigade Unit came screaming towards them.

Izzy saw Dylan's cousin, Amy, and her parents rush down the road. They spoke with the Zhaos in Chinese until the first Fire Brigade engine reached them, and everyone stepped back, except Mr. Zhao who hurried over and began to talk to the fire officers streaming out of the vehicle.

Dylan turned to Izzy. "You know who did this, right?"

Izzy already felt cold. Now her temperature dropped another five degrees.

"No, it can't be Adam."

But she could hear the lack of conviction in her own voice. Maybe Adam had pushed Elaine down the stairs... and tried to kill the Zhao family too.

"Wake up, Izzy. He's got a screw loose. I'm going to tell the cops about him as soon as they get here."

Izzy shook her head, but no words came. What could she say? Dylan was right.

"I better help my dad."

He ran over to Mr. Zhao as a second Fire Brigade engine arrived. Izzy backed towards the footpath, so she wouldn't get in the way. Amy followed a minute later. Her face looked even paler than it had earlier. Her eyes were wide with shock.

"They say it's arson," Amy said. "But who would do such a thing?"

Izzy said nothing.

Instead, she ran to her car.

Chapter 58

Tess left Gareth rubbing his wrists and feeling sorry for himself. She swept out of the house, stopping at the end of the driveway to read the message again.

The impossible message from Kate.

Meet me at Izzy's house. Now.

Some sick fuck had Kate's phone and was using it to mess with her. She had a suspicion of her own about who killed Kate, and she wondered if it just might be true. What she didn't understand was Izzy's connection.

The safest thing to do was leave everything to the authorities. However, having ditched her idiotic boyfriend, Tess felt giddy. Giddy and very curious. She decided she'd look into the text message, then continue on to the Garda Station to report everything. Her suspicions about Kate's murder and everything she knew about Gareth's activities too.

As she stood there, a train rumbled past. The damn things never seemed to stop. Its noise prompted her to move.

She walked towards Izzy's house. What was she going to find there?

I'll keep a distance, Tess told herself. *I'll just take a look and see what's going on.*

And something was definitely going on in the area. She heard sirens and caught the smell of smoke.

After all the stress and fear, Tess was amazed at how relieved she felt to be rid of Gareth. She wondered whether she had ever loved him or if she had simply settled for him.

The relationship was over now and that was what mattered.

She straightened her back and felt a thrill as she reached Izzy's road. The smell of smoke was stronger here, and she could see the smoke rising over nearby rooftops.

Tess continued on.

*

Adam watched the building burn from the back.

Seeing Izzy walk off with the Asian guy had made Adam incandescent with rage, more furious than he could put into words.

But Adam knew where to find the guy. That little prick wasn't stealing his girl.

Adam had lost quite a bit of blood before he cleaned himself up in his van, put on his jacket again to hide the bloody bandages, then went to the shop and got some matches, cloths and bottles of spirits.

Starting fires was fun. He used to do that a lot back

in Maryhill, long before the likes of Ruth and Izzy came along.

When the lights in the Chinese building went out, he jumped the wall into the back garden again, then used four Molotov cocktails to get the party started.

A thirst for vengeance grew as he stood in the shadows of the garden and watched the flames surge and the smoke billow.

He hoped everyone in the house was killed, but he'd settle for Izzy's new boyfriend.

Adam sat on his ass in the garden.

After a while he heard screams and shouts. Music to his ears. When he was sure the fire was going strong, he jumped the garden wall again and got into his van.

He pointed it towards his apartment.

Adam's work in Dun Laoghaire wasn't yet done. But there was something he needed to get from home.

Chapter 59

Izzy pressed her foot down on the accelerator. Her little Fiat tore through the Saturday night streets. She passed people clustered around bars, clubs, and takeaway restaurants. Drunken laughter and shouting exploded everywhere.

An icy breeze came from the broken window and blasted the side of Izzy's face, making her even colder than she would otherwise have been.

Confronting Adam was risky, but she wanted to see him one last time. She had to know if he'd started the fire.

If she looked him in the eyes and asked him, she'd know if he answered truthfully.

Wouldn't she?

The place wasn't just a shop. It was a *home*. So if Adam started that fire, he meant for people to die. Izzy wondered if he was really capable of such a thing.

Adam was sick. Controlling and cruel. But Izzy couldn't face the possibility that he was a murderer. What would that say about her? That she was dumb enough to be taken in by a killer? She wouldn't be the first.

For the millionth time, Izzy thought of Ruth. Had the Scottish girl been taken in by Adam too? Had he killed her and moved on, eager to find another sucker?

Who knew?

Even the Scottish court seemed uncertain.

Not proven.

The apartment complex appeared ahead. Izzy shunned her usual parking spot in front of the building, and ditched the Fiat outside the next block, so Adam wouldn't see it if he was around.

Within her, a battle was taking place.

She needed to see Adam. At the same time, she never wanted to see him again. She suspected he was a killer, but desperately wanted proof that he was not. It was enough to make her crazy.

She stepped out of the car and walked briskly across the tarmac. Her breath misted in the night air.

Seeing no one, she let herself into her old building. She took the stairs, pushed through the door to the familiar, dim corridor.

The usual hum of the lights came from overhead. She forced herself to continue to the door of Adam's apartment.

After a moment's hesitation, she knocked.

A bitter taste filled her mouth as she waited for the door to open. Her ears strained for the sound of movement from within, but she heard nothing.

She wondered if Adam had gone to hospital to get

his wound taken care of. If he had any sense, he would have gone straight to the Accident and Emergency Department. But if he'd had any sense, he wouldn't have sliced his arm open like that in the first place.

The image of his mutilated flesh shot into her mind. Vivid red blood against pale skin. Dark water lapping against the pier's side.

And Dylan's stunned face.

There was still no sound from inside the apartment, so Izzy slid her key into the hole. She swallowed as she turned the key.

Gingerly, she pushed the door. She was half-expecting Adam to rush out at her. He didn't. There was still only silence and stillness.

Izzy stepped inside.

The lights were on, but Adam was nowhere to be seen. Closing the door, Izzy walked across the sitting room. She paused by the kitchen area, which smelled like stale take-away. The bin was overflowing, the sink full of dirty dishes.

That was more alarming than anything else.

Adam was so organised, so neat. In her time living with him, Izzy had never seen the bin overflow, had never witnessed him leaving dirty dishes unwashed. He controlled the dishes the way he tried to control everything else.

Curious now, she checked the cupboard over the sink, where he kept canned food in meticulously neat order.

Now there was chaos. Tins of tomatoes, beans, and

fruit were all mixed up and some lay on their side. Someone who didn't know Adam would not have been shocked by the disorder. But Izzy had never seen such a sight in Adam's place before. That, even more than him carving *IZZY* into his arm, told her that Adam was melting down.

She closed the cupboard, then moved to the bedroom. She needed to take her passport. Izzy was surprised to see a black holdall sitting on top of the bed.

Izzy had never seen the bag before. It looked full and somehow ominous, though she couldn't have said why.

She walked to the bedside drawer. There was no sign of her passport inside. Adam must have taken it.

She cursed under her breath, then turned her attention to the holdall. What was inside? She grasped the zip and opened it. A motley collection of items came into view. They sent her pulse racing even faster.

A blindfold, a bottle of bleach, cable ties, a couple of knives, duct tape, a gag, a length of rope, a hammer, and a small axe.

It was a murder kit.

Izzy's breath quickened at the sight.

Everything Dylan had said was true. Adam was a killer. And he was planning to kill *her*.

Perhaps torching Dylan's home was only one part of the night's fun.

It was then that she heard a faint sound from the next room. Someone had just entered the apartment.

Chapter 60

Gareth Gillen spat a loose tooth onto the carpet at his feet. He was going to need a lot of dental work. Was that provided in prison? Because prison was probably where he was going.

He'd stolen from Tess. He'd used illegal money-lending services. What else? He wasn't even sure what other laws he had broken, though there might well be more.

Gareth kept pacing his study, moving in a tight circle around his bloody tooth. He didn't bother picking it up.

Running his tongue around his mouth, he found another loose one. The twins had really done a number on his mouth, the bastards.

He checked his watch again, noting its cracked face.

Where was Tess? How long would she be? He'd expected her to be back by now. The Garda Station wasn't far.

For a moment, Gareth entertained the notion that Tess might have changed her mind and had mercy on him.

He quickly dispelled that idea. Tess came to decisions quickly and firmly, and she stuck to them. If she said she was going to report him, then that was what she was going to do.

He couldn't take the suspense anymore. Waiting for the Gardaí to come, for Tess to arrive back. It wasn't supposed to end like this. He paced a bit longer before deciding he'd head to the Garda Station himself to see what was happening.

He got a damp cloth and cleaned the worst of the blood off his face, then slipped on his coat and headed outside, his shaky legs carrying him to George's Street.

Passing Fitzgerald's pub, he wondered fleetingly if Robert Murphy was inside. It was Friday night. Not everyone's life was imploding like Gareth's. There were happy-go-lucky people everywhere, having fun.

Gareth plunged his hands deep into his pockets to warm them and kept walking.

Flashing lights came into focus farther down the street. The Fire Brigade was dealing with a burning building. He gave the scene a wide berth.

Gareth wanted nothing more than to go to bed, and find, when he woke, that the previous couple of days had been a dream.

But that wasn't going to happen.

He pushed on. The Garda Station was a modern three-storey building next to an identical structure which housed the District Court.

Gareth made his way past a couple of patrol cars

parked out front and entered the station. The room inside was empty.

Gareth pressed the bell on the unmanned counter. He waited for someone to appear, trying his best to ignore the missing person posters on the wall.

RING ONCE, said a sign. Gareth waited and waited. No one came. He hit the bell again. Still no one came so he hit the bell a third time.

The door behind the counter burst open.

A big meaty Garda roared, "What's this? Are you trying to wake the dead or what?"

Gareth shook his head. He spoke again, trying to enunciate clearly despite his ruined mouth. "I'm looking for my partner. Her name is Tess."

"Tess?"

"Is she here?"

The officer shook his head. "No, we haven't had anyone dropping in tonight. Not voluntarily." He cocked his head, narrowed his eyes. "Why was she coming here?"

"Um, never mind." Gareth backed away from the counter and stepped outside before he was asked anything else.

Tess had never got to the station. So where was she?

The end of his exchange with Chisel Cooney came back to him.

The house isn't mine. It belongs to Tess.

Then we need to talk to her too.

He'd never forgive himself if Tess got hurt because

of him. She was guilty of nothing except choosing Gareth for a partner.

He'd assumed that she was safe, that Cooney wouldn't do anything to her.

What if he was wrong?

Chapter 61

Izzy had experienced distress, apprehension, and anxiety during her months with Adam. The longer they'd lived together, the more she saw through his charm, and the more worried she felt about their future.

She had felt fear too, but never like this.

The sound of someone in the next room sent a wave of terror through her. For a moment she stood staring at the murder kit which Adam had prepared. Then the spell broke and Izzy moved fast.

She had to or she'd die.

She stepped away from the bedroom door so that Adam wouldn't see her from the next room.

As quietly as she could, she moved to the wardrobe. The door creaked slightly when it opened. Izzy clenched her teeth. There was nothing she could do. It was the only place to hide.

She pulled the door the rest of the way open. The wardrobe was packed with clothes. Mostly Adam's, and some stuff Izzy had left behind.

She stepped into the wardrobe, squeezing herself

between the hanging coats, trousers, and shirts, sitting on the wooden base, her knees tight to her chest so that she fitted.

Footsteps moved across the sitting room.

With a swallow, Izzy pulled the wardrobe door inwards with her fingertips. The interior of the wardrobe darkened. There was nothing to grab on the inside of the door, so she couldn't get the door to shut fully. She had to make do with pulling it in most of the way and covering herself with a jacket, though that wouldn't fool Adam if he looked.

She made herself as small as possible as Adam came into the bedroom.

He muttered under his breath. A constant stream of filthy, angry words. He was right outside. Only a thin layer of wood separated them.

Blood pounded in Izzy's ears, impossibly loud.

She was sure he'd hear it.

Looking through the crack, Izzy caught a glimpse of Adam's back, which faced her way. He moved to the side, disappearing from view.

Izzy closed her eyes.

I'm a stone. I feel nothing.

She clasped the sleeve of a jacket that hung over her.

What was Adam doing? If she opened her eyes, would she find him standing in front of the wardrobe, looking in the crack?

She squeezed her eyes shut even tighter but despair began to give way to anger. How dare he make her feel like this? She'd done nothing wrong. What made him think he could make her life hell? Terrorise her? Stop her moving on?

She wasn't his possession.

Perhaps she should confront him. Dive out of the wardrobe and scream in his face, *Get out of my life.*

A tickle began to irritate her throat. A coughing fit? *Oh, God, no. Not now.*

She opened her eyes in time to see Adam pass in front of the crack in the door. He exited the room, crossed the next one.

The apartment's front door opened and closed.

He was gone.

Izzy finally let herself breathe. She wiped her face with her hand. Some survival instinct prevented her from moving at once. She waited to see if he was really gone, unable to shake the feeling that it might all be a trick.

Perhaps Adam was still there, waiting for her to emerge so he could take his revenge.

She waited for what seemed an eternity. Perhaps it was only ten minutes. At the end of that time, she had still heard nothing.

She pushed the door open and blinked in the sudden brightness of the bedroom. While she had been folded in the wardrobe, her limbs had grown stiff. She got out and stretched.

Now the coughing fit came. Thank goodness she had held it off long enough. She coughed until her lungs hurt, then straightened up, her face pink.

Glancing out the bedroom door confirmed that Adam was really gone. She looked at the bed.

The murder kit was gone too.

Chapter 62

Adam brought his van to a screeching halt on Izzy's street. His phone beeped for the second time as he killed the engine. Another text message. His blood boiled with pent-up rage. Reading the text, Adam knew there was only one way for this to end. He hoped he wasn't too late.

He grabbed his holdall and got out of the van.

His mind flashed back to Ruth, in Glasgow. The state her body was in when the police came to his house.

She shouldn't have pushed him. She made him do it.

Adam hadn't killed her. She'd killed herself. All the same, he regretted her death more than anyone. Ruth shouldn't have defied him, dumping him, and making him look like a fool in front of his friends.

No woman could tell him Adam that things were over. He decided when a relationship had run its course.

Although he'd stabbed her thirty-seven times, Ruth herself was the only one to blame. She shouldn't have wound him up.

Adam moved through the darkness like a shadow. Excitement blended with rage. His boots made heavy sounds as he ran down the road to Izzy's house.

He got there and stopped, decided to take a different tack. He ran down the lane that led to the back of Izzy's house.

The element of surprise. That would be better.

Everything would end now.

*

Robert was restless, more and more so as the night went on. After half an hour in bed, he gave up on sleep. He padded downstairs, intending to fix himself a nightcap.

He had had some crappy days recently, but this was worse than most. Getting a fire extinguisher discharged in his face had been no fun. Melanie had thrown the damn thing at him once it was empty. Gave him a nasty bruise on the shoulder, but at least it hadn't hit him in the gob.

As he descended the stairs, Robert rubbed his shoulder. It was still sore, though it hurt less than his pride. If he had any pride left.

Years of watching Louise run around behind his back were starting to take their toll.

He wondered again if he should leave her.

The problem was that he didn't think anyone else would put up with him and being alone was worse than anything else.

He made his way to the front room. The curtains were still open, so the room was not completely dark.

Robert glanced outside, saw nothing. He took a drink as he stood gazing out. He was about to return to bed when a man came running down the road, headed to Elaine's house.

Robert was about to turn away when he recognised the jacket the man was wearing. Green with yellow bands.

It was Robert's jacket.

"Son of a bitch," he said.

He hurried up the stairs to Louise's bedroom.

"You're never going to believe this shit—" Robert said, opening the door. He broke off when he saw that she wasn't there.

*

Gareth staggered the whole way to the Ale House, half a mile from Dun Laoghaire. It was the dingy bar where he had first met Chisel Cooney. The Ale House was a rough place and the first time he went there, he'd been afraid for his safety. This time he was only worried about Tess.

Poor Tess. Gareth had no interest in another woman. Even when Kate had thrown herself at him the previous night, Gareth experienced no temptation. His teenage crush was history.

When he fixed her a Martini, it was obvious that she was trying to seduce him. Gareth wasn't sure why at the time, but now that her husband had come out as a woman, he figured that must have something to do with it.

She'd been so obvious, rubbing his thigh with her

foot, then leaning over and getting right in his face, trying to get him hot before she leaned in to kiss him.

But he'd been unresponsive, and she'd quickly grown irritated.

"What's wrong with all you guys?" she said.

She stormed out of the house without finishing her cocktail, leaving Gareth to ponder the question.

Now he knew why Kate hadn't turned him on. Robert was partly right. The stress of the money situation had got to him lately. But the larger reason was that he loved Tess. And he was damned if he was going to let anything happen to her.

Conversation died when Gareth entered the Ale House. The place was half-empty. Gareth noticed again that most of the customers were of a certain type. Men in their twenties, thirties or forties.

They were all looking at him. Gareth was sure he resembled a beaten dog. A grim determination drove him on, though. He walked straight across the room to the door which led to Chisel Cooney's 'office'.

"Hey," the barman called. "Hey."

Gareth ignored him.

He opened the door and stepped inside.

Chisel Cooney sat behind a desk, his teeth chomping down on a big cigar. His golf club leaned against the desk. Its head was still spattered with Gareth's blood.

The twins stood on either side of Cooney. Gareth stifled a shudder at the sight of them. At the side of the room, Cooney's solicitor lounged in an armchair.

His nostrils were circled with white powder, as he leaned over a glass table covered in lines of cocaine.

"Well, well, well," Cooney said. "This is an unexpected pleasure."

"Where ith Tethh?" Gareth said.

Cooney laughed, looking from one twin to another. "What the fuck did teacher boy say? Did anyone catch a word of that?"

Everyone broke out laughing.

Gareth tried again, enunciating more clearly. "Tess. Where is she?"

He crossed the room quicker than they probably expected, grabbed Cooney by his T-shirt, and pulled him so close their noses almost touched.

"What have you done with her?"

Cooney's face twisted into a scowl.

"You better—"

Gareth punched him hard. "Tell me where she is."

The twins grabbed him, pulled him away.

"Teacher boy grew a pair of balls," said Cooney's solicitor.

One of the twins hit Gareth across the face. A sledgehammer blow that nearly knocked his head off his shoulders.

Cooney fixed his clothes.

"I didn't touch your lady friend. Not yet," he added. "That's one mistake. Second mistake is you touched me. You shouldn't touch me. I told you before. It's about respect." He turned to the twins. "Take care of teacher boy. Bury him in the usual place."

Chapter 63

The little Fiat's engine sputtered as it reached Dun Laoghaire, as if warning Izzy to stay away. Instead of heeding the message, she urged the car onwards.

The Fire Brigade was still working on the main street, Izzy saw. The flames had died down but smoke still poured out of the building, and firefighters continued to hose the place down. A crowd had gathered on the street to watch. Izzy supposed the neighbouring houses had to be evacuated until the blaze was brought under control.

She ditched the car at the side of the road and ran over to Dylan. He was standing alone now, staring grim-faced at the ruin of his home.

His face lifted when he saw her. "Are you okay? You didn't answer your phone. I called you three times."

"I'm okay, but I think Adam is going to do something terrible."

Anger clouded Dylan's face. "He already did something terrible."

Izzy glanced at the burning building. "You're right. But he's not finished."

"Did you talk to him?"

Izzy shook her head. "Where are your parents?"

"I convinced them to go to Amy's house. It's freezing out here. I don't watch them catching hypothermia."

"Good," Izzy said. She figured that the Fire Brigade wouldn't be finishing any time soon. "There's no point in you standing here all night either. Come with me."

Dylan looked reluctant.

"What about the house?"

"Fires take time to put out. I'm thinking you were right about Adam. I'd like to talk to you, tell you what I saw. Then I'll get my head straight and we can go to the authorities."

After a moment's thought, Dylan nodded. "Alright. Let's do it."

He followed her to the Fiat and got in alongside her. They were silent as Izzy drove to her house. She applied the handbrake, got out, and headed up the path to the house. Dylan walked next to her.

"You smell like smoke," she said.

Dylan nodded. "All my stuff, all my parents' stuff, gone."

His handsome face looked crestfallen. Izzy paused, then threw her arms around Dylan. After a moment, he hugged her back.

"I'm just glad no one was hurt," Izzy said. "That's the main thing. And you're lucky you have family nearby."

"I guess so."

He didn't sound particularly grateful. Maybe it was too soon to expect him to count his blessings.

They went inside the house.

"Can you put the kettle on? I want to use the bathroom."

Dylan said, "Sure."

He disappeared towards the kitchen while Izzy climbed the stairs. As usual, she shuddered, thinking of Elaine's death.

What would Elaine have thought if she knew all the stuff that Izzy had been through in the last twenty-four hours?

In the bathroom, Izzy splashed cold water on her face. It seemed like a year since she'd been in bed, trying to sleep. And it felt like a decade since she arrived in Dun Laoghaire.

She planned to have a cup of tea, tell Dylan what she had seen at Adam's apartment, and talk over what they would say to the officers at Dun Laoghaire Garda Station. Her brain was a jumble, and she needed to sort out her thoughts.

After giving her face a final splash of water, she dabbed her cheeks dry with the towel. She opened the mirrored cabinet above the sink, thinking she'd use her eyedrops before joining Dylan. As the door swung open, she saw a reflection in the mirror.

Izzy screamed, spun around.

A woman was lying in the bath tub. It was Tess. Eyes open, staring vacantly. Under her dark suit, her blouse was drenched with blood.

She was obviously dead.

Izzy scrambled out of the room. It felt like a thousand spiders were crawling all over her.

She shouted down the stairs.

"Dylan?"

There were footsteps in the hall below. But it wasn't Dylan who appeared at the bottom of the stairs.

It was Adam.

Chapter 64

Adam had come around the back of Izzy's house, the holdall slung over his shoulder. He was starting to like back gardens. The walls were no obstacle. Adam had a lean, athletic body, powerful arms, and he was a good climber. Had been ever since he was a kid. Years ago, he used to like jumping from balcony to balcony in his tower block. 'The Spider-Man of Maryhill' they called him.

He was over the wall in a moment.

The lights were on in the house, but the curtains were shut, so he couldn't tell if anyone was inside.

He got his tools out of his pocket and picked the lock.

Then he counted down from three and opened the door. It didn't make a lot of noise. Even if someone was in the next room, they might not have heard him. Sure enough, there was no reaction when he went inside.

Adam closed the door behind him. He stood still a moment and listened. There was movement upstairs. And footsteps on the ground floor.

Adam peered around the door frame.

The Asian guy was in the front room, scowling like his dog had just died. At that moment, he pulled out his phone and turned his back on Adam.

A deadly mistake.

Adam moved fast. He didn't open the holdall. The sound of the zip would have ruined the surprise. He picked up a paperweight from the dining room table. It was a big ball of marble. Very solid.

The other man was still engrossed in his phone.

He had no chance.

Adam came up behind him, drew back his arm and swung the paperweight through the air. It hit the side of the man's head with a crunch. He crumpled on the floor as a shout came from upstairs.

"Dylan?"

The sound of another man's name filled Adam with rage.

He went to the stairs.

Chapter 65

Izzy stared at Adam at the bottom of the stairs. The holdall she had seen in his apartment was slung over his shoulder. His murder kit.

"You killed Elaine," she said.

She tried to shout but her words were choked with emotion.

Adam shook his head slowly. His voice was a low growl when he replied, "No, I didn't."

"You're lying. You killed Ruth, Elaine and Kate. And now Tess."

"I didn't touch Elaine – or Tess or Kate, whoever they are. But Ruth?" He paused. "Ruth had it coming. Just like you."

Izzy's stomach lurched. He'd really done it, killed his ex as she feared.

Adam's muscles tensed.

He was about to spring up the stairs. Izzy couldn't move a muscle. She was frozen, waiting for Adam to move.

Someone else got there first.

A figure rushed out of Elaine's bedroom. It was Louise. She grabbed Izzy by the arm.

"Quick," Louise said.

What the hell was she doing there?

Louise dragged Izzy down the landing as Adam's footsteps pounded on the stairs. He was coming. Fast.

"Where?" Louise asked.

Izzy hurried past her, leading the way to the spare bedroom.

As soon as they spilled into the room, Izzy slammed the door and turned the key in the lock. She was grateful for the solid walnut door.

Still, her pulse was racing and she felt like her head might explode.

Breathing hard, she turned to Louise.

"What are you doing here?"

Chapter 66

Adam gaped as Izzy's neighbour appeared next to Izzy at the top of the stairs. That woman was meddling again, just like when she accosted him outside the house.

Nobody had permission to stick their nose in Adam's business.

Just ask Ruth.

He'd make Louise pay.

He'd make both of them pay.

As Louise and Izzy ran down the landing, Adam hurled himself up the stairs. He'd only gone up the first step when his leg was pulled out from under him.

He flopped on his belly, chin hitting the wood hard. He flipped onto his back and saw the Chinese guy holding onto his leg.

Adam kicked out with his free leg. The blow connected with the other man's hand, forcing him to release Adam.

Adam scrambled to his feet.

The Chinese guy looked dazed. He backed away as

Adam advanced on him, heading back to the front room.

"You should have stayed down," Adam said as they passed through the doorway.

"Back off."

The guy backed into the side of the couch. A trickle of blood ran down the side of his head.

"Make me, Jackie Chan."

"I'm warning you."

"Come on, tough guy. Come and get me. How's the family?"

The guy's eyes flared with anger. "Don't you dare speak of my family."

Adam said, "But I love crispy Chinese meat."

He feinted a punch from the left. When the other man blocked it, Adam stepped in and hit him from the right. The undercut knocked him on his ass. He was definitely out for the count this time.

Chapter 67

Izzy heard muffled sounds coming from downstairs. It sounded like a struggle was taking place. More than one voice. She hated to think of Dylan facing off against Adam.

She watched as Louise walked to the window and peered out the gap between the curtains.

"What are you doing here?" Izzy asked again.

Louise turned to face her. "I saw a prowler, so I wanted to check if you were okay. The door was open."

"Why were you in Elaine's room?"

Louise came closer. "I was looking for you. I think Adam did it. I think he killed Elaine."

"Me too."

"There's only one way to be sure. Elaine's diary. Do you have it?"

"Yeah, but I'm not reading it now! We need to get help."

"Where is it?"

Izzy caught the flash of a bracelet on Louise's wrist. Her brain tingled with a sense of déjà vu.

"It's in my bag," Izzy said. "But now *really* isn't the time."

"It's evidence! Whatever happens, we have to pre-serve it." Louise looked around the room. "Is your bag in here?"

Something half-remembered teased the edge of Izzy's consciousness.

Why was she was thinking of bracelets? She walked to the drawers and opened the one where she was keeping her bags. She took out Elaine's diary.

"Is there anything incriminating?" Louise asked. "At the end, I mean? Anything about Adam?" She pulled out her phone. "You check it and I'll call 999."

Izzy wondered if Louise was hysterical. Who cared about the diary at a moment like this? But she opened the diary on the last page, thinking maybe it did say something interesting.

Standing next to the bed, she flicked through the pages till she got to the bit she'd read earlier.

December 5th

The Scotsman came by this afternoon. He said I'm poisoning my niece's mind against him. That would be some achievement given that she's ignored me for a week. In any case, all does not seem well in paradise. I hope she gives serious consideration to breaking the engagement.

The Scotsman told me in no uncertain terms that I should stop calling with Izzy 'or else'.

Izzy read the next bit.

Update

I couldn't tolerate it any more – not after Adam's visit. While he was here, I pretended not to know anything, but he stared at me as if he could read my mind.

<u>The fact is that I saw the face of Louise's mystery man – and it's Adam – Izzy's Adam.</u>

I've tried to tell Izzy what's going on but she still refuses to take my calls. I'll keep trying but in the meantime I decided to give Robert Murphy a clue what his wife is up to.

I wrote a note, snuck out and stuck it under the windscreen wiper of his car. I told him to ask Louise who Adam McGregor is.

Hopefully that will do the trick.

Second Update

I've had some rotten luck. Louise must have seen me putting the note out. She marched over here with it in her hand and demanded to know what I was up to. When I said I knew about her and Adam, she denied the affair and made some silly excuse about buying pastries from him. She must think I was born yesterday.

Although I loathe confrontation, I let her know that I was not happy with things. I even shut the door in her face.

I'm a nervous wreck now. I'll try calling Izzy again tomorrow. Also I'll try to get Robert Murphy alone so that I can tell him about Louise.

Izzy looked up. She saw that Louise wasn't calling for help. In fact, she had put her phone away and was holding a strip of leather in her hand. Izzy had a bunch of them in the drawer. She used them to make handbag straps.

She gave Izzy a hard shove, knocking her onto the floor.

Crouching down, Louise pushed Izzy onto her belly and wrenched her hands behind her back. The pain was excruciating.

"What are you doing?" Izzy screamed.

She felt Louise bind her wrists together with the strip of leather.

Louise pulled Izzy up into a sitting position against the side of the bed. Her face had changed. Izzy saw a predatory expression in it that was new and terrifying.

"What are you doing? Let me go."

"Thanks for showing me where the diary was. I've been searching the house for more than half an hour."

Louise and Adam were an item.

Izzy cold hardly believe it.

"You had an affair with Adam?"

Louise smiled. "Where do you think he disappeared to all the time?"

Chapter 68

Louise and Adam had met down by the pier one day. Louise had gone there to get an ice cream. Adam was standing near the ice cream stall smoking a cigarette. Liking what she saw, she went up to him.

"Got a spare?"

Adam put a fresh cigarette in his mouth, lit it, then handed it to her. He had that smouldering bad boy vibe that she liked so much. The stubble, the lean, hard body. Not to mention the accent and that scar.

"I like a drink when I smoke," she said. "I'll allow you to buy me one."

"You're a forward one, aren't you?" Adam said.

They went to the nearest hotel and had a drink in the bar. It didn't take much prompting for Adam to open up. The first thing he mentioned was his girlfriend.

"Izzy's an absolute psycho. And her aunt hates me too. I came over here to talk some sense into the old bird, but she won't give me the time of day."

Louise was surprised to learn that her neighbour Elaine was the aunt in question. She had a vague memory of a young woman visiting Elaine once in a while.

"Izzy is telling lies about me. Both of them are."

He seemed really depressed.

"Sexy guy like you, you'll find someone else," Louise said.

"You mean you?"

There was a gleam in his eye. Louise took a sip of her drink before replying. "Hardly. I'm married."

"I won't tell your husband."

Louise smiled. There was a long pause, bubbling with delicious tension.

"It can only be once," Louise said. "I'm not leaving Robert."

"Did I tell you to leave him?"

They chatted some more, letting the anticipation build, and then Adam went and booked a room. A sense of giddiness overcame Louise as they went upstairs. She couldn't recall the last time Robert had whisked her off to a hotel.

Louise thought she'd drank enough but Adam insisted that they each have a glass of Champagne. They sat by the window, looking out over the sea.

Soon afterwards, they tried out the bed.

Adam wasn't a considerate lover and Louise liked that. He pushed her down on the bed face-first, then shoved her skirt up around her waist without any tenderness. It was shocking and unpleasant and so unlike Robert.

Adam didn't hang around afterwards. He left first

and Louise followed ten minutes later, hoping none of her friends would see her.

Despite agreeing that it was a one-off, Adam was back at the ice cream stand the next day. So was Louise.

This time, they went to her house. Robert wouldn't be home for hours. She let Adam have her in her own bed, with Robert's things around them. As soon as Adam had satisfied himself, he was gone. This time, he took Louise's phone number. He also took a T-shirt of Robert's, holding it proudly like it was some kind of prize.

"He might notice it's missing," Louise said.

Adam laughed. "That's his problem."

They met regularly after that. Always for a brief tryst and always at a time and place of Adam's choosing. The few times Louise suggested a venue, Adam shot her down.

Louise didn't mind. But she was irritated that he still hadn't left Izzy, despite insisting she was a psycho.

"You're the one who said this was to be a one-off," Adam said one afternoon in early December.

"Well, it hasn't turned out that way, has it? I thought your relationship was over."

"You said you aren't leaving your husband."

"Now I'm thinking about it. Wouldn't it be nice to spend more time together?"

"Aye," Adam said. "But not before Christmas. The timing is terrible. Elaine is a nightmare. She's telling Izzy all kinds of things about me. Filling her head with lies. I can't leave. It would look bad, like she's right about me."

"What's she saying?"

"This and that," Adam said with a shrug. "Poison! These rich women are all the same. Looking down on the little people."

Louise stroked his chest. "You're hardly little. And is Elaine rich?"

Adam shrugged. "She has that house. It's far too big for one person. Must be worth something."

Louise nodded. She and Robert were renting. They'd never managed to get on the property ladder. Even meeting rent was a struggle, especially now that Louise was out of work.

That night she Googled Adam and learned that he had been tried for his girlfriend, Ruth's, murder.

A few days later, when Adam came to Louise's house, she asked him about Ruth. She waited till after they'd had sex as she knew Adam would be calmer then. He'd been getting more abrasive as time went by. Liable to raise his voice at the slightest provocation.

Adam became animated when she mentioned Ruth. "The coppers were just looking for a scapegoat. Thank Christ they didn't convict me. They could have, you know. The whole system is rigged against the little guy. I wouldn't have been surprised if they'd stitched me up. Happens all the time."

"So you didn't hurt Ruth?"

"I had nothing to do with her death, God help her."

"You swear?"

"Aye. She was a nutjob, but I never laid a finger on her. Anyway, that's long in the past. Good riddance to her."

Louise was surprised to feel a frisson of anger. Some awful part of her had *wanted* Adam to be responsible for the death of the girl.

Ever since she'd been very young, Louise had known that she had more intense emotions than her peers. There was something different about her. She didn't kill stray animals or anything like that. But she could be headstrong, and sometimes got in trouble for taking games too far. She was very young when she realised she needed to repress that side of herself, because people were unnerved when they saw it.

"Izzy sounds like a loser," Louise said. "I don't know why you're with her."

She heard the slap and her head jolted to the side, but it took a moment for Louise to realise that Adam had struck her.

"Keep your nose out of my business."

He got out of bed while Louise was still frozen in shock, and got dressed in silence. Before leaving, he grabbed Robert's green jacket with the yellow stripes.

"I'm taking this," Adam said.

Then he left.

That afternoon, Louise's emotions were in turmoil. Shocked at Adam's violence, depressed by his lack of affection, and irritated by her husband, who kept asking what was wrong with her.

"I'm just sick of not working," Louise said.

"How's the job hunting going?"

The truth was that Louise despised looking for work, so she simply hadn't done it.

"Fine," she said. "I expect I'll get something soon."

After Robert had gone out to the pub, Louise went to their bedroom. She kept the light off and stared out at the dark street. She felt miserable.

Perhaps Adam would come back? No, twice in one day was too much to hope for.

Her cheek still stung where he'd hit her. Robert, being his usual oblivious self, hadn't even noticed the mark.

She'd always thought that if a man hit her she would never forgive him, so it confused her that she still wanted Adam. But the fact was that she did, and desperately.

She was looking out the window when the door of Elaine's house opened, and Elaine came out. She craned her neck from side to side, in a way that made Louise pay attention. Then Elaine darted across the dark street with an envelope in her hand.

She went over to Robert's car and slipped the envelope under the windscreen wipers. Then she scurried back to her house, like she was scared of being seen.

Louise went straight out there. Baxter followed, wagging his tail, as she marched out to the car and snatched up the envelope. She tore it open and pulled out the sheet of paper inside.

Ask your wife who Adam McGregor is, was written inside in spidery letters.

A wave of hot rage washed over Louise.

Elaine had been spying on her. She must have seen Adam coming and going, and, of course, she knew who he was. The guy was dating her niece.

They hadn't been careful enough. Or rather, Adam hadn't. It was he who had insisted on coming to Louise's house. Now everything was going to fall apart.

Louise crossed the street and banged on Elaine's door. Baxter stood next to her, his tail still wagging.

The door opened a crack.

"What do you want?" Elaine said.

"You don't look happy to see me."

Elaine began to sputter some excuse.

"Cut the shit. What's this?" She brandished Elaine's note.

The older lady fell silent. Then a certain rigidity came over her features.

"You know what it is. I'll be talking to Izzy too, believe me. If she wasn't at work, I'd call her right this minute. But I'll tell her first thing in the morning, you can count on that."

"What do you think you know, Elaine? I buy pastries from Adam. That's it. There's nothing underhand going on."

Elaine shook her head. "What you do is your business but I won't let you make a fool of my niece."

"You've got it wrong—"

"Goodnight," Elaine said in a curt voice. She had the door shut before Louise could say another word.

Louise went home and fumed. She couldn't let

Elaine expose her and Adam. Robert would never for-give her. Not this time. And Adam would be furious that his thing with Izzy was ruined. He'd blame Louise, and she'd lose Adam too.

She couldn't let that happen.

Chapter 69

Izzy stared at Louise in horror, as if seeing the woman for the very first time. She looked different. Not at all like the friendly lady who had welcomed Izzy to the neighbourhood. Her eyes burned with a fire Izzy had not seen before.

Izzy struggled to free her hands.

She wanted to get away. But with her backside on the floor, her back to the bed and her hands out of action, she couldn't even get to her feet. And even if she could, what then? Adam was right outside the door.

Louise pulled a steak knife from her jacket. The bracelets on her wrist shook with the movement.

Izzy's eye fell on a turquoise one.

She finally remembered what had been annoying her. The tickle at the back of her brain. Something Tess had said, when she was driving Izzy home.

That bracelet... Never mind. It's probably nothing.

At the time, her words had made no sense. Neither had the shocked expression on Tess's face. Now Izzy realised what Tess had noticed, and the train of thought it had sparked. Because Izzy recognised the bracelet too. Kate had been wearing it the previous night.

Tess had been far ahead of her. She'd seen Louise wearing the same bracelet Kate had been wearing when she died. Louise just happened to have it the next day... A strange coincidence. Was that why Tess was dead in the bathroom? The vague suspicion could have bloomed into something more if Tess's sharp mind had kept turning it over.

Izzy said, "You had an affair with Adam? You killed Kate and Tess? And—"

"I killed Elaine." Louise ran her finger along the knife blade and nodded to herself. "I did."

Izzy heard footsteps pound up the stairs and down the landing.

"Open up," Adam screamed. He pounded on the walnut door but it was reassuringly solid.

Louise hardly seemed to notice the sound. She met Izzy's gaze.

"It was basically an accident."

Chapter 70

On that December night, Louise had been at home, fuming after Elaine shut the door in her face. Louise was thinking of how to deal with her, when she remembered the key to Elaine's house.

Two years earlier, when they were on friendlier terms, Elaine had asked Louise to mind her cat while she went to Milan for a week. Louise had got a copy made so that she and Robert would each have one, as Robert had a habit of losing things.

The cat had died a while back, but Louise still had the copy of the key. In fact, she had the original too, as Elaine had said to hang onto it in case she ever locked herself out of the house, perhaps while sleepwalking.

Louise dug out one of the keys and decided she'd give Elaine a scare.

Soon Robert came home from the pub. Louise waited until he had gone to bed, then grabbed her favourite steak knife and snuck out of the house.

It was late by then. From the street, Louise could see that the lights were all off in Elaine's house. She crossed the road and let herself in.

She walked around the ground floor in the dark, stalling, thinking of what she should do. She was tempted to mess with Elaine. To move things in the house and see if she noticed. How funny would that be? Elaine would freak out. Maybe she'd think she was going mad.

She had sleepwalked a few times, a fact that Louise had already fed to Dee while making her promise not to tell another soul. She knew that only made Dee more desperate to spread the rumour.

Louise was standing in the sitting room, pondering what she might do, when she heard a creak. She turned, just as something hard smashed against her head.

She staggered into the fireplace.

Turning quickly, Louise realised two things. It had been a vase that broke on her head and Elaine was in the room. The dim glow from a streetlamp outside cast an orange glow on her face.

Elaine said, "Subtle as ever."

Louise touched her head. She could already feel blood matting into her hair. She had the thought that she shouldn't get blood anywhere. That would be evidence.

She got to her feet and wiped her fingers on her jumper. Then she assumed her most innocent voice.

"What are you doing, Elaine? I just—"

"You just what? I know what you're just up to."

"Don't ruin my marriage."

"What about my niece? I won't let her marry the Scotsman. That's all there is to it."

"I don't want them to marry either. Maybe you and I can figure something out."

"If you think I'm going to scheme with you, you're very much mistaken. Now get out of my house."

Elaine strode out of the room without waiting to see if Louise complied. Maybe she was scared and wanted to put some distance between the two of them. But the superior way she carried herself annoyed Louise.

She hurried after Elaine, caught up with her at the bottom of the stairs.

"Please, Elaine."

She put a hand on the older lady's elbow, but Elaine shook it off and started up the stairs.

When Louise grabbed her again, a new look came over Elaine's face. Alarm.

"Let go of me," Elaine said.

Pulling away, she climbed the steps quickly.

A pulse of adrenaline shot through Louise. This was her only chance to shut Elaine up. She hurried up the stairs.

At the halfway point, they struggled. A tangle of arms and fingers and grunts and gasps. Louise wanted to hurt Elaine. But, in the struggle, she ended up getting a punch in the mouth.

Elaine scrambled towards the top of the stairs. Clearly she'd call for help if she got to a phone, but Louise was right behind her and now she was furious.

At the top, she grabbed Elaine and tugged her as hard as she could.

The older lady sailed through the air. Out into space.

That part seemed to happen in slow motion. Their eyes locked. Elaine's were comically wide.

Then everything sped up.

Elaine fell, hit the stairs. She rolled and tumbled and grunted as the air was forced out of her lungs.

Down she went, head over heels.

Near the bottom, there was a snap as her neck broke. She lay in a heap at the bottom of the staircase.

"Oh my god." Louise put a hand to her mouth. "Elaine? No."

Even as the words came out, Louise realised she was acting. Performing a role. But there was no audience, and, after a moment, she snapped out of it.

Although she had been tempted many times over the years, Louise had never killed anyone before. Had never watched anyone die. It was more marvellous than she had dreamed, and all the sweeter for how long she had repressed the urge. An incredible sense of power bolted through her. Louise had never felt so alive.

She found a cloth, dampened it, and wiped the banister where she'd touched it. She descended the stairs carefully, stepping over Elaine's body, and checking the house for any traces that she had been there.

Louise tidied up the broken vase in the sitting

room, put the fragments in a bag and took them with her when she let herself out.

She crossed the empty street, so joyful that she could hardly contain herself. Baxter welcomed her home with a wag of the tail. She disposed of the vase, cleaned the gash on her head, and went to bed with a light heart, all her problems solved.

Over the next few days, the waiting was hard. Louise began to wonder if anyone would ever notice that Elaine was dead. Even Izzy didn't come to see her.

The day after Elaine's death, Louise waited till midnight, then went over to Elaine's house. She knew this was risky, but some dark impulse drew her back. She wanted to make sure that it had really happened, that it wasn't all a dream.

Elaine still lay motionless on the wooden floor, her neck twisted, and her limbs splayed.

Louise was the only person in the world who knew, who could come and look at the body and do whatever she wanted to it.

Louise texted Dee the next day and told her she was worried about Elaine. Said Elaine had been sleepwalking a lot lately and Louise hadn't seen her for days. She knew the message would be passed on to Paula, who would already know that Elaine had not been to work.

On the fourth day, the body was found.

Louise hadn't told Adam anything. He tended to be suspicious of anything that didn't have his approval and killing Elaine certainly didn't have his approval.

Louise waited days to see what his reaction would be. She couldn't call him. Although she had his number, he'd forbidden her from using it.

He called *her*. She didn't call him. That was how it worked.

So, she waited and she watched. An ambulance came and took the body away. Dee had heard through the grapevine that the Gardaí were satisfied that Elaine's death had been accidental. There would be no post-mortem and the funeral could proceed without delay.

It was all so perfect.

Louise couldn't resist going to the ceremony. The service was small. It just showed how little Elaine would be missed.

Louise saw Adam with Izzy. She took some satisfaction from the fact that Izzy wasn't much to look at. She was gaunt and miserable looking, exactly like a little mouse.

Louise approached them after the service and offered her sympathy. Izzy seemed lost in a world of her own. She barely registered Louise's presence.

Adam noticed though. His eyes blazed when he saw her.

I did this for you, Louise thought.

It was almost true.

Chapter 71

Something strange happened as Izzy listened to Louise giving her account of Elaine's death. She felt tears in her eyes. Not many and not big ones, but it was the most her glands had managed in a year. Finally, despite her illness, Izzy cried for her aunt.

"Elaine was a good woman," Izzy said.

Adam tried the handle, then pounded on the door. "*Open up.*"

Ignoring him, Louise advanced on Izzy. The knife she held had a wickedly sharp blade, which gleamed in the light of the bedroom.

"Elaine should have kept out of my business."

"I'm going to break this door down," Adam shouted. He kept banging on it, hard. "Stay away from her, Izzy. She's crazy."

Both of them were crazy. Adam and Louise. One killer in the room with her and another outside the door. Where was Dylan? Izzy hoped he was calling for help. She had to stall for time.

"What about the others? Why did you kill Kate?"

Louise opened her mouth to reply. Just then Adam gave a particularly brutal kick to the door.

"This is all your fault, Adam," Louise shouted.

He gave a howl of frustration. Fresh blows rained down on the door. It sounded like he was kicking it now. Adam let out an exasperated groan. "Jesus. What are these fucking doors made of?"

"Walnut," Izzy whispered.

It almost made her smile. But she didn't doubt that he'd break it down soon.

She kept working to get her hands free.

Chapter 72

Adam kicked the door close to the lock. He was desperate to get inside. He regretted ever getting involved with Louise. How dare she think of killing Izzy? Izzy belonged to him. If anyone was going to kill her, it would be Adam.

That was why he came here with his kit.

He'd got a taunting text message from Louise as he drove to Dun Laoghaire.

I'll make sure Izzy never comes between us again.

After they'd slept together a few times, he started to see her stubborn side. She liked to play at being the bored housewife, but he saw that she wasn't good at obedience. Not really.

That was when he decided he wanted nothing more to do with her. She was hard to shake though.

He'd always wondered if she had something to do with Elaine's death. Adam certainly hadn't been involved, though a few times he'd stood outside her office, and her house, thinking about wringing her neck.

The night she died, though, he'd been visiting

another of his girlfriends. He liked to rotate them. It kept things interesting.

Now, catching some of what Louise said to Izzy through the door, it turned out that his suspicion about Louise had been correct.

*

Louise thought constantly of the day the affair had ended. It was soon after Elaine's funeral. She went to Adam's workplace, which turned out to be a bit of a dive, not at all like the grand venture Adam's description had conjured up in her mind. McGregor Fine Foods turned out to be a small kitchen in a grotty city centre building.

When she went inside, she only found Adam and two members of staff in dirty aprons.

The kitchen itself wasn't dirty. Everything was neatly arranged, in typical Adam fashion. But the equipment looked old and worn, and the place was rather pathetic. Maybe it was the miserable, uninspired atmosphere of the place, but Louise doubted the company would ever amount to anything.

Adam's face went tight when he saw her. "What are you doing here?"

"I wanted to see you."

He grabbed her by the elbow and pushed her out the back door. Louise found herself in an alley that stank of rotting food.

"We can't meet," Adam said.

"Why not?"

"I can't afford any suspicion going my way," Adam said. "Not after what happened to Elaine."

"But it was an accident. You didn't have anything to do with it. Did you?"

Louise did her best to keep a straight face but inwardly she laughed at the irony of the question.

Adam scowled. "Of course, I didn't, you mad cow."

"Don't call me a cow. I want to see you."

"Izzy's just lost her aunt."

"Aren't you happy? You're one step closer to inheriting that nice big house."

"We're not married yet," Adam said.

His focus on Izzy was beginning to get seriously irritating.

"Well, hurry up and marry her. Or forget about her. I don't want to wait any longer. I can break the news to her, if you like."

Adam pushed Louise against a steel bin. His fingers squeezed her throat until she struggled to breathe.

"Don't mess with me, Louise."

As his fingers tightened, she clawed at his face, dragging her nails across his cheek. It only made him squeeze tighter. As she was on the point of losing consciousness, he released his grip. Gasping for oxygen, she fell to the ground.

Adam looked down at her like she was a piece of trash.

"Don't come here again."

Then he was gone, with the clang of a steel door slamming shut.

Furious, she made her way home and vowed to never think of Adam again. She promised herself and she had done her best to keep that promise, until Izzy turned up the previous afternoon.

It was Adam's shouting that drew Louise's attention. She'd been about to bake herself a nice apple pie to treat herself. She'd gone to the front of the house to fetch her phone. She'd heard it ping a moment earlier and was sure it was one of the book club ladies.

After Elaine died, Louise had felt the need to build a support group, a little community that would confirm her good character if it was ever questioned, though she didn't expect that to happen. And it gave her a chance to feed Dee any more rumours she liked.

The librarian and her mother had been a great help in blackening Elaine's name. Now everyone in the area thought of her as a freak who tumbled down her stairs while sleepwalking.

As Louise scooped up her phone, she heard shouting and looked out the window. Adam was across the road, banging on Elaine's door. Louise felt confusion for a moment, then watched as Adam came tearing down the steps of the house and smashed the window of a car parked outside. Then he got in his van and drove off.

A wisp of a girl stepped out of the house a moment later. Louise recognised Izzy from the funeral. Today she looked less like a mouse and more like a drowned rat.

Izzy and Adam must have had some kind of fight.

Louise hated herself for thinking it, but maybe she had a chance with Adam again.

She had to find out more.

Grabbing her umbrella, she hurried across the road to where Izzy was standing by her car. The girl looked rather dumbstruck. Almost immediately, she broke out in a fit of coughing.

Although disgusting beyond belief, the coughing fit gave Louise a great excuse to invite Izzy over so she could extract more information from her.

They'd only just sat down when Robert came in and interrupted, waving that box of dog dirt around.

In any case, Louise had already got some idea what happened. Izzy had walked out on Adam, and he was furious. Mad because he wanted to get the house or mad because he cared about the girl? Louise wasn't sure.

The girl was surprisingly plain, and that gave Louise hope. Izzy didn't even look healthy. There were dark circles under her eyes, and her bones were clearly visible through her face and hands. She made no effort at all with her appearance, wearing scruffy jeans and a tacky fake-leather jacket, and no make-up or jewellery.

Almost as soon as she arrived, Izzy said she was leaving. Louise had to think of something. She wanted to keep tabs on Izzy and see what she was up to.

So, she invited her to the book club.

Chapter 73

Izzy listened speechlessly to Louise. Her voice was flat and unashamed. She might as well have been reading a dictionary. Her expression only became more intense when she mentioned Adam.

"You killed your friends," Izzy said. "Not just my aunt."

"It's not like I had a choice," Louise said.

"Because of the diary."

"Exactly. I had to protect myself. I was almost enjoying the book club meeting until you said Elaine kept a diary. And, worse, you had found it. You had the damn thing right there in your handbag. I had to find out if Elaine recorded our confrontation the day of her death. If anyone learned about that, I'd have been a suspect. The death would be looked at again, and this time it might be reclassified as a murder. A post-mortem examination might show that there had been a struggle. I knew I had to get the diary."

"Then Robert came along and kicked Kate out," Izzy said.

Tess had stormed off after Kate. Clearly, there was something she wanted to discuss with her.

Louise said, "I watched Kate go. She'd taken the diary with her, so I had to follow her and retrieve it. But I couldn't let anyone see me behaving suspiciously."

Izzy thought back, looking at everything in a new light. "After Melanie and Dee left, you walked me home."

"Yes. I wanted to make sure you actually went there. It only took a minute. As soon as you closed her door, I hurried home and checked on Robert. He'd retired to the spare room, where he likes to listen to music and get drunk. I went outside again, caught up with Kate and Tess on the East Pier, but stayed out of sight."

"What then?" Izzy asked. She couldn't help it. She needed to know. As she listened, she kept wriggling her hands, trying to loosen the leather strap that bound her. She had to get free.

Adam bellowed as he flung himself at the door again.

Louise said, "I hurried across the road, and went around the outside wall of the pier, where the old cannon is. A very suitable landmark. From there, I could overhear Tess and Kate without being seen. Tess clearly wanted something, but Kate wasn't co-operating. Eventually Tess gave up and stormed off."

"Then what?"

Louise shrugged. "I did what I had to do."

Chapter 74

After Tess went home, leaving Kate on the pier, Louise approached the gap in the wall. She peered around the corner. Kate had both her own bag and Izzy's slung over her shoulder, and she was walking back towards land.

Louise checked again that no one else was around. When Kate drew close, Louise stepped out in front of her.

Kate gave a little gasp of surprise.

"What the hell are you doing here?"

Louise tried to appear unthreatening. She put on a concerned voice. "I came to make sure you got home okay."

"Got home okay?" Kate sneered. She came closer and they both stepped through the gap in the wall. "What are you doing sneaking around?"

"Nothing." A moment's silence. "It's not a bad night."

Louise walked down the path past the cannon, leading Kate closer to the sea.

"Are you kidding?" Kate looked around. "It's freezing. The wind would cut you in half."

"Is that Izzy's bag?"

Kate looked at it as if she had forgotten she was carrying it.

"This? Oh, yeah."

"I can give it back to her if you like."

"I'll return it myself."

Give me the damn diary.

"Are you sure? It's no trouble."

Louise reached for the bag, but Kate stepped out of her reach. Kate stared at her. That was when Louise realised she had given herself away. She'd sounded too enthusiastic, and Kate had picked up on that. It was a pity she wasn't stupid.

"What's so special about the bag? Why do you want it?"

"I don't."

"Secrets and lies. I've had more than enough of them today, Louise."

"I just want to help."

Kate fixed her eyes on the dark horizon. "Everyone around here has an agenda."

"Give it a rest. I only want to help. Izzy is probably worried about her bag."

Kate backed away, towards the edge of the path. Sharp rocks glistened in the darkness below.

Louise said, "Give it to me."

"Why do you want it so much?"

Ignoring the question, Louise made a grab for the

bag, but Kate pulled away, and Louise succeeded only in snagging Kate's bracelets. One of them flew off her wrist and fell on the ground.

Kate gave a little squeal of pain. She was on the very edge now, pressed against a low wall.

"Don't be difficult, Kate."

"You're the one acting like a maniac."

"So give me the bag."

Louise grabbed it and they struggled. Kate was strong, stronger than her, but unsteady on her high heels. The alcohol had made her reactions slow, her movements clumsy.

Louise smashed her keys into Kate's mouth. There was a spurt of blood and Kate screamed.

While she was distracted, Louise grabbed Izzy's handbag. She threw it on the path behind her. In the struggle, Kate dropped her own bag too.

"What's your problem?" Kate glared at her. "What's in the bag that's so important?"

"It doesn't matter." Kate backed away and Louise followed. "I'm sorry but I can't let you go now."

"What are you talking ab—"

Louise rushed forward and clawed at Kate's eyes. The actress backed away in surprise. Her legs hit the low wall behind her and she lost her balance. A hard shove propelled her over the edge.

For a moment Kate was suspended in space. Her arms reached out. Her eyes scoured the heavens for mercy but found none.

She let out a scream, but it was cut short when her

body hit the rocks below. She rolled under the dark waves and was gone.

This was even more fun than Elaine's death.

Louise jogged back the way she'd come, scooping up Kate's bracelet and the two handbags as she went.

Robert was still listening to music when she got home. Louise hid the handbags in her usual hiding place, on the top shelf of the laundry cupboard. She powered Kate's phone down and removed the battery so that it couldn't be traced.

She made sure she looked okay, then opened the door of Robert's room and said goodnight to him. Barely looking, he gave her a sleepy, "Night."

She had a shower before bed, safe in the knowledge that no one but her would ever read Elaine's diary.

In the morning, Louise was up early. She was in an excellent mood. After a quick breakfast, she retrieved Izzy's handbag from the laundry cupboard and took out the diary. She flicked through it, eager to see if she was mentioned in it.

While she read, she slipped on Kate's bracelet. A bright turquoise one that went great with her own copper-coloured jewellery.

On the last page, the diary ended on November first. Louise stared at it in horror. There was nothing of interest in this volume.

She had murdered Kate for nothing.

Chapter 75

Bang.

An axe's head suddenly broke through the door to the landing. Only a little of the blade was visible but that was enough to convince Izzy he'd get through the door soon.

Adam had been silent for a minute, and Izzy had presumed that was because he was tired from his efforts to break down the door, but it was more than just that. He'd been getting some equipment from his murder kit.

The axe's blade disappeared.

Adam grunted. Then roared as the axe sank into the wood a second time.

Bang.

Izzy kept struggling with the strap binding her wrists. It was loosening but she needed something to snag it against.

Meanwhile, Louise paced in front of her.

What was her plan? How did she expect to walk away from this? Izzy was afraid of the answers to those questions. Louise wasn't about to let Izzy go and neither was Adam. Two murderers had their sights on her.

She hadn't a chance.

But she wasn't going to give up.

Chapter 76

With panic, Louise had realised that if Elaine was an enthusiastic diarist, she would have continued her scribblings in another volume. Presumably it was still in the house.

Louise needed it, but she couldn't go across the road and let herself into the house. Not in broad daylight. Anyone might see, and Izzy was probably at home.

Just then, her phone had beeped with a text message from Dee.

Girls, Kate is DEAD!!!!!

With her rage increasing by the second, Louise went to wake Robert up. She was in a foul mood, and she wanted to take it out on someone.

Louise found him lounging in bed. She woke him up and let him know Kate was dead. He didn't look awfully sorry for kicking her out of the house.

It was a relief when he took Baxter for a walk. He'd be back soon, though.

She was staring out the window when she saw Adam walk down street. He went up to Izzy's door and rang the bell. When there was no answer he took out his phone, clearly trying to call her too.

Louise felt sick looking at his drawn face.

Did he love Izzy so much?

Louise couldn't help herself. She hurried across the street to confront him. Her mind quickly came up with an excuse for talking to him, in case any of the nosy neighbours saw.

She was standing up for her new friend, telling Izzy's abusive ex to leave the poor girl alone.

Louise reached the opposite kerb as Adam came out of Izzy's gate.

She said, "What do you think you're doing?"

He scowled. "Don't use that tone with me."

Louise hated him at that moment, but she had never seen him look so handsome.

"Still chasing Izzy? I'm starting to think you love her."

He stepped closer, spoke in a threatening growl. "I've already told you."

"I know. You want the house. Is it worth it?"

"Have you ever been poor, Louise?"

"I'm not rich."

He gave her an ugly smile. "But you're not *poor*. Not the way I've been. You wouldn't know what it's like."

I might know soon enough. She and Robert couldn't afford rent on one salary. They were burning through what little savings they had.

"I need to talk to you. We have a problem."

"*I* don't," Adam said.

Louise watched in amazement as he turned his back on her.

"Don't walk away from me," Louise hissed. "Elaine kept a diary."

"I don't give a toss," Adam said, still walking.

Louise watched him, fury building within her. He hadn't even *listened*. She went home, slammed the door and screamed. Baxter crawled under the kitchen table. He watched her warily, ears flat to his head.

She'd almost had enough of Adam.

She needed to get the diary covering Elaine's final days. And if Adam didn't do something about Izzy soon, Louise would handle that too.

In the evening, when Louise walked Izzy to Dee's house, it was all she could do not to grab Izzy and squeeze the life out of her. She hated her that much. But Louise was practiced at hiding her true feelings, so she smiled and talked nonsense about the local architecture.

Louise hadn't had a chance to sneak into Elaine's house all day. She couldn't risk it in daylight. And Robert was hanging around at home. He hovered next to Louise constantly, no matter what room of the house she went to.

She felt like screaming.

She'd have to get the diary that night.

Louise had watched the outline of Izzy's face as they walked past the People's Park. What a horrible little face. Louise hated her eyes, her mouth. In con-versation, Izzy was dull and nervous. And she seemed to have coughing fits all the time. Every time Izzy coughed, Louise backed away. She hated sickness and sick people. Louise wondered if the girl was dying of some awful disease. She certainly hoped so.

More than anything, Louise wanted to kill Izzy, but she was worried about Adam's reaction. He might never forgive her.

When she got to Dee's, she decided to tell everyone a little about Adam. Maybe he deserved to feel the heat. That would remind him that she had power. And it would encourage Izzy not to take Adam back.

So Louise told the women about Ruth.

It was amusing to see Dee and her awful mother drool over this juicy morsel. Tess seemed too preoccupied to care. Then a suspicious expression came over her face. She was looking at Kate's bracelet on Louise's wrist. What a curse it was to have observant friends. Why couldn't they just be dummies?

Louise would have to deal with her later.

She planned to leave first and sneak into Izzy's house before Izzy got home. Tess ruined that by storming off early and Izzy had followed her.

Louise made her own excuses soon after they left. She went home and paced in her bedroom. Louise knew she had to wait until Izzy was asleep before she sneaked into Elaine's house.

Thankfully Robert had retired to his bedroom early and Louise didn't think he'd come out again before morning.

Louise watched the lights go out across the road as

Izzy went to bed. She waited a little longer and then took Elaine's key and hurried over.

As quietly as she could, she let herself in and began to search for the diary. Clearly she hadn't waited long enough, however.

She was in the sitting room, examining the book-shelf, pulling out volumes and squinting at them in the dim light, when a book slipped from her hand and hit the floor. Louise froze.

Maybe Izzy wouldn't wake up. Maybe she'd go back to sleep. Then a fox began making a racket outside.

"Holy shit," Izzy shouted.

Louise tiptoed towards the door as an upstairs light came on. She sneaked to the hall. Izzy was coming. Louise didn't dare close the door in case it made a sound.

She just pulled it over, then hurried outside and across the street. She was even able to sneak past the fox without disturbing it. The faint smell of smoke carried on the night air.

When she got home, she ran straight into Robert.

"What are you doing up?" she said.

"What are you doing *outside*?" he countered.

"Just checking the porch light. It's been flickering lately. Did you notice? It seems okay now. I tightened the bulb."

Robert said nothing.

"Well, goodnight," she said, brushing past him.

Louise went to her bedroom and gazed out the

window. That had gone badly, but Louise would have to try again.

She had a stroke of luck when Izzy left the house. Where was she going? Louise waited a while and was glad she had. Izzy came jogging back. Instead of settling down for the night, she got in her car and drove off.

Louise didn't know what Izzy was up to but suspected it might be something to do with Adam.

Suddenly she had an idea.

A way to kill three birds with one stone.

Tess had recognised the bracelet Louise took from Kate. Louise was sure of it. And that meant that Tess had to go. The woman was too sharp. She'd figure things out eventually.

It would be hard to engineer another accident. Better to just kill her and cast guilt onto someone else. Someone like Izzy. That would get both of them out of the picture.

Louise decided she'd lure Tess to Izzy's house, kill her there, and take Elaine's diary while she was at it.

Everything would be nice and neat.

Louise fetched Kate's mobile phone from her handbag in the laundry cupboard. She used it to text Tess, knowing the lawyer would be intrigued.

Then she hurried across the road to wait for her.

Chapter 77

It was a lot to take in. If Izzy hadn't seen the crazed look on Louise's face, she might have wondered if her neighbour was capable of the things she described.

Izzy said, "So you waited here for Tess and killed her?"

"I had to," Louise said. She made it sound like the most natural thing in the world. "Tess was like a dog with a bone. She'd never have stopped till she got the answer."

The door shook again as Adam continued to tear into it was his axe. Izzy heard his ragged breathing.

While Louise's attention was distracted, Izzy braced her legs and pushed herself up, rising slowly from the floor as her back pressed against the bed. With an excruciating effort, she rose to a standing position.

"I'm coming," Adam shouted.

Izzy backed away towards the corner of the room. There was nowhere else to go. The leather strap holding her wrists together had loosened, but her hands were still not free.

"Where do you think you're going?" Louise said. "Don't get any stupid ideas."

The edge of the chest of drawers was nearby, and at about the right height. Izzy stood in front of it and used the corner to snag the leather strap around her hands. Louise walked across the room, knife raised.

"You should stop," Izzy said. "Your plan didn't work. Everyone knows now."

"Not everyone. Just you and your boyfriend. That's only two more bodies." Louise gave an icy smile. "I don't know why Adam cares so much about you."

"He doesn't. He only cares about himself."

Adam screamed and hit the door again with his axe. Izzy just knew he was going to break through it any second. Louise stared at the door.

Meanwhile, Izzy worked frantically to free her hands, tugging and tearing, rubbing the strap against the chest of drawers.

Success. The strap went slack as it broke.

Izzy shook her hands free and grabbed the strap.

A final devastating blow of the axe left a gaping hole in the door. Adam's arm sprang through. Izzy watched, petrified, as his hand groped for the door handle.

He found it, turned the key and the door opened.

Louise moved out of his reach and grabbed Izzy, got behind her and held the knife to her throat. She didn't seem to notice that Izzy's hands were free.

If Louise's eyes looked crazed, Adam's were even more so.

"Izzy belongs to me," he said. "Don't do anything stupid."

"Don't come any closer," Louise said.

Adam stepped forward.

"I thought you wanted me. Now you want me to stay back? Make up your mind," he sneered.

Louise squeezed Izzy tighter. "I thought I'd get Izzy out of the way. Send her to jail for Tess's murder. We can still do that, maybe. We just need to get rid of her boyfriend too."

"The Asian lad isn't her boyfriend. I am."

Adam's face was purple with rage.

Louise pushed the blade against Izzy's throat. Izzy held her breath, not daring to move even slightly. She had never been so terrified in all her life.

Adam said, "She's mine, Louise. I decide what happens to her. Nobody else. Got it? I get to decide if she dies."

"I might slit her throat," Louise said.

"It'll be the last thing you ever do."

"We can't let her live."

Just then, Izzy broke out coughing, which made Louise loosen her grip. Izzy had forgotten Louise was a germophobe. She turned her head and coughed right in Louise's face. A look of disgust crossed Louise's features. She let go of Izzy and turned her face away.

Izzy used that moment to hurl herself at the open doorway. She dodged the axe as Adam swung it at her. She felt the blade pass over her head. She whipped the leather strap across his face.

He grunted, dropping the axe and raising his hands to protect himself.

Izzy scooped Elaine's diary up from the floor, ran out the door and down the landing. She swung around the banister and prepared to dash down the stairs.

She stopped.

A man was blocking the way.

Chapter 78

Dylan emerged slowly from a dark fog. He was in a world of pain and his head felt like it had been cracked open like an egg. He was lying in a heap on the floor. It took a moment for him to orient himself.

Izzy's house. The struggle with Adam.

When Dylan touched his hair, his fingers came away bloody. Not a lot of blood, but enough to confirm that he'd been clobbered.

Shouts came from upstairs. A bang, a scream.

Dylan staggered to his feet. His first instinct was to rush upstairs but the logical part of his mind told him to ring for help first.

He took out his mobile and dialled 999. He crossed the room while the recorded message played. As soon as he was put through to the operator, he began speaking rapidly.

"I need help quickly. I was attacked. I think my girl-friend is being attacked now."

A calm woman's voice replied. "What's your ad-dress?"

Dylan was giving it to her as he walked to the hall.

At that moment, the front door opened, and a man Dylan didn't recognise walked in.

*

Robert Murphy used one of the spare keys to enter Elaine's house.

He had seen a suspicious-looking man heading towards Elaine's property. The one who was wearing *his* jacket. A terrible suspicion was creeping its way up Robert's spine.

After he found Louise wasn't in bed, he looked in her secret hiding place. Robert wasn't stupid. He knew she had secrets. Usually, he tried to convince himself that he was better off not knowing.

Maybe he was.

Tonight, though, he was in the mood for the truth.

On the top shelf of the laundry cupboard, he found two handbags and a diary. After a quick glance at it, he figured out that it had belonged to Elaine. A lot of the entries spoke about work she was doing for the County Council.

He wasn't sure why Louise had it. The fact that she was hiding it didn't reassure him either. He figured it was all connected to the man wearing his jacket.

Who was this guy, though?

Was Louise sleeping with him?

Robert was quite drunk and didn't feel like reading any more of the diary. Instead, he made his way across the road, the spare key in one hand and a bottle of beer in the other.

He knew he shouldn't be following the mystery man into Elaine's house. He needed answers, though.

Someone upstairs was yelling and banging on a door.

Robert saw a suspicious-looking Asian fellow in the front room. Was this the man Louise had been cheating on him with? He wasn't wearing Robert's jacket now, but he could have taken it off since coming inside.

Robert's mind filled with wild imaginings. Maybe Louise and Izzy were having a threesome with this guy?

"Where's my wife?" Robert demanded.

The Asian fellow gave a confused look. Robert saw that he was on the phone.

No doubt he was calling friends for backup.

"Oh, no you don't."

Robert swung his beer bottle at the guy, who dodged the blow, but dropped his phone.

"Hello? Are you there?" a woman's voice said from the phone.

Robert stomped his foot on the screen. It gave a satisfying crunch as it broke.

"You idiot," the guy said. "I was calling for help."

"I bet you were."

Robert swung the bottle again. It flew harmlessly by the guy's nose, spilling foam across the floor.

The guy threw himself at Robert. A hard blow hit him in the chest, driving the air from his lungs.

Despite being winded, Robert lashed out too. One

blow caught the guy on the chin and knocked him down.

Robert hurried to the stairs to see what the hell was going on above his head.

Chapter 79

What the hell was Robert Murphy doing blocking the stairs? There was a moment of terror when Izzy wondered if he was trying to stop her leaving because he was working with Louise. But that didn't make any sense. According to Louise's explanation, Robert knew nothing about the murders.

"Get out of the way," Izzy shouted at him.

She started down the steps, moving as quick as she could, still holding the diary like a good-luck omen.

"Is my wife here?"

Yeah. The crazy bitch is right behind me, Izzy thought.

But she didn't waste her breath. Just kept moving down.

Adam's heavy footsteps pounded down the landing. Louise's lighter steps followed. Robert started up the stairs, his broad shoulders leaving no room on either side.

Izzy was blocked in on all sides.

"Louise?" Robert called. "Are you up there?"

"Get out of the way!" Izzy screamed.

She couldn't stop. She knew she was dead if she did.

So she kept descending the stairs, moving so fast her feet barely had time to grip the surface of the steps.

Izzy was halfway down when Adam caught up with her. He grabbed her shoulder.

She shrugged his hand off and hurled herself at Robert since the idiot wouldn't get out of the way.

The only way was through.

Robert grunted when she hit him, then tumbled back, hands flailing. Izzy fell against him and the two of them tumbled down a few steps. Robert took the brunt of it.

They ended up in a tangled heap two steps from the bottom.

There was no time to waste.

Adam was still coming. His strong hands were clenching and unclenching, speaking of untold violence.

Louise was right behind him, pulling at him, trying to get his attention.

Ignoring her, Adam jumped over the banister and landed on his feet in the hall. A few steps took him to the bottom of the stairs, blocking the way to the door.

"Adam, wait." Louise's voice was shrill now. How could she be so scared of losing a maniac like him?

"Game over," Adam said. "Give up, Izzy. You live if I let you live."

Izzy extricated herself from Robert and got to her feet. She clutched Elaine's diary behind her back.

She stepped over Robert and moved closer to Adam.

A broad grin broke out on his face. "It's over. You know you belong to me."

She was close enough to smell him now. Sweat mixed with hate.

He grabbed her wrist.

Izzy said, "No, Adam. I don't."

She spun in a circle. The movement tore Adam's hand loose. She brought up her free arm and as she completed the circle she smashed her elbow into his face.

He groaned and wobbled on his feet.

Before he could recover, she drew back her other arm and swung it in a huge arc, putting every scrap of strength she had into it. She was gripping Elaine's diary tight, feeling the weight of its pages, the weight of the past. Its spine smashed into Adam's face.

His head snapped to the side.

His eyes rolled up in his head as he lost balance and banged his head against the wall. The third blow. Game over.

Adam crumpled on the floor.

Izzy hunkered down over him and checked that he was out cold.

"Now it's over," she said.

A small brown booklet poked out of Adam's pocket. Izzy pulled it out, saw that it was her passport. She placed it in her pocket, stood up and stepped away from him.

A few steps up the staircase, Louise was wailing

hysterically as she tried to get past Robert. He was holding her to him. She reached past him with one arm, trying to reach out to Adam, who lay unmoving on the floor.

"You okay, Izzy?"

She spun around to find Dylan. The side of his face was bloody.

Relief washed over her. "I'm fine. What happened to you?"

On the stairs, Louise gave a final moan, then buried her face in Robert's chest and fell silent.

Dylan said, "Your ex clocked me on the head. Then that idiot on the stairs interrupted my 999 call. And *he* attacked me too. It's like National Crack Dylan's Skull Day."

Izzy slipped her arm around him.

A moment later, the scream of sirens filled the night. Izzy opened the front door as a patrol car and an ambulance pulled up outside. Flashing lights filled the hallway, bathing Izzy in their glow. Officers and medics jogged up the steps.

She couldn't wait for them to get Adam out of there.

Chapter 80

A week and a half after 'the book club murders', as everyone was calling them, on a mild day that marked the beginning of March, Elaine was (for the second time) lowered into a grave at Deansgrange Cemetery.

Izzy watched as the coffin disappeared into the ground. She felt strong today and hoped this was a sign of her health improving.

Mr. and Mrs. Zhao had been sending Izzy a steady stream of meals to help her recover her strength, together with more bags of pungent medicine, which hadn't got any easier to swallow. At least the stuff seemed to be helping.

All this while the Zhaos chased their insurance company over the fire which had destroyed their home.

Izzy was impressed with the large crowd that had gathered to pay their respects. The sight of so many people gave her a lift. And the graveyard itself looked better this time. In December, the place had been so overgrown with weeds that some graves were not even accessible. Izzy was relieved that the gravediggers had been busy since then, cleaning the place up, cutting back the grass and weeds.

It felt like order had been restored in some small way.

Dylan took Izzy's hand and gave it a squeeze. He looked so handsome in a black suit and tie and a white shirt. And he'd been a rock of support during everything that had happened.

She squeezed back, glad to have him next to her.

Amy stood on Izzy's other side, looking elegant in a long black dress. She rubbed Izzy's back, a strangely reassuring gesture. Izzy couldn't remember the last time she had felt so safe.

Dylan's parents stood a short distance behind them. Both of them were dressed in white. Mrs. Zhao held an incense stick.

After Father Peter Brennan said a final prayer by the graveside, people began to move off.

"Let's go," Izzy said, squeezing Dylan's hand.

"Sure."

They kept holding hands as they walked.

Once Louise's actions became known, the State Pathologist had been asked to exhume Elaine's body and perform a post-mortem examination.

The Coroner and the Gardaí were getting a lot of criticism for not requesting one first time around. An opposition politician had called it 'an example of the outrageous incompetence which thrives under the current government', turning the whole thing into a political issue. Izzy didn't care about the politics, but she had come to realise that rumours about Elaine's sleepwalking had influenced that decision – rumours which Louise had fed to Dee, who in turn spread them all around town.

Izzy walked down the path lined with vibrant yellow daffodils and bright pink tulips. A passenger plane passed overhead, cutting across the pale blue sky.

Although the post-mortem, by itself, had not been conclusive, it had revealed possible signs of a struggle and minor defensive wounds. Those, in conjunction with Louise's confession, meant that Elaine's death was now definitively classed as a murder.

This time, when Elaine was buried, everyone knew what had happened to her and who was responsible for it. That meant something.

It also meant something that Louise and Adam were in custody pending their trials. There was little doubt that both of them would be going to prison to serve lengthy sentences. Never again would Adam appear out of nowhere, never again would he stalk or terrorise Izzy. The relief was incredible.

Outside the gate, Izzy greeted a few of the mourners she hadn't spoken to earlier. Hannah from the diner, and her boss, Mr. Romano, were there. So was Stephanie Long.

Izzy wished she had got to know Kate and Tess more. Gareth Gillen, Tess's boyfriend, had disappeared the night Tess died, which had led to all kinds of wild rumours.

As if listening to her thoughts, Dee Philips appeared. She was side by side with her mother, Paula.

"Did you hear about Billy Cooney?" Dee said. Izzy had heard a rumour that Cooney was responsible for Gareth's disappearance. The story, as it was told, though, was that there wasn't a scrap of evidence against the man everyone called Chisel.

"No, and I don't want to hear it," Izzy said.

Dee ignored her. "Guess where he moved?"

Izzy said nothing. The rumour was that Cooney had planned to take Tess Smith's house, as payment for a debt Gareth had accumulated. Izzy had no idea if there was any truth in it, and she didn't much care.

"Do you give up?" Dee said. "Cooney has only gone and moved into Melanie's old place. We saw him moving in last night."

Izzy sighed. "Dee, I don't like gossip. I don't want to hear it. I don't want to spread it. Now, if you'll excuse me, I'm leaving."

As Izzy turned away, she heard Dee take a little gasp of surprise. It almost made her laugh, but she kept a straight face as she walked away, arm in arm with Dylan.

"Nice!" Amy whispered with a giggle as she caught up with them. "But it's true. You know that guy is distant cousin of Melanie's? He really did move into her house. And apparently the cops are watching him like a hawk. They have an unmarked car parked outside the house, and they're just waiting for him to make one tiny slip, so they have a reason to arrest him."

Izzy said, "I suppose he'll keep his whistle clean."

They stopped at the edge of the road. Amy looked from Dylan to Izzy. "There's a little food at our house, so I expect you both to come straight there."

"You shouldn't have gone to any trouble," Izzy said. By now, she knew that when Amy said there was a little food, she meant that there was a feast big enough to feed an army. "I know how busy you are, what with taking over the salon."

Melanie and Tom had left town after all that had happened in the area. The house had been sold faster than Izzy would have thought possible. Amy had taken over the running of the salon in Melanie's absence and she hoped to buy it eventually.

Amy said, "It's no trouble. I've taken the day off."

"Why? There's no need."

"Of course, there is. We need to celebrate your aunt and give her a proper send-off. See you both back at my place. No excuses!"

Amy walked to her car while Izzy and Dylan headed the other direction, to Izzy's Fiat.

Just then, she caught sight of Fr. Peter Brennan. She was surprised at the sadness in his face, having never before seen a priest get teary at a funeral.

"Do you need a lift, Father?" she asked.

"No, thank you, Izzy. I have a lift arranged."

Izzy thought of the way Elaine had spoken of this man in her diary. And there was the photo of him and Elaine in Elaine's bedroom.

"You were close to my aunt."

Fr. Peter nodded. "As you know, we were all very fond of her."

Something told Izzy he was fonder of Elaine than most. She gave his hand a quick squeeze, then got into her car. Izzy didn't start the engine immediately. She needed a little time to let everything sink in.

Elaine had been *murdered*. Now that fact had been recognised and Elaine had been laid to rest in that knowledge.

After a moment, Izzy turned to Dylan.

"You look so handsome in a suit."

"Of course, I do."

She laughed.

His parents were staying with Amy's family, but Dylan and Izzy had become inseparable, and he was basically living with her now. It was wonderful finding him at the house when she came home from work, and she loved greeting him when he returned from college, or from scouting for new premises for his parents' business.

He was studying hard for his MBA too, hoping to make some money, and make his parents proud.

"Amy is so kind," Izzy said.

"What do you mean?"

"Inviting me to her place. Preparing food. The way she came today, took time off work. She treats me like I'm part of the family."

Dylan gave her arm a playful punch. "Will you knock it off? You *are* part of the family."

She'd lied to him, the day they met. He had asked

if she had any ambitions. She had said no, but it wasn't true.

She had a huge, impossible ambition: to have a family.

Maybe not impossible.

Dylan wrapped his arms around her, but it was his words which felt like the warmest embrace.

Chapter 81

Stephanie returned to Dun Laoghaire after Elaine's burial. Attending had been a mark of respect and a way to say goodbye, not only to her former neighbour, but to the recent turbulent days. She hoped she could put them behind her now.

Not wanting to be alone, she stopped off at a café on the main street. The enticing aroma of coffee hit her in the doorway. She nodded a greeting at the waitress and sat down at a table just inside the door.

The last couple of weeks had been rough. Kate's death had hit her harder than people seemed to think, especially Kate's parents. Though they no longer blamed Stephanie for their daughter's death, they still acted like she'd committed *some* indeterminate crime.

And that hadn't been all. Although a few of her colleagues had been supportive about her coming out as a woman, many more turned out to be prejudiced. Stephanie heard people gossiping about her, and complaints had been made when she used the ladies' bathroom.

"I'm damned if I'm going to share the bathroom

with a tranny," Stephanie had overheard a woman from accounting say. And Stephanie didn't want to use the male toilets. The company's solution – that Stephanie should use the special needs toilet, until they figured out what the hell to do – had pleased no one, especially not Jack from HR, the only staff member who used it, and who had enjoyed having his own private toilet for the last four years.

Stephanie's parents were struggling to accept the news too. They'd said how much they loved her, no matter what, and Stephanie knew they meant it, but their frown lines and distracted expressions told Stephanie they were still trying to make sense of the news.

To make herself feel better, she had applied some lipstick today, and her new haircut – at Amy Zhao's place – had given her a greater sense of confidence. She had started hormone therapy too, but it would take time for that to kick in.

"Hey there," came a voice.

Maggie Connell, Stephanie's principal from Saint Brendan's Secondary School, was standing next to the table. She hadn't seen her old principal for years.

"Mrs. Connell? What are you doing here?"

The principal smiled. "I was just passing, and I saw you." She lowered her voice. "I heard about your transition."

"Yeah, well, it's not turning out so great."

"Can I join you?"

"Sure, Mrs. Connell." Stephanie gestured to the

chair opposite her. She'd always admired her former principal, but she was the last person Stephanie expected to come and congratulate her.

"Call me Maggie. I've actually been meaning to get in touch," the principal said, sitting down.

"Why?"

"I thought maybe you could visit the school and give a little talk."

"What?" Stephanie thought it was a joke at first, but Maggie's expression said that it wasn't. "Let me tell you about me. My wife freaked out and now she's dead. My in-laws treat me like I killed her, even though they know I didn't. My parents love me, but they don't know what to think about me being trans. People I work with avoid me like the plague. The gossip mills are churning out shit and I'm just feeding it. I'm so confused, I don't even know how to feel about myself half the time. I want to fucking die. I'm all alone and I'm going through hell. Why the fuck would anyone want to hear me talk?"

By the time she finished, Stephanie's heart was racing. Beads of sweat had broken out on her forehead, and she felt like crying.

Maggie said, "Because maybe some of them are going through it too."

A waitress interrupted them. She gave Stephanie a smile, then opened a notebook and held her pen poised to write.

"What can I get for you ladies?"

It took a moment for the word to register in Stephanie's brain. *Ladies.* Had the waitress really said that?

"Latte for me," Maggie said.

"I'll have a cappuccino," Stephanie said.

"You ladies want anything with those coffees? *Alfajores* maybe? They're our specialty dessert."

"Ooh," Maggie said. "I'll have one of those."

"Wonderful. And for yourself?"

Stephanie swallowed. "Uh, yeah... same for me."

"Coming right up."

The smiling waitress moved away but Stephanie stayed frozen. *Ladies.* She'd been called a lady. She couldn't believe it.

For the first time in a long time, Stephanie wondered if things might eventually get better.

*

Robert Murphy clipped Baxter's leash onto his collar and led the Labrador out of the house. Robert couldn't help grumbling as they set off on the usual route. He felt like people were laughing at him even more now than they did before.

Before, people thought he was a bad-tempered cuckold and a drunk. Now they thought he was bad-tempered cuckold and a drunk who didn't even know his wife was a killer.

"God damn fucking psycho bitch," he muttered.

How was he supposed to know?

Robert knew Elaine was being laid to rest today, but he didn't want to be there, surrounded by all those mocking bastards.

"Bunch of grade-A douche nozzles. Aren't they, boy?"

Ignoring him, Baxter trotted along happily, sniffing everything within reach. Robert envied him. What a simple life dogs had. Eat, sleep, play. Nothing more to their days than that. And unlike people, they were loyal.

The low sun blinded Robert momentarily.

"Fucking sun," he muttered.

He knew he'd been grumpier the last week and a half but who could blame him? Louise was in prison awaiting trial for murder. Her nutjob of a lover was too.

Louise was on her own now. He wouldn't be visiting her. Robert wasn't going to be a chump any more. Screw that. It was his life, and he was damned if he was going to compromise on another thing.

They passed a woman on the footpath at the end of De Vesci Terrace. She gave Robert a look that passed from his shaggy beard to his bulging belly and back.

"What's your problem?" Robert shouted. "So I'm carrying a couple of extra pounds. So what? Go suck a lemon."

She hurried past.

Robert led Baxter on down the footpath, past a car with a guy sitting in it. The man looked out the car window at Robert.

Robert said, "The fuck are you looking at?"

A few steps down the road, he paused to unclip Baxter's leash. As soon as the dog was free, he ran into the nearest garden. Robert turned his back and whistled to himself.

Melanie had moved out of her house the previous week, which was a shame. With her gone, Robert didn't need to bring Baxter here anymore, but the damn dog had got so used to their routine, he didn't want to relieve himself anywhere else.

Anyway, who gave a rat's ass? The place was empty now. Might as well use it as a dumping ground, pun intended.

Robert laughed. Pity he hadn't saved that one for the guys down the bar. Oh, well. He'd try to remember it for tonight.

"Hey, get out of my garden."

Robert stepped closer to the gate of Melanie's old house. An ugly-looking dude, dressed all in black, was running at Baxter with a golf club raised. Poor Baxter was trying to finish his business, but his neck was craned around behind him, nervously watching the guy approach.

Robert shouted, "Stay away from that dog."

The guy looked up. "This yours?"

Robert stepped through the gate. The guy looked vaguely familiar. "Yes, he is. Don't interrupt him when he's doing his business. Baxter is very sensitive."

"This is my place now. No dog can shit in my garden. It's a matter of respect."

"Well, tough titties, dick head. Baxter likes this patch of grass."

The guy moved fast. He'd crossed the few metres

to Robert in a second. He was fast with the golf club too. It hit the side of Robert's head with the force of a train.

Robert's head exploded.

He dropped to the ground, his head hitting the concrete path.

If he hits me again, I'm dead, Robert thought in amazement.

But another blow never came. Through his daze he heard a second man's voice.

"Let's go, Billy."

"I'm not going anywhere with you."

There was a metallic click. Robert looked up and saw a guy handcuffing his attacker. It was the person he'd seen sitting in a car a minute ago. He was a cop? For some reason, Robert found that hilarious and he cracked up laughing.

When the laughing fit eased, he rolled onto his back and gazed up at the sky. Baxter came over. He licked Robert's face, then lay down beside him.

"Good boy." Robert put his arm around his dog and looked at the sky again. A single wispy cloud eased across the heavens. The vastness and incomprehensible nature of the universe struck him. He sighed, then turned to Baxter, and said, "Seriously, though, can you believe that shit?"

THE END

Acknowledgements

Sincere thanks to my brilliant first readers: Awais Khan, Sarah Faichney and John Gorevan, who provided me with valuable feedback that vastly improved this book.

Thanks also to all the readers, bloggers, librarians, booksellers, fellow authors and other assorted book-loving folk, who make it so rewarding to write stories.

Alan Gorevan is an award-winning writer and intellectual property attorney. Visit www.alangorevan.com to learn more.

By the same author:

NOVELS:
Postcards from San Michele
The Book Club Murders
The Kindness of Psychopaths
Better Confess
Out of Nowhere

NOVELLAS:
Hit and Run
The Hostage
The Forbidden Room

SHORT STORY COLLECTION:
Dark Tales

ANTHOLOGY:
The Thriller Collection *(contains The Forbidden Room, The Hostage, and Hit and Run)*